# Lying to a Lord

The League of Eligible Bachelors

Mindy Burbidge Strunk

Cover Design: Blue Water Books



Publisher's note: This is a work of fiction. Names, places and incidents are a product of the author's imagination. Locales and public names are sometimes used for atmospheric purposes, but any resemblance to actual people-living or dead, to businesses, companies, events, institutions, or locals are coincidental.

# Chapter One

London, Late June 1815

Lady Mariah Thornbeck hadn't always despised dogs. While she had never cared overly much for them, she'd not hated them until her sister-in-law and former best friend, Sarah, brought home Lady Guinevere, a pug that was just as ill-natured as its owner.

Horses, on the other hand, Mariah could appreciate. They were helpful—pulling carriages and working in the fields. And they looked quite noble doing it.

But a dog? What purpose did it serve? They were nothing more than a nuisance that chewed up her slippers and scared woodland creatures.

The little pug nipped at Mariah's ankles. She stomped her foot and growled, sending the animal scurrying behind the butler. Its retreat did nothing to temper Mariah's scowl as she slowly yanked each button on her spencer through its hole, taking far longer than was necessary.

Maxwell, the family's butler, stood in front of her with her bonnet and gloves in hand. "Are you nearly done, Lady Mariah?"

Mariah sighed, looking up as she secured the last button. There was little else to delay her. "Yes. I am finished."

A yip drew her attention back to the pug cowering behind the butler. She glared at the animal. "Where is Sarah? Why can she not take this beast for a walk? It is *her* dog."

"Lady Stoke is busy overseeing preparations for the ball tonight. You're the only one with nothing else to do." Maxwell bent down and picked up the dog, obviously as vexed by it as Mariah.

While she didn't believe Maxwell had intended the slight, it cut that everyone in the house thought her so completely purposeless as to only allow her to walk the dog. "Why can't a servant take her?"

"The servants are all busy." Reginald, her older brother and the Earl of Stoke-on-Trent, stood on the landing with his arms folded across his chest. "Lady Guinevere needs her exercise, else she will be intolerable for the whole of the evening."

*Exercise won't prevent that,* Mariah thought angrily. "But Lady G dislikes me so. And I cannot say the feeling is not mutual." She glared at the dog again.

Reginald smiled. "Then perhaps you should take this opportunity to become better acquainted. I'm certain once you know each other better, you will become fast friends." His voice softened, and he came to stand in front of her. "We all have responsibilities, Mar. And this is yours for today. Please, do not make it more difficult than it need be."

"Very well." She huffed, grabbing the dog from Maxwell. "Where is the leash I asked for?"

"Leash? Why should you need a leash?" Sarah emerged from the ballroom, concern knit across her brow.

"I intend to attach it around Lady G's collar—to keep her from running away."

Sarah frowned, looking at the dog rather than Mariah. "You shouldn't need one. She will walk alongside you." She looked up at Mariah's face and Mariah looked away. Sarah looked as though the need to tether the dog only added to the list of Mariah's deficiencies.

Mariah let out a snort. "She does nothing of the sort. When last I took her for a walk, she let out after a squirrel. I ruined a perfectly lovely gown trying to catch this mongrel. She will be on a leash, else I shall not take her." She folded her arms across her chest and pushed her hip out in challenge. Perhaps if she let the dog have her head, she would chase something and be lost forever. Surely Mariah's slippers would thank her for giving the little beast its freedom.

Reginald let out a sigh. "Very well. If it means Lady Guinevere receives her exercise, then I suppose the leash won't harm her. Just do not let her pull at it too tightly."

Mariah rolled her eyes and put the dog on the floor.

Maxwell stooped down next to her and handed her the leash, taking over the position of holding the animal still. Mariah fastened the long strip of leather around the dog's collar.

Once it was secure, she grasped it tightly. "Come along, Lady G. Let us see this task completed. I should like to have plenty of time to ready for the ball." Her stomach gave a small lurch as she thought about who might be in attendance. She'd heard Lord Heatherton had sent his acceptance, and she intended to look her best for him.

She had endured nearly the whole of the Season without him as he escorted his mother on a tour of the continent. He'd only returned a month ago and had kept to the cardrooms for most of the events. He danced with her the few times Reginald had enlisted the help of his friends in saving her from dancing with undesirable men. But that had been the extent of it. Lord Heatherton never asked her to dance of his own accord. Indeed, he had spent very little time with her outside her brother's company.

The Season was very nearly over. There were few balls

remaining, and this was one of her last chances to draw his attention.

Mariah was determined that Sarah would not be the only one to marry this Season.

She looked over her shoulder, flicking an annoyed glance at Sarah before turning her gaze to her maid. "You will be joining us, Miriam?" There was more bite to her voice than she had intended, but she could not help it. Sarah and her demanding dog simply made Mariah's blood boil.

Her maid nodded, following several steps behind.

Maxwell opened the front door and Mariah didn't miss the slight uptick of his lips as she stepped out onto the landing. "Have a pleasant walk, my lady." Was he laughing at her?

Mariah raised her chin and offered a pert smile. "Indeed, I shall." She gave the leash a little tug. "Come, Lady G."

They headed down Hill Street toward Hyde Park. She only hoped she could finish the task before the fashionable hour caused the walkways to swell with people. The last thing she wished was to be seen walking a dog. It was such a lowering duty meant for the likes of a servant. Not the daughter of an earl. Perhaps she should hand the leash over to Miriam. She glanced back at her maid, whose gaze stayed on the walkway in front of her.

If she stayed to the side paths, rather than those used for being seen, Mariah could avoid most people—at least those of consequence.

Lady G pulled at the leash and then let it go slack as she sniffed at the trees and bushes they passed. Mariah tugged the dog away, only to have her pull at the leash until they neared the next tree.

Mariah huffed. At this rate, they would never reach the park. She stopped walking as Lady G sniffed thoroughly at the ground. Lawks, there were hundreds of trees in the park. What if Mariah did not return home in enough time to dress for the ball?

She glared at the dog. She knew Sarah would never let her discipline the mongrel. Which meant Regi wouldn't allow it either. But what could they do if Lady G slipped away when the gate was ajar? Perhaps if she loosened her grip on the leash, the dog would pull free. Surely they would not expect her to chase after it. Not when Sarah was so concerned about Mariah doing only what was proper.

They reached the park in what must have been a record for slowness. Mariah lowered her head, looking at the ground on the off chance she should see someone of her acquaintance.

Lady G continued to pull on the leash, and Mariah felt vindicated. She'd been correct. If not for the leash, the pug would be running off to cause who knew what kind of mischief.

A flock of birds stood in the path, pecking at whatever had fallen from the overhanging tree. Lady Guinevere barked and pulled harder on the leash.

"Stop it this instant, Lady G," Mariah snapped.

Lady G continued to bark, and Mariah dropped her head lower. Leave it to the little cur to draw undue attention to them with her incessant barking. She picked up her pace, allowing Lady G to dictate the speed. The faster they walked, the sooner the dog would tire, and they could return home.

They rounded a corner of the path, and Mariah picked up her skirts as she nearly ran to keep up. She had wanted the dog to tire quickly, but perhaps this was a bit excessive. "Lady G, you really are the devil himself!" She kept her eyes trained on the path directly in front of her.

"Oof." Mariah collided with a solid form and stumbled backward.

Strong hands clutched at her upper arms, keeping her upright. "There now, miss. My apologies. I did not see you there."

Mariah tucked her chin to her chest as her cheeks

warmed. She knew that voice. Indeed, she listened for it at every party and ball she attended or any time Reginald's friends came to visit. Normally, she would be thrilled beyond words to see Colin—that was how she thought of him, no matter how improper it was—but normally she did not have the spawn of Satan biting at her ankles.

"Are you injured, miss?" Colin asked.

Mariah shook her head. "No, my lord. I'm well." She murmured, hoping he might not recognize her. Was it too much to hope he would simply tip his hat and be on his way without ever seeing her face? It was humiliating to be seen walking the dog. What would he think of her?

He dipped his head and looked up, catching her gaze beneath her down-turned bonnet. "Lady Mariah? Is that you?"

She let out the breath she'd been holding and lifted her head to meet his blue-gray gaze. Gracious, he was handsome. His eyes were one of her favorite things about him. They always seemed to have a sparkle about them, as if he had only just heard a good joke. Indeed, they were the first thing that drew her to him when she was only a girl.

Smiling falsely, she died a little inside. Gads, what he must think of her. He would surely tell Reginald of this incident at the ball tonight. They were best friends, after all.

Colin kept a firm hold on Mariah's arms. "Lady Mariah, it's a pleasure to see you."

She looked down, hoping against hope that the earth would open to swallow her up. But solid ground laid beneath her feet. Well, drat the earth. "And you, my lord."

She looked up again, only to realize how close they were standing to one another. What would it be like to kiss Colin? As much as she wished for it—and she had wished for it for years—she knew it was not proper. And she was trying to be more aware of propriety. If for no other reason than to avoid another lecture from Sarah.

Taking a step back, she stumbled on the leash Lady G had wrapped around both their legs. Colin pulled her closer toward him, keeping a grip on her arms. They were so close together, Mariah could feel the heat from his skin through her long gloves. In a word, she was in heaven.

# Chapter Two

Lord Heatherton tightened his hold on her arms, and she breathed in the scent of bergamot, rosemary, and clary sage soap that she always associated with him. "We seem to be in a bit of a hobble, do we not?" He smiled, but Mariah could not readily decipher if it was forced or not. "Perhaps if I lift my leg out, it will loosen the leash and we may both step free."

He lifted one foot out of the leash noose. Lady G continued to run around them, barking and nipping at the tips of Colin's tailcoat. Colin wobbled on his foot, tightening his grip on her arms—for his sake this time, not hers. The space he freed up from removing his leg was quickly tightened away.

Mariah looked from the crazed dog back to the man in front of her, her humiliation only rising.

*That was it.* When she returned home, she would indeed leave the back gate open so the little demon might have its freedom at last. Or perhaps it was more accurate to say that Mariah would be the one finally free.

She knew she was thinking unreasonably. Lady G was a *dog*. But Mariah saw little choice in the matter. This mongrel was ruining everything. Mariah had planned for a month—years, if she was being completely honest—trying to gain this gentleman's attention, and now Lady G had surely muddled it all.

His brow creased as he concentrated on disentangling himself from Mariah and the leash. Once he was free, he bent and held Lady G still as he unwrapped the leash from around Mariah's legs.

She often dreamed of Colin being before her on bended knee, but never had it been for this reason.

If she had not been completely mortified, Mariah might actually have enjoyed the undivided attention. But alas, she could not.

Once Colin freed her from the leather bonds, she stepped away from him reluctantly. "Thank you, my lord. I do not know what I would have done without your assistance." She glanced down at him and gave a fleeting smile that she felt not in the least.

To Mariah's utter shock, Colin stayed hunched down, scratching Lady G behind the ears and mumbling words of endearment. Was he rewarding the animal for her deplorable behavior?

He looked up at Mariah and she was even more surprised not to see anger or annoyance in his gaze. Indeed, a large grin turned up the corners of his mouth. "I didn't know you had a dog, Lady Mariah."

Heat burned her cheeks. She opened her mouth to tell Colin this devil-dog was not hers when he continued. "I had never thought of you as one to enjoy the company of a dog." His brow creased in thought, and he returned his gaze back to Lady G. In a slightly lower voice, he mumbled. "Interesting."

Mariah straightened, and her frown increased at the slightly offensive statement. What was interesting and why would he not think her a dog lover? Why would he assume she wasn't? Had she ever said something to him to make him believe she was not?

She paused. Which version of her did he prefer? Would he

like her better if he thought her partial to dogs? Or would he prefer she was not?

Her shoulders dropped as an uncomfortable thought struck her. Lawks. Could Colin be a dog lover?

She stared harder at him, trying to decipher his preference. Judging from the way he scratched and cuddled the animal—speaking to it in hushed tones—Mariah conceded he must, indeed, like them. Why else would he pay the beast such attention?

She took another step back. How did she feel about such a revelation? Did this change her feelings for him? Could she even tolerate someone who enjoyed the company of a beastly mongrel so much?

A deep burning filled her belly, and her irritation grew. Could she be jealous of a dog? She shook off the thought. What a ridiculous notion.

Lady Guinevere turned in his arms and pawed his chest, licking his chin. Colin laughed and Mariah gagged. Why was he letting the animal so close to his face? It was vile. She tilted her head to the side and watched for a moment.

Vile, but also somewhat endearing.

Although, her tender feelings were likely brought on by Colin's genuine, unguarded smile rather than anything Lady G had done.

But it set her to thinking. She'd had no use for the little cur up to this point, but perhaps she could use Lady G to her advantage. "Me? Not fond of dogs? Why should you think such a thing? I quite adore them." The untruth flowed from her lips like the Trent in spring. And the look of approval on Colin's face only made her continue with the ruse. She stepped closer and ran her hand awkwardly down Lady G's back. "What a good dog you are, Lady G."

Colin laughed. "Lady G? What does it stand for?"

Mariah tilted her head to the side and giggled lightly. Unlike Sarah, Mariah knew how to flirt with a gentleman. "Her full name is Lady Guinevere. I didn't name her," she hastened to add, lest he think she had come up with the ridiculous name. "She is actually my sister-in-law's dog. I only offered to bring her with me on my walk because I have spent little time with her of late." Her voice came out higher than normal, but would he notice? And if he did, would he realize it was a sure sign she was lying?

Perhaps she should just tell him the truth. He would still find her appealing if she did not like dogs, wouldn't he?

She eyed him as he dragged a stick back and forth across the ground in front of her, Lady G chasing it and growling. He was completely taken with the animal.

Mariah drew in a breath. *In for a penny, in for a pound.* This was the first time he had looked twice at her, and she had no intention of giving that up. This was her chance to show him she was the proper match for him.

She dropped and put her hands on either side of the dog's face. Praying the cur would not lick her, Mariah brought her face close to Lady G. "And I have missed you, have I not, Lady G." She spoke as she would to a small child or perhaps even a baby. Did dogs like to be talked to in such a way? Mariah had no notion, but both man and beast seemed pleased with it, so she carried on.

But when she saw a certain look in Lady G's eyes, Mariah pulled her head back. The last thing she wanted was the little devil's tongue to find her face.

She stood back up and straightened her gown. Leaning down, she scooped the dog into her arms, and scratched at her ears as she had seen Colin do.

Colin reached forward at the same time and their hands brushed against each other, making her cheeks warm.

Colin pulled his hand away. Had he felt it too?

She lowered the pug to the ground. "I take it you also like dogs, my lord?"

He nodded and clasped his hands behind his back.

"Indeed, I have three pointers at my estate in Shropshire. I miss them when I'm in Town."

Three dogs? What a miserable thought. Although, they must surely behave better than Lady G.

"How diverting. I should love to meet them someday." Mariah frowned. Did one really meet dogs? It seemed rather absurd. "If you're to bring them to Town, of course." She could not have him thinking she wished to be invited to his estate, even though that was precisely what she wanted. But it was simply not proper to have him think that is what she wished.

"Of course." They set out walking without either of them saying more.

A squirrel scurried down a tree, and Lady G let out a bark and tugged at the leash, catching Mariah off guard. The dog pulled free and ran full tilt toward the bush where the frightened squirrel fled. It was just as she had imagined only moments ago. Only now, it seemed Mariah could not allow the dog his freedom. What would Colin think if she did? "Come back here, you little devil!" she growled under her breath.

Hurrying over to the bush, she picked up the end of the leash and tugged. Nothing happened. Was she going to have to go into the bush to fetch Lady G?

Mariah reached into the foliage, trying to feel for the dog. Twigs and branches pulled at her hair and spencer. "You little . . ." She glanced over her shoulder and saw Colin watching her. "You silly little dog." She said through gritted teeth. "Leave that poor creature alone." It seemed an eternity, but finally, she managed to pull Lady G free.

Running a hand down her stained and wrinkled skirt, she smiled up at Colin, hoping he did not notice how irritated she truly was. "While I have enjoyed our short walk, I believe it's time to return Lady G to Sarah. After all her excitement, I'm certain she will barely make it home." She smiled. "But I'll see you at the ball tonight, will I not?"

Colin pulled his top lip between his teeth, and Mariah wondered if he was trying not to laugh. Did he think her little jaunt into the bushes humorous? He must think her utterly absurd. Drat Lady G and her unruly behavior.

She tried not to scowl as she lifted a hand to her head. Leaves and large tufts of hair stuck out in every direction. Curses, she must look a fright. It was no wonder he was laughing at her.

"Indeed, I shall be there. Nothing could keep me away." His eyes twinkled more than usual.

While Mariah enjoyed seeing this side of Colin, she didn't enjoy being the cause. "Until tonight." She murmured through clenched teeth. Dipping into a curtsy, she turned and tugged Lady G toward Hill Street.

Once she was certain she was away from the park and Colin's twinkling eyes, she picked up the pug and shoved her into Miriam's arms. "Please take her before I set her free to roam the streets of London."

Mariah stared into the mirror as Miriam placed the last tiny rosebud into her braids. She did not know where her maid had found buds that perfectly matched the color of Mariah's gown. But she was grateful for it. Surely, this was the night that Colin would notice her. Especially after their interaction in the park that afternoon.

She placed a hand on her stomach to quell the waves rolling about inside her.

She stood up and ran a hand down the front of her skirt, turning her head one way and then the other as she examined the whole effect. It was quite pleasing. But would Colin agree?

"Have a lovely evening, my lady." Miriam did not smile as she gathered the discarded clothing and moved toward the dressing room. But that was not unusual for the girl. She rarely smiled, which was just how it should be with a servant.

"I am certain I will." Mariah gathered up her reticule and checked to make certain her fan was inside. Draping the laces over her wrist, she lifted her hem and moved out into the corridor. Walking quietly, so she would not disturb Reginald or Sarah—they would likely feel the need to lecture her about something—Mariah hugged the opposite wall and tiptoed past the doors of their chambers.

But the voices coming through the crack in Sarah's door stopped Mariah in her tracks. What were they saying? Did they speak about her when they were alone?

Moving across the hall, she leaned in toward the open door. The voices ceased and Mariah tipped her head to peer inside.

Her brother and Sarah stood close together, his head bent low toward his wife.

Mariah's nose turned up. Lawks, she had caught them not only in an embrace but in the midst of a kiss. Mariah's stomach burned. She moved to take a step back when voices sounded again.

"What was that for? *Not* that I am objecting." Her brother's voice was soft and happy.

"I simply needed to borrow a little courage to help me through the evening."

Reginald lifted a hand to her cheek. "You need not be anxious, my love. This evening will be a great success. The most notable of the *ton* will be in attendance."

"That is what I fear." Sarah dropped her gaze to the floor.

"That they accepted the invitation is already a mark in your favor. Can you not see that?"

Sarah shook her head. "No, I cannot. They only accepted so they might be present to watch me fail. This is my first time hosting an event, and my mind was not fully on the task. Not with the news of my mother's health." She sighed. "You know people will be watching and criticizing my every decision and move."

Reginald dropped his forehead to Sarah's. "There will be nothing to criticize. I will be at your side the whole of the evening, making certain everything runs smoothly."

Sarah guffawed. "Then they will simply say it went well because of you."

Reginald sighed. "Everyone is not waiting for you to fail, Sarah. You must put such thoughts from your mind, else you will drive yourself mad." He intertwined their fingers. "I have complete faith in you." He dropped another kiss at her temple. "Come, let's enjoy the evening together before you depart on the morrow."

"Perhaps I should leave now. What if my mother's condition has worsened?"

Reginald shook his head. "Your father said she was ill. He did not indicate it was serious yet. And you know your mother. She would be disappointed if you did not attend your own ball."

Sarah wrapped her free hand around his arm, hugging him tightly to her. "You are right. I must put it from my mind and enjoy the evening. I have prepared as well as I could. There is nothing else to be done. Besides, it would be terribly improper for me to leave before the ball was over."

Mariah clapped a hand over her mouth as a laugh worked its way up her throat. Apparently, Sarah could not stop talking about propriety, even when she was alone with her husband.

Sarah looked up into Reginald's face, her brow drawn low. "I only wish Mariah was at my side, also."

Mariah flinched at the sound of her name. They did speak of her when they were alone.

"She will come around, my love. Just give her time." Reginald sounded weary.

"It has been nearly five months, Reginald. How much longer will it take before she forgives me?"

Reginald shook his head and growled. "You should not be seeking her forgiveness. Rather, she should seek it from you. You did nothing wrong. Indeed, I am sure you saved her from certain ruin."

Mariah's hands clenched into fists at her side. When would they stop insisting that she had done something wrong? She had simply taken a turn with a gentleman. She placed a hand on her stomach as the familiar pang of fear twisted, and she looked at the ground. She did not like to think about that night at Vauxhall.

Mariah pushed the pain away and lifted her chin. Reginald would surely have listened to her explanation if Sarah had not poisoned him first.

They turned toward the door, and Mariah jumped back to the other side of the corridor. Without thinking, she hitched up her skirts and hurried toward the staircase. Racing down them, she didn't slow until she reached the landing below.

Once there, Mariah stopped and allowed herself the chance to think over what she had just heard.

Sarah was nervous about the evening? That was certainly a surprise. Lady Perfectly Proper was concerned about something other than Mariah. That was a new development.

If Mariah were the vengeful sort, she might just have planned something to help Sarah's concerns come true. But Mariah was above such pettiness. She would not be so cruel to her sister-in-law. Even if Sarah had no qualms about treating Mariah in such a way.

# Chapter Three

Colin Burke, the Earl of Heatherton, stepped from his carriage and looked up at the front of the London Townhouse of the Earl of Stoke-on-Trent.

Formerly, when he arrived at 15 Berkeley Square, he would have thought only of his friend, Stoke. But after his walk in the park that afternoon, it was Lady Mariah he now pictured.

He grinned at the memory of her hair in stunning disarray—her face the picture of masked irritation. She had done her best to look amiable. But he knew it likely she wished to be rid of her unfavorable walking partner. At least at that moment. She surely did not wish the animal away for good. Not when she so clearly adored it.

He looked at the windows dotting the front facade. Was one of those windows hers? Tilting slightly to the side, he tried to catch a better view of the upper floors. He shook his head of the thoughts. What was he thinking? He was not looking to leg-shackle himself as Stoke had done.

Besides, he'd known Lady Mariah since she was a child. He had danced with her occasionally over the last few years. But he'd never seen her as anything other than Stoke's sister.

Never as an eligible young lady. He never looked at any lady as eligible, because that implied he was looking for a wife. Which he wasn't. He might ask Lady Mariah for a set, but he would spend the rest of the evening in the cardroom. Just as he always did.

He tugged on his waistcoat and ran a hand through his hair. The front door opened as he approached, and a footman ushered him inside.

Colin had been inside Stoke's home often enough that he didn't need to admire its fineness. However, his gaze moved to the upper-floor landings of its own accord. Colin grunted. It was simply curiosity. Not because he wished to see if Lady Mariah was about.

"Lord Heatherton, we are so pleased you are joining us this evening." Stoke's wife smiled cordially—as any well-trained hostess would—and reached out for his arm. She drew him toward the small line of people greeting the guests. Lady Stoke stood next to her husband, but she motioned around him to the other person in line. Colin could not help but grin as Lady Stoke made the introduction.

"I'm certain you have met Lady Mariah." Lady Stoke gave him a small push in that direction and turned to the next guest.

"Heatherton, how are you this evening?" Stoke looked at him with slightly widened eyes. "I am glad you were not otherwise engaged."

Colin smirked at his friend. "And miss seeing you in utter misery? I should not have missed it for all the jewels in the Tower."

Lady Stoke paused in her conversation. "Miserable? Why should you believe my husband to be miserable, my lord?" Her brow drew down into a *v* between her eyes and she darted a glance at Reginald.

"It has nothing to do with your ball, my lady. It is simply balls in general. They are rather intolerable." He leaned in close. "Although, I should think Stoke will have an easier go of it tonight. There will be no mothers setting their eyes on him as a match for their daughters." He winked at her. "You have seen to that."

Stoke rolled his eyes and pushed Colin toward Lady Mariah. "Thank you for your help, Colin." He turned slightly to Lady Mariah. "Mar, are you not happy that Lord Heatherton has graced us with his presence?"

Colin grinned down at Lady Mariah. She was wearing a pale pink gown which brought out the rosiness of her cheeks. Her blond hair was no longer home to sticks and twigs, but rather tiny rosebuds and pearls. While the pearls were fetching, Colin could not deny he missed the twigs and leaves just a little. They had made her seem more approachable—more likable. While he had never disliked Lady Mariah, he could not say he had ever discovered anything about her to make him desire to learn more.

She pouted when she did not get her way, which was a quality he rarely found endearing, and he had never once heard her thank a servant. Perhaps that was why he had been so surprised to discover her fondness for dogs. She simply had not seemed the sort to care about small creatures. Or any creature, for that matter.

But if he had been wrong about the dog, was it possible he was also wrong about other things? Had he simply misjudged her?

She tilted her head to the side. "Indeed, Regi, I am most happy to see him here tonight."

He bowed deeply. "Lady Mariah. You look well this evening. May I attribute it to your exercise this afternoon?"

Her face deepened in color—which was rather fetching—but she gave a tittering laugh as she flicked her gaze to her brother. "Yes, Lady G always gives me plenty of exercise."

Colin twitched slightly. That laugh was enough to send any man running toward the cardroom. Why had he not noticed it at the park? Perhaps she was simply nervous this evening. "I hope I'm not too late to claim your supper dance?" He would dance the one set and feel no regret for spending the rest of the evening in the cardroom.

Lady Mariah smiled, her lashes fluttering. "No, you're not too late." She moistened her lips, drawing Colin's attention.

Why had he never noticed them before? They were just the right amount of plump and pink. He shook the thoughts from his mind and pulled his eyes up to hers. What was he thinking? He had no interest in following Stoke into the parson's mousetrap. Especially not in the same Season!

The candlelight sparkled in her brown eyes. "It's still available, my lord."

Colin dipped his head. "Then consider it claimed, my lady."

The next guest nudged him, and Colin moved into the ballroom. Lady Stoke had done a fine job of decorating. Enormous bouquets of white and pale pink flowers contrasted against the deep brown of the wood-paneled walls.

He moved around the perimeter of the room taking note of those in attendance. The ball was already a well-attended crush, which didn't come as a surprise. Stoke was not without influence.

"You do not look to be enjoying yourself."

Why had he never noticed the pleasant tone in Lady Mariah's voice? There was much about Lady Mariah he hadn't noticed before. It was as if the park encounter had opened Colin's eyes to something he'd been blinded to before. While her fondness for dogs had made him curious, it was the complete imperfectness of the situation that had made him take more notice. He had never seen her so adorably flustered. "On the contrary. Your sister-in-law has done a fine job on her first ball. It is already quite a crush."

Lady Mariah looked out across the room. Her hands clasped in front of her. "Yes, I'm certain Sarah will be happy with the turnout. She feared everyone had returned to the country by now."

Colin frowned. "But there is still a fortnight before Parliament closes for the summer."

Lady Mariah lifted a shoulder in a slight shrug. "Yes, well, Sarah is returning to Staffordshire on the morrow. And if she is returning to the country early, then she reasons surely everyone else must be also." She rolled her eyes as if she thought the notion absurd.

"And when are you quitting London, my lady?" Was she leaving early as well? He did not know why he cared—other than simple curiosity.

"I'm to stay with Reginald until he has finished in Parliament."

Colin nodded, oddly relieved. "I'm glad to hear it. Perhaps we will meet again in the park when you are out with Lady G."

A look he could not place flitted across her face, but a sad smile quickly replaced it. "Regretfully, Lady G will travel to Stoke-on-Trent with Sarah."

"I'm sorry to hear it. You will surely miss your walks with her."

Lady Mariah's lips turned down in a practiced pout. "Indeed. I do not know what I shall do without her. Thankfully, we shall only be apart for little more than a fortnight."

Colin nodded. He could sympathize with her gloom. It had been months since he'd seen his pointers. "Perhaps we could take a turn about the park . . . simply to keep you from feeling too lonely." His brow creased. Why had he mentioned a walk? Would Lady Mariah interpret his offer as something more than a friendly gesture? From his experience, when a lady thought a man was interested, it changed their interactions. And not usually for the better. He did not wish to give her ideas that were not possible.

She turned her head toward him and tipped it to the side. "Why Lord Heatherton, what a marvelous idea."

Mr. Roundy appeared from the crowd and approached Lady Mariah. He bowed. "My lady, I believe I claimed this set."

She curtsied and lifted her hand.

Colin watched with curiosity as they walked toward the dance floor. Did Lady Mariah enjoy Mr. Roundy's company? He was a decent enough man, but he lacked the spirit and gumption for the likes of Lady Mariah.

Lord Berwick sidled up next to him. "Colin, there you are. Cort and Rags were asking after you. They expected to find you in the cardroom."

Colin clasped his hands behind his back. "I was just speaking to Lady Mariah."

"Are you to forsake cards this evening?" Ben glanced toward the dance floor. "Mr. Roundy seems to have her full attention at present."

Colin shook his head. "No, of course I'm not abandoning the cardroom. I was just about to find my way there. I have already noted several matrons looking my way. And they have that look in their eyes."

Ben chuckled. "It is why you should not even venture inside the ballroom." He shook his head. "Did you forget everything about Society while on your tour of the Continent?"

Colin smirked. "I didn't forget how to best you at cards, if that is what you are wondering."

Ben grunted and turned back toward the ballroom doors. "What were you speaking to Lady Mariah about, anyhow?"

"I asked her for her supper dance."

Ben looked at him with utter confusion. "And why would you do such a thing?"

"She is a safe and amiable partner. If I dance with her, I need not feel guilty when Lady Stoke asks how I enjoyed the ball. I can say with complete honesty that I enjoyed myself very much."

Ben scoffed. "I may do the same, and yet I have not set the precedent of dancing."

They reached the doors to the entryway and Colin glanced back over his shoulder. Lady Mariah smiled prettily at Mr. Roundy. Was the man interested in her?

"I am certain all the gents have arrived by now. Although, I doubt we will see much of Reg this evening. He is too busy watching over his wife."

Colin put his thoughts about the ballroom and those within it from his mind. If he was to have any success at the tables this evening, he would need to keep his mind on his cards.

# Chapter Four

MARIAH KEPT TO HER ROOMS UNTIL SHE WATCHED THE carriage—with Sarah and Lady G—disappear down the street.

She was free! Releasing a sigh, she pulled open her door and left her chambers in search of her brother. With Sarah gone, surely Regi would have time for her again. It had been months since they had done anything together—just the two of them.

But just where was Reginald? Mariah knew he would be home, for he would not have left for the club before Sarah had departed. She rolled her eyes. How would he kiss his lovely wife goodbye if he were not home when she left?

He had surely already eaten breakfast with Sarah, which meant he would likely be in his study.

Mariah made her way down the corridor. When she arrived at his study door, she rapped two times.

"Enter," Reginald called.

Mariah pushed open the door and stepped inside the dimly lit room. The curtains were still drawn over the windows, keeping out the bright morning sunlight. "You are not mourning the departure of your wife, are you, Regi?"

Mariah crossed her arms over her chest and pushed out her hip.

Reginald looked up from behind his desk. "And why should you believe I am in mourning?"

Mariah nodded to the closed curtains. "Your study is so dark. I should think if you were not melancholy, you would open the curtains and allow some sunshine in."

Reginald shook his head. "While I do already miss my wife immensely, the curtains remain closed to keep the heat of the morning out. If I don't, this room will be deuced unbearable by afternoon."

Mariah smiled sweetly. "But that should not be a problem. I thought we might go on an outing this afternoon. Just the two of us."

Reginald sat back, his elbows resting on the arms of his chair, his fingers interlaced. "Oh? What did you have in mind, Mar?"

Mariah sat in the chair across from his desk and lifted a delicate shoulder. "I do not know. I thought perhaps we could decide that together."

Reginald eyed her, as if he were deciphering a riddle or charade. Since marrying Sarah, he seemed rather taken with charades. Mariah didn't see the appeal. "Surely, you had something in mind." His lips pushed out slightly.

"I still have yet to see the Peerless Pool. Or perhaps we could go to Gunter's for ices."

Reginald nodded slowly. "I suppose an ice would be agreeable this afternoon."

Mariah leaned forward in her seat. "But what about the Peerless Pool? May we go there also?"

Reginald frowned. "I am not certain the Peerless Pool is the most proper place for a young lady to go."

Mariah let out a growl. "I am dashed sick of all this talk of propriety. You and Sarah have hardly let me out of your sight this entire Season. I am not asking to go bathing. I simply wish to walk around the pool—see what all the talk is about."

"If you do not wish to hear about propriety, perhaps you should not use words like *dashed*." Reginald raised a brow then shrugged. "I suppose it would not be too improper for you to walk around it. Although, I do not think it will be as amiable as you are expecting. There are certain times of the day, if the wind is just right, when the smell can be a bit unpleasant."

Mariah's shoulders dropped. "Why must you ruin everything for me? Can I not discover things on my own?"

Reginald held up his hands in front of him. "I'm sorry. I did not intend to ruin it for you. I simply wish for you to have the proper expectations."

"You need not protect me from everything, Reginald. I do not need you to be always watching out for me. I am not a child any longer."

Reginald raised a brow. "Some of your recent decisions and interactions may have indicated the opposite."

Mariah opened her mouth to disagree, but Reginald held up his hands again. "I do not intend to argue with you, Mar. What time do you wish to leave this afternoon?"

Mariah slumped back in her chair. Why did all their interactions of late seem to end in an argument? Because of Sarah. It always came back to Sarah. Mariah and Reginald had had a very amiable relationship, until Sarah came along. "Why do we not set out at two?"

Reginald smiled at her, for the first time in what felt a very long time. "Then I shall be back to fetch you at two." He pushed his chair back and stood. "I find I am looking forward to our outing, Mar. You are right, it has been much too long since we have done something just the two of us."

Mariah stood from her chair, the anger and disappointment she'd felt so much of late, lifting off her shoulders. "I shall make sure I am ready." She tilted her head to the side. "Where are you off to now, Regi?"

"I am to meet the gents at Brooks's." He gave her a wry smile. "It seems they have a similar complaint as you—that I have not spent as much time with them as usual."

Mariah nodded, a small burning sensation filling her stomach. While she would never admit it, she envied Reginald and the relationship he had with his friends. Mariah had never had many friends. In truth, Sarah had been the only close friend Mariah had ever had. She swallowed painfully past the lump in her throat.

But that was neither here nor there. She raised her chin, focusing instead on what Reginald had said. It seemed she was not the only one who was displeased with Sarah and the role she had taken in all their lives. Mariah turned toward the door. "I shall see you at two." She looked back over her shoulder just before she rounded the door frame and stopped. "And Regi?"

He looked up from the papers he shuffled on his desk. "Yes, Mar?"

"Thank you. I am most excited about the prospect of our afternoon."

He grinned. "As am I."

Mariah tucked her fan into her ridicule, knowing it would be needed in the stifling June heat. She had not realized before coming to London how truly displeasing London could be in the summer. While summer was warm in the country, it felt as if the closeness of the buildings in London simply radiated the heat, making it feel far hotter than it truly was.

She had told Reginald she had no plans to bathe, but would he stop her from dipping her toes in the water? Surely he would understand that she was simply doing so to cool off.

And Sarah would not be there to lecture her on propriety.

Mariah frowned. Although Reginald seemed to have taken to lecturing her nearly as much as Sarah did.

She shook those thoughts aside, not wishing to start off their outing on a negative note.

Looking at the clock on the mantle, she took one last look at her reflection in the mirror, then turned and left her bed chambers. Her pale blue gown was just right for a walk about the Peerless Pool. And her straw bonnet, while likely not proper for a walk in Hyde Park, was perfectly proper for ices at Gunter's.

Reginald was already waiting for her in the entryway. He glanced up as she came down the stairs. He smiled. "Mar, just in time."

She took her spencer that Maxwell held out to her. "Enjoy your outing, my lady."

Mariah fastened the buttons and smiled. "I have every intention of enjoying myself."

Reginald took his beaver from the butler and gave a slight dip of his head. "Thank you, Maxwell. We shall be back before teatime." He shoved his hands in his gloves and looked over at Mar. "You remember that we have the Batemans' card party tonight and the Cleverlys' ball on Sunday evening?"

Mariah scrunched up her nose. "I do not know why you had to accept Mr. Cleverly's invite. Especially not when we had an invitation from Lord Dumont."

Reginald sighed. "It was not so many months ago that you wished for me to introduce you to Mr. Cleverly."

Mariah raised her chin. "And did you not say he was not a proper man for me?"

"I never said he was not proper. I simply said I did not wish for you to make his acquaintance."

Mariah stared at him in confusion. "If it was not his impropriety, why did you not wish for me to meet him?"

Reginald lifted his arm for her to take, leading her out the front doors to the waiting carriage. "He is just not the sort of man I wish for a brother-in-law." He glanced over at Mariah. "And if you will remember, I was on my way to speak to Sarah. Introducing you to Mr. Cleverly was not a pressing matter at the time."

Mariah felt her anger rising again. How was it that Sarah could ruin Mariah's afternoon with Reginald when she was not even in London? Just how far did her reach extend?

The carriage ride to Old Street was quiet, both of them seeming content to stay in their own musings. Mariah was certain if she opened her mouth, Reginald would just find something else to find fault with. Thankfully, most of the traffic seemed headed in the direction of Hyde Park.

The carriage stopped and Reginald swung down to the walk, waiting to hand Mariah down.

Once they were both on the walkway, Reginald clasped his hands behind his back, and they made their way around St. Luke's Hospital. The walkways were not as crowded as those in Hyde Park, but it seemed the warmer weather had brought many to seek the cool waters of the Peerless Pool.

Reginald looked ahead, but Mariah knew his mind was working. "I know you have something you wish to say, so why do you not simply say it?"

Reginald shook his head. "Because I know how it will end."

"What do you mean, you know how it will end?" Her voice came out slightly shrill.

"Because lately our conversations always end the same, Mar."

"Then what you have to say has to do with Sarah?" She could not help the disdain in her voice.

Reginald shook his head. "You see? I have said nothing and already you are arguing."

Mariah stopped and put her hands on her hips. "I would not have to argue if you did not always take her side."

Reginald released a sigh. "I do not always take her side, Mariah—only when you are in the wrong." He guided her along a narrow path through many trees and bushes before they emerged onto the walkway surrounding a large pool. Marble stairs lay at one end, with several marble enclosures dotting the sides.

"Mariah, I am just going to say it because I am tired of your constant belittling of Sarah. She misses you. And she longs for you to return to your previous friendship." He shook his head again. "Lud, Mariah. How many times has she apologized? And in truth, she is not even the one who should be apologizing."

Mariah let out a rueful laugh. "And just why not? Is Lady Perfectly Proper too perfect to need to apologize?"

Reginald looked at her with a bland expression. "I do not believe my wife is perfect, nor does she believe it of herself. However, as much as you wish not to admit it, she did you a great service at Vauxhall."

Mariah balled her fists at her side but dropped her gaze to the ground. "That is where you were both wrong. I was in no danger. I do not need you to protect me. And I certainly do not need Sarah to." Her stomach churned at the lie.

Reginald reached over and gently gripped her by the arm, pulling her to a stop. "You are very naïve if you believe you were in no danger. Muckrake had already led you to the darkened paths. It was only a matter of moments before he did something you would not recover from if Sarah had not discovered you when she did."

Mariah did not need Reginald to recreate that night for her. Her memory was quite capable of doing it on its own. She raised her gaze to meet his. "While I still do not agree, that is not even my biggest grievance. Why could she not leave it be? Why must she lecture me on propriety at every chance she gets? She acts as if I was the one whose London lodgings were above a shop in Cheapside, rather than her. I am the daughter of an earl, not her. I do not see why she thinks herself so far above me now."

Reginald dropped his hands to his side but continued to stare at her. "Perhaps if you thought of someone besides yourself for once, you might understand the answer to your question." He turned away from her. "But then thinking of others has never been one of your stronger suits, has it?"

Mariah took a step back, his word striking her almost as forcefully as if it had been his hand.

"Perhaps it would be best if we did not speak for the remainder of our walk." Reginald turned from her and made his way through the groups of people clustered around the edge of the pool.

Mariah stayed rooted in place. How could he say something so unkind to her? Something so untrue? He acted as though she never did anything for or thought of anyone else. Which was completely untrue…was it not?

# Chapter Five

The ride back to Berkeley Square was as quiet as the ride to Old Street, but much more tension filled the carriage.

Mariah still could not believe the things Reginald had said to her. She could not believe Sarah had turned him so against her.

The carriage stopped in front of their home, and Reginald helped her down. She moved toward the front door but stopped when he called her name.

"Are we not to go to Gunter's for ices?"

Mariah looked down at her hands, unable to look him in the eye after his cruel words. "I do not believe I have the stomach for Gunter's today."

Reginald walked over and lifted his arm to her. "After our conversation about it this morning, I find I can think of nothing else. Perhaps by the time we have walked down the street, you will have changed your mind."

Mariah watched as their carriage disappeared down the alleyway leading to the mews. "Where shall we sit? You know Gunter's will be crowded. And you have just sent away the carriage."

Reginald motioned to the front door, as it opened and a

footman stepped out with the rug draped over his arm. "I realize it may be a little unconventional, but I thought perhaps we could eat our ices alfresco." He smiled at her as if he had not spoken the cruelest words she had ever heard only moments ago.

Mariah shrugged. "If that is what you wish." And then she added, "I should not like to think only of myself." She smirked at him as she continued across the street.

Reginald paused for a moment but then continued walking as if he had not heard what she had said. But she knew he had. And it did not make her feel better. Indeed, the twist in her stomach only seemed to tighten more.

Berkeley Square was just as crowded as the Peerless Pool had been. They walked through the crowds lining the low fence toward the center of the small park, and Reginald unfolded the blanket, spreading it out on the ground under a large tree. A waiter hurried past them with a tray of ices in his hand. On his way back toward the shop, Reginald stopped him.

"Excuse me, might we have ices delivered?"

The waiter gave an exasperated sigh. "There are many before you, sir."

Reginald nodded. "I do not wish to imply we are more important than others waiting. If you could let me know when our turn has come, I would be much obliged."

The waiter nodded and hurried off across the street, disappearing through the door of Gunter's tea shop.

Reginald lowered himself down to the ground. He leaned back on his hands, his legs stretched out before him and his ankles crossed. "In the shade, the heat is not so oppressive."

Mariah stepped onto the edge of the blanket and kneeled down, spreading her dress out to cover her and keep it from wrinkling too badly. She unbuttoned several buttons on her spencer and waved a hand in front of her neck. "Yes, the shade does help a small bit."

"Stoke, is that you?"

Reginald stiffened beside Mariah. He looked up as a shadow passed over them.

Lord Muckrake smiled down at Mariah. "Lady Mariah, it is a pleasure to see you. I do not believe I have seen you since our evening at Vauxhall."

Reginald flicked a glance at Mariah. Her face warmed. Why, of all days, had today been the day they saw Lord Muckrake? It was almost as if his presence somehow made Reginald's earlier assertions true. Not that they weren't, but Mariah would never admit to it.

She smiled tightly up at Lord Muckrake but then scurried to her feet when she noticed where his gaze was focused, hurriedly fastening the buttons on her spencer as she did.

"Lord Muckrake, I did not know you were still in London."

He pulled his eyes up to her face. "I did return to my estate for several months as I had business to attend to. But I could not miss the final events. They are usually the most well-attended crushes of the entire Season."

"Are you to attend the Cleverlys' Ball on Sunday evening?" Mariah asked. The Cleverlys were not considered one of the higher-ranking families in society, so she was hopeful Lord Muckrake would have declined such an invitation. If he had received one in the first place.

"Cleverly? His is not a ball I should consider as well attended. I opted to attend Lord Dumont's card party instead."

Mariah feigned disappointment. "Oh, that is a pity. I fear we shall not have each other's company this evening."

Lord Muckrake raised a brow. "Perhaps, you would accompany me to Mr. Warrington's musicale on Monday evening?"

Reginald shot to his feet before Mariah could reject Muckrake's invitation. "I'm sorry, my lord, but we have already sent our acceptance to Lord Perryweather's musicale. It would be improper to send regrets now."

Lord Muckrake dragged his gaze to Reginald. "I did not invite you along, Stoke. As long as one of you attends Perryweather's party, there will be no improprieties."

Mariah wrung her hands in front of her. How was she to get out of it? She must think quickly. Had she not just told Reginald she did not need his protection? Now seemed a good time to prove it. But how?

"Good day, Lord Stoke," Colin moved in next to Reginald from out of the crowd behind them. He looked at Lord Muckrake, and his nostrils curled. "Muckrake," Colin said with disdain.

The man smirked at Colin. "Heatherton, I heard you were back in London."

"If only I had heard the same about you, I should have taken better precautions to avoid you." Colin sneered.

Reginald sucked in a breath and drew himself up to his full height. "I am afraid I cannot allow you to escort my sister to Mr. Warrington's party. It simply is not possible. You see, Lord Heatherton has already engaged her for Lord Perryweather's party."

Colin's head jerked around to look at Reginald, but he did not object. Did that mean he was amiable to the idea? A warmth spread across Mariah's chest.

But then just as quickly her stomach twisted. Reginald had once again saved her. And this time she did not even need it. She had a plan, but he had not allowed her to use it.

She smiled at Lord Muckrake. "Yes, and I am already scheduled to perform. I could not possibly back out now."

"You are not to play your harp again, I hope. That instrument is dreadfully out of fashion." Lord Muckrake simpered.

Mariah's eyes widened at his insult.

He shrugged. "I suppose it is not to be, my lady. At least

not on this occasion. But perhaps we shall see each other again before you return to the country."

Mariah dipped into a curtsy. "I can hardly wait, my lord." She said through gritted teeth. Her face ached from the effort it took to continue smiling cordially. When would the gentleman take his leave? Colin was here and she would prefer to spend her time speaking with him.

Lord Muckrake strode away, quickly disappearing into the crowd of people. He was barely out of sight when Colin turned on Reginald. "What the devil do you think you are doing?"

The scowl on his face did not look like that of a contented man. But what was he so displeased about? Surely it was not about Reginald's claim that he would escort Mariah to Perryweather's party, was it? A knot formed in her throat. She had thought she was making strides with him.

Reginald lifted a hand. "Calm yourself. You need not really escort her. But I had to say something to keep that rake away from Mariah. I did not intend to use you. But when you arrived, I saw the opportunity and I could not pass it up."

Colin dipped his head to one side, still scowling at Reginald. "But what will he do when I show up and I do not have Mariah with me?"

Reginald waved his question away. "Not to worry. Muckrake has accepted an invitation to Mr. Worthington's. He will never know that we lied." He grinned and patted Colin on the arm. "You see, there is nothing to worry about."

Mariah looked between the two of them. *But I know,* she wanted to scream. She knew now that all her plans had failed. He wanted nothing to do with her. But why? Why had Colin been so adamantly opposed to escorting her? What must she do to get him to see her for what she was? See that she was perfect for him?

She rubbed a finger at the spot between her brows. What

of their interaction in the park and then at the ball? She had thought perhaps she had finally drawn his attention.

She stood staring up at him from beneath her lashes. Perhaps she needed to handle the situation without gloves.

She grinned. She simply needed to flirt with him to draw his attention back to her. After all, he was used to being a bachelor and paying the ladies no mind. It seemed a habit he might have difficulty breaking. She simply needed to give him a reason to break it.

She released a breath. It was a good thing she knew exactly what to do. Sarah might not have been any good at flirting, but Mariah was surely a proficient.

Reginald motioned to their rug on the grass. "We are waiting for ices. Would you care to join us?"

Colin grinned. "Indeed, after hearing you mention this morning that you were bringing Lady Mariah to Gunter's, I admit I came in hopes that I might join you." He dropped to the rug and stretched out his legs in front of him, leaning back on his elbows. "I have not had an ice the whole of the Season. But I find the idea quite pleasing."

He glanced over at Mariah and his mouth ticked up in a smile. Was he only anticipating the ice? Or was he just as excited about the company? Perhaps he was not so unaware of her as she had imagined.

Colin tugged at his cravat. "I cannot imagine the devil himself could be this hot on his throne in Hades."

Mariah let out a giggle, her eyes wide with shock. "Oh, my lord. That is truly a terrible thing to say. Especially in front of a lady."

Colin's brow creased, and he looked from Mariah to Reginald.

Mariah flicked a glance at her brother. His brow creased also, but not in the same confused manner as Colin's. He was wearing his thinking expression.

Slowly, Reginald's brow rose. Could he tell what she was

doing? Mariah wasn't certain, but she had wondered if Reginald might not have overheard some of her teaching techniques with Sarah. And knowing Sarah, she had likely told Reginald everything Mariah had ever told her.

But she did not care if Reginald knew. He would discover her partiality for Colin soon enough. And perhaps if he knew, he might actually help her in securing the affections of his friend. He owed her that little bit, did he not?

# Chapter Six

Colin looked at Lady Mariah. Why was she making it seem as though he had just said something so very untoward? Perhaps his comment was not appropriate for the ballrooms, but they were among friends, seated on a blanket in the park. It was not so very improper. And why was she giggling at what he had said? He disliked giggling very much. It was so disingenuous.

From the way Reginald looked at his sister, Colin thought he might agree.

But Colin smiled tightly at her simply because he did not know what else to do. However, he quickly looked away, not wishing for her to misinterpret the smile as something it was not. The park was crowded, which he should have expected. Although, even with all the people standing or milling about, Colin could see some of the *Ton* had already taken their leave of London.

Men stood about the perimeter of the park, waiting for their purchases to be delivered by the waiters. Carriage after carriage lined the streets as the ladies waited inside for their snacks.

Colin had to admit that Reginald had the right of it.

Sitting on a blanket in the cool grass under the shade of a large maple tree had to be better than sitting in the stale air of a carriage. He glanced over at Lady Mariah. Even if he had to endure a giggling girl.

She caught him staring at her, and he looked away quickly. Where had the lady from Hyde Park gone? There had been no giggles then. Although, she'd rather had her hands full. He grinned at the memory.

But even at the ball, she had not been the giggling girl sitting beside him then. "Reg, did I remember you saying you were to attend Cleverly's ball on Sunday?"

Reginald nodded. "And I have never been happier to have accepted an invitation." He glanced over at his sister. "Perhaps I approached this Season's invites completely wrong."

"Oh? How so?" Colin shifted onto one elbow and leaned onto his hip.

Reginald flicked a glance into the crowd. "I should have been accepting all the least desirable events. Then I should never have had to worry about Mariah accepting a set with Lord Muckrake." He shook his head as if disgusted he had not discovered the answer sooner.

Mariah released an exasperated sigh. "But Regi, you would not only be keeping me from Lord Muckrake, but from all the other desirable gentlemen as well."

Reginald shook his head. "I completely disagree. We are to attend Mr. Cleverly's, are we not? So are Berwick and Colin. Indeed, all of the gents will be there. Are you calling them undesirable?"

Mariah's eyes widened, and she flicked a glance at Colin. "Of course not." She giggled again.

Colin looked away and rolled his eyes. Lud, was the giggling to be a constant thing? It was annoying, and he doubted he could stand it for an extended period of time. He looked toward Gunter's, wondering how long it would take for their ices to be delivered.

Lady Mariah stopped giggling and sobered. "I am sorry, my lord, if you mistook my meaning." She pulled the side of her bottom lip between her teeth and looked over at her brother. "But it is not as if your friends are truly eligible, Regi. Perhaps you should not count them among the available gentlemen I am to encounter." She looked up at him from beneath her lashes. She meant something by it, but he could not tell if she was hiding something from Reginald or from him. But what would she have to hide from him?

Colin pushed to his feet, tired of sitting and waiting for the ices to come. It seemed things were only becoming more awkward the longer he sat with Reginald and Lady Mariah—or rather her giggles.

"I'm tired of sitting about waiting. I believe I shall take a turn about the park while we wait." He shook one leg and then the other, getting the pinpricks in his feet to go away.

Lady Mariah pushed to her feet as well. "May I join you, my lord?" She hurriedly asked. "I believe we are of the same mind." She smiled sweetly up at him, her eyelashes fluttering.

Colin raised a brow. Hang it all. How was he to escape the giggles if she was to take the turn with him? He narrowed his gaze at her. "Have you something in your eye, my lady?" He did not believe that was the problem. But neither did he wish to admit that Stoke's sister was flirting with him because it made no sense. Why should she flirt with him? Had she not just stated that none of Reginald's friends were looking for marriage? Was not Colin in that group?

Ladies only flirted with men they were seeking an attachment with. And she knew he was not available.

He blinked several times at her. *She was Stoke's sister.*

Colin looked at Reginald, hoping his friend would intercede. But he did not seem of a mind to help.

Colin released a heavy sigh. "Very well, you may join me. But we shall stay to this side of the park," he directed his words to Reginald, wanting him to realize that Colin had no intention of taking Mariah into a position that might be compromising.

Reginald smiled up at him. "I cannot think of anyone I should feel safer escorting Mariah."

Colin scowled at Reginald. Was he trying to play matchmaker? Colin shook that thought from his mind almost as quickly as it came. Reginald would not try to match Colin up with his sister. Just because *Reginald* had embraced matrimony, did not mean he would try to force the rest of them into it.

Colin clasped his hands behind his back, not wishing to give Lady Mariah any reason to believe that he might be interested in her as anything more than the sister of his best friend.

They walked towards the center of the park, as the perimeter of the park remained crowded with gentlemen waiting for their ices to be delivered.

"It appears we were not the only people to desire a cool snack this afternoon." He did not speak the words to Mariah, looking straight ahead as they walked.

"Yes, it seems all of London is waiting on an ice."

Had she just moved closer to him? Perhaps she was simply experimenting, trying to see what would happen. Surely she was interested in someone else. Colin had done nothing to give her the idea that he wished for an arrangement.

"Are you eager to return to Staffordshire?" He asked. It seemed a safe topic of conversation. And hopefully one that would not elicit any giggles. "I suppose you are anticipating seeing Lady G again."

"Oh, yes. Lady G." Lady Mariah laughed, but it was more of the uneasy sort than the giggle-y sort. She released a heavy breath. "While I am eager to escape the oppressiveness of the London air, I am not eager to return home. Especially not now that Sarah is living there."

Colin glanced over at her. "You do not care for your new sister-in-law?" He knew the two women had had some kind of disagreement, but he was interested in Lady Mariah's view of it. "Reginald led me to believe the two of you were good friends."

Mariah lifted his shoulder. "Once, perhaps. Until she married Regi."

"You did not wish for the match?"

"At first, I did. I thought it would be wonderful to have a sister." She pushed out her lips in a pout. "But she does not act like a sister, rather a most disagreeable governess. Where she once was fun, now all she worries about is propriety."

"I have no sisters," he frowned. "Or brothers, for that matter." He often thought of Reginald as a brother. Indeed, he was the closest thing Colin had to a brother. He could not imagine them ever being at odds with each other. At least not enough to force them to become enemies. But perhaps it was different between brothers than sisters.

"I cannot offer you any advice." Colin scratched at his earlobe. "Although I am not surprised that Lady Stoke is concerned about propriety."

"Oh?" Lady Mariah looked at him with raised brows.

Colin shrugged. "She surely married far above what she ever thought possible. I imagine such an increase in status must leave her feeling overwhelmed and, at times, inferior. I should think propriety is a very important thing to her."

Lady Mariah opened her mouth to offer what was sure to be an objection but closed it before she allowed any words out.

Colin glanced back over his shoulder. "Ah, it looks as though the waiter has found your brother. Perhaps now we will get our ices." He motioned toward Reginald. "Perhaps we should return."

Mariah nodded, but kept her gaze trained on the ground in front of them. He was uncertain what he had said to make her so pensive, but it seemed a prudent idea to figure it out as it seemed it and Lady G were the only subjects that would keep her from giggling.

They both walked back to where Reginald sat on the rug.

The waiter had left, presumably to fetch the ices Reginald had purchased.

"How was your turn?" Reginald asked.

"The crowds are much sparser towards the center of the park." Colin dropped to his knees and positioned himself on the rug next to Reginald.

He watched as Lady Mariah gracefully sat, spreading her gown out over her legs that were curled up beneath her.

"What about you, Mar? How did you enjoy your walk with Lord Heatherton?" A hint of a smile turned Reginald's lips.

"It was very pleasant. Except for those times when we ventured out from beneath the trees." She seemed to look everywhere but at Colin. Had he said something wrong? Was she angry with him? He shrugged his shoulder. Why did he care, aside from him not liking to be the source of contention? Except, perhaps, when it came to Rags. But then, who did not enjoy contending with Rags?

"Was there any trouble in sending Lady Stoke off?"

Reginald shook his head. "No. She and her maid were ready earlier than I had thought." Reginald sighed. "I only wish I could have returned with her. I dislike the thought of her traveling so far without protection."

Lady Mariah let out a guffaw, but then snapped her mouth closed. When Reginald looked at her pointedly, she spoke. "I am certain she will encounter no problems, Regi."

Perhaps speaking of Lady Stoke was not the most prudent idea. It seemed both brother and sister became agitated at the topic, although for completely different reasons.

Finally, after what seemed a rather long and tedious time, the waiter returned with a tray of ices. He gave one to each of them, along with a spoon. "When you finish, please wave me over and I shall return the dishes to the shop."

Reginald withdrew several coins, but Colin stopped him before he could place them in the waiter's hand. "I invited myself on this outing. The least I can do is pay for the refreshment." He handed over several coins to the waiter before Reginald could object. "Thank you. I know you must be near bedlam, with the size of the crowd."

The man looked at the coins in his hand, a quick smile turning his lips. "Thank you, sir." Then he hurried back across the road to the shop.

"There is pineapple, pistachio, and lavender-flavored ices." Each small glass bowl held the fruit-shaped ice, except for the lavender, which was shaped as a flower. But in the heat of the afternoon, all the ices were already drooping.

"Lady Mariah, I believe you should be the first to pick." Colin gestured toward the bowls.

"I should like the pineapple unless someone else wishes to have it."

Reginald reached down and handed her the pale yellow ice and a spoon. He then looked at Colin. "And which one do you want?"

Colin narrowed his eyes at Reginald. It was a tricky situation.

Would Reginald take the one Colin said he wanted just as a joke? Or would it be better for Colin to offer Reginald the first choice? Either way, it seemed likely one of them would end up with an ice they did not want.

"Why do you not pick first? After all, I am the one imposing on your outing."

Reginald grunted. "It's no imposition, I promise you. But if you insist, I believe I shall take the lavender."

Colin released a breath and grinned. It was just as he had hoped. The pistachio ice was his.

Lady Mariah sat quietly eating, a pensive look on her face. What occupied her mind so completely that she could not laugh or giggle? Again, he wished he knew so he might employ it in the future.

# Chapter Seven

COLIN SETTLED HIMSELF IN A CHAIR ACROSS FROM REGINALD'S desk. Rags, Ponsy, and Ben took the seats to Colin's left and Charlie and Cort to his right. Each man held a glass in their hand. The room was silent for a moment as they all settled into their chairs and sipped their brandy.

Colin released a breath, feeling at home among the men he'd called friends since they were boys at Harrow. He pulled at his collar, loosening his cravat just enough to be comfortable, and leaned back in his chair. "Since you married, Reg, we have spent more time in your study than we have at the club. Perhaps we should let our memberships go."

Cort crossed one leg over the other and twisted his glass around on the arm of the chair. "I am not forfeiting mine just yet." He cleared his throat, a confident look on his face. "I have my chair there just to the right softness." He wiggled around in his seat. "Which I cannot boast of this one."

Reginald cast a bland look at Cort from over the top of his glass. He turned his gaze to Colin. "How was your turn yesterday afternoon with Mariah? What could you possibly have to speak about with her?"

Colin didn't lift his eyes, focusing on the liquid in his glass.

What was he to say? It was not as if he could tell Reginald that they had discussed how Mariah disliked Reginald's wife. He took another sip, hoping to delay the conversation. Had they discussed anything else?

He looked up and smiled. "We were discussing her anticipation of seeing Lady G when you both return to Staffordshire." He tilted his head to the side. "Perhaps I'll invite her to walk in the park a time or two. Just to help her along."

Reginald lowered his glass to the desktop and stared at Colin. "Whatever are you babbling about? Mar . . . sad Lady G has left?" He let out a chuckle. "You must be in jest."

In jest? What was that supposed to mean?

Reginald's eyes widened slightly. "If you believe the story that Mariah has any affections for that animal, I have a rare treasure I wish to sell you."

Rags let out a guffaw, and both Cort and Ben's lips twitched. Ponsy and Charlie looked at Colin pityingly.

Colin scooted back in his chair, sitting stiff backed. "What do you mean, *if I believed the story*?" He shook his head. "I saw her affection for the animal myself when she walked with it in the park. There was a moment of frustration when the dog became tangled in a bush, but that was to be expected. All other indications were that she was in earnest."

A smile spread across Reginald's face.

"What? Why are you smiling like a jackanapes?" Colin's skin felt moist and itchy.

Reginald shook his head. "I had simply never believed Mariah suitable for the stage. But it seems I may have been wrong." He threw his head back and laughed. "Mariah *loathes* Lady G. She did nothing but complain and scowl at the creature when Sarah brought her home. Indeed, that very morning before their walk in the park, I saw Mariah stomp her foot and send the dog scampering to safety behind Maxwell's legs."

Colin narrowed his eyes. A slow-burning sensation

simmered in the pit of his stomach, moving outward until the whole of him was hot. "You are saying she played me for a fool?"

"Surely not." Reginald shrugged, but his grin remained. "Did you fawn over the animal as you do with your pointers?"

"I do not fawn over my dogs, Reg." Colin shifted in his seat, not liking the amused expressions on all of his friends' faces.

"Yes, you do. It's rather unseemly." Rags looked bored with the conversation.

Colin slapped his hand down on the arm of the chair. "I can't believe I fell for it," he growled through gritted teeth.

"Come now. I cannot imagine she meant any harm. She likely didn't wish to disappoint you when she learned of your affinity for dogs. I assume you told her of your pointers?"

"And telling her of my pointers is permission for her to trick me?"

"Why would she wish to trick you? Have you earned her ire?" Ben asked from the next seat over.

"No. That turn in the park was the first time I have uttered more than three sentences to her at a time. Even when we danced, I hardly spoke to her."

Cort chuckled with the glass at his lips. "Yes, it certainly sounds as if you have done nothing to earn her displeasure."

"Then you are on her side? Just because I have had little to say to her, you believe she has a right to lie and deceive me?"

"Since when did a woman need an excuse to lie and deceive?" Rags added.

Reginald sighed. "I cannot imagine she set out to lie to you. My sister may be a lot of things, but malicious is not one of them."

"Then why did she do it?" Colin lurched from the chair, unable to sit and think at the same time. He needed to do something—exercise the anger brewing inside him.

"Perhaps she was flirting? Mariah believes herself very proficient in the subject."

"Since when did lying become a means of flirting?"

Reginald leaned back in his chair, lacing his fingers together behind his neck. "Don't be an idiot. Saying she had something in common with you—that is the flirtation."

"But she has nothing in common with me. Why would she assert it if it were not true?"

"How should I know? I am not an expert on the female population."

Charlie cleared his throat. "You are the only one of us married, so I believe that makes you the most qualified among us to make an assumption."

"That's rather pitiful," Ponsy leaned forward and placed his glass on the tray on Reginald's desk.

"I don't know about the rest of you, but I know plenty about women. How do you think I have avoided them for so long?" Rags drained the rest of his drink and looked expectantly at the rest of them.

"No, Rags, I believe it is your personality that has kept them at bay. It has nothing to do with your knowledge." Cort grinned widely at Rags.

"You're a nodcock, Cort." Rags growled.

"Before we descend into a round of name-calling, why do we not just accept that none of us are particularly knowledgeable when it comes to women?" Reginald held up his hand.

Colin opened his mouth and Reginald shot him a look.

"Even when that woman is my sister. Trust me, if I knew why she did half the things she does, my life would be much easier. And perhaps she would not be at odds with my wife."

Colin clasped his hands behind his back, not feeling any better after Reginald's stumbled excuses for his sister. Lady Mariah had treated him very ill, and he could not let it stand. He had to do something. Something to show her he knew of her deceit and would not stand for it.

He stared at his friends. Although, he could not help but wonder why she had cast her devilish plan on him. Why not Cort or Rags? They were both rather irritating, albeit in completely different ways. Why him? Was it simply because he had met her in the park? If Cort had been the one to happen upon her, would he be the one in this position now?

Regardless of why or how he had become her chosen target, it did not matter. He would see that he brought her down a notch or two. He would show her he was not the kind of person who she could just trick and play with on her whim.

But what could he do? He could not simply approach her and tell her he had discovered her ruse. No, he needed a plan. One that was just as devious as she was.

"Come now, Colin. Don't be angry with her." Reginald leaned forward in his chair, his elbows resting on the desk.

A grin spread across Colin's face, and he snapped his fingers. He knew exactly what he needed to do. "Not to fear, Reg. I don't get angry," he leveled his stare at his friend. "I get even."

"Oh, no." Reginald jumped up from his seat and scooted around the desk. "I don't like that look in your eyes. What do you have planned, Colin?"

Colin dropped his head to the side with a dull look on his face. "You have nothing to worry about. I'm a gentleman. I will do no harm to your sister."

Reginald shook his head. "I do not feel comforted by your words."

"I wouldn't either," Ben agreed.

Colin glared at Ben over his shoulder, then turned back to Reginald. "I give you my word as a gentleman, Reg. No harm will come to Lady Mariah—"

Reginald opened his mouth.

"Or to her reputation."

Reginald's shoulders relaxed, and he stared hard at Colin for a moment before he returned to his seat and sat down. "I suppose Mariah has a bit of recompense coming and as long as you promise no harm to her or her reputation, I will not stand in your way."

Colin raised a brow. "Did you really believe I could do her harm?"

Reginald looked sheepish. "I suppose not. Although Mariah has a knack for making me do things I never thought possible."

Charlie laughed. "Hmmm. I thought it was your wife who did that."

Reginald grinned. "Perhaps she does too. But the things Sarah drives me to do are much more diverting than Mariah's."

Not for the first time, Colin regretted missing the first half of the Season when Reginald and Sarah had fallen in love. Had Colin been there, perhaps their little league would not be down a member.

Reginald shrugged and looked back at Colin. "It is as I said in the park yesterday. I trust you."

Colin grinned at his friend. If Reginald knew the plan, he would likely not feel such relief. But Colin could not feel any remorse for what he was about to do. After all, Reginald was not completely innocent. He had excused his sister's behavior repeatedly. And it seemed only proper Colin should punish them together.

# Chapter Eight

MARIAH DESCENDED THE STAIRCASE ON HER WAY TO THE breakfast room. She walked past the entryway table, stopping to examine the bouquets of flowers. They had been there for three days, but still, she did not tire of seeing and smelling them. She grinned as she rubbed a petal between her fingers. At least ten bouquets filled the table. Mr. Weebly, Lord Pingree, Mr. Roundy, and Mr. Cleverly. Every gentleman she had danced with had been represented—except one.

Colin.

Mariah didn't know why he had not sent a bouquet. Was it because he felt the flowers were unnecessary because she was only Reginald's sister, or was there some other reason? Even Lord Ragsdale had sent her flowers after being forced to save her from Lord Muckrake several months ago.

She nearly turned away when a flower caught her eye. It was a new bouquet. But when had it come and who could it be from? She smiled coyly.

Tilting and twisting her head to the side, she noticed a cream-colored card tucked among the arrangement. Her pulse picked up as she dug into the flowers, careful not to destroy the delicate petals.

She released a triumphant sigh as she withdrew the card and saw the name scrawled across it. *Lord Heatherton.* Colin was represented after all. It was vexing he had not signed it with his Christian name. But it made sense that he would not because she might not be the only person to see the card.

She hugged it to her chest as a tingle skittered over her skin. She knew the flowers were simply an expectation and likely meant nothing, but she could not help her excitement.

He'd been less conversant when they danced at the ball, and he had not spoken to her after they ate their ices in Berkeley Square. But Colin never had been one to talk overly much. Especially while dancing. She had watched him enough over the years to know that much to be true.

She lifted the card and her heart slowed as she read. There was only an apology for the lateness of the flowers and the usual pleasantries. It was nothing special. *She* was nothing special. As she tossed the card on the table, she noticed writing on the back. Looking side to side, she flipped the card over and read the message.

*Be so kind as to meet me in the park at two at our usual place. I have a surprise.*

*H*

Mariah didn't even try to contain her excitement. *A rendezvous with Colin*! She let out a delighted squeal. *H* was not as intimate as Colin, but it was better than his full title.

It was more than she'd hoped for. It was wholly improper. Some might even call it scandalous, which only made Mariah want to go more.

Sarah would surely disapprove. But Sarah was not there to lecture her any longer.

A shiver ran through Mariah's body. *A surprise*? What kind of surprise could he have for her? She could not think what it might be. But she surely intended to be at the park precisely at two to find out.

"Good morning, Lady Mariah." Maxwell stepped out from a side corridor.

She discreetly tucked the card into the cuff of her sleeve. "Good morning, Maxwell." She turned toward the butler, trying to keep her excitement in check. There was no need for the entire house to know of her rendezvous with Colin. "Maxwell, when did this bouquet arrive?"

Maxwell squinted, trying to see the bouquet in question. "They came just this morning, my lady."

Mariah nodded, grinning like a ninny. She needed to school her features better, else her secret would be out before the meeting ever took place. "It is better late than never, is it not?"

"Indeed, my lady." Maxwell looked at her with the barest hint of a creased brow. "You received many lovely bouquets."

Mariah glanced over, her gaze focusing on the small bouquet from Colin. "Yes, I did."

Maxwell bowed to her as he moved off in another direction.

She moved to the breakfast room and filled her plate. Then, sneaking up the back staircase, she took it to her room. She did not wish for Reginald to join her. He would surely notice her shaking hands and breathless voice.

Positioning herself on the window seat, she placed the tray on the opposite end. She stared out the window at the street below as she picked at the roll in her hand and thought about the surprise Colin promised. She had no notion what it could be. Would it be more flowers? She scrunched up her nose. While she rather enjoyed flowers, she had ample bouquets on the entry table. Although, if the flowers were from Colin, she would graciously accept them and bring them up to her room to enjoy. Still, flowers seemed to show a certain lack of imagination. And she could not imagine Colin lacking in anything.

She released a sigh. Sometimes she wished she and Sarah were not still at odds. Indeed, more than sometimes she wished it. She missed Sarah—missed having someone to talk to...to confide in. With her fight with Sarah and her mother gone, Mariah was quite alone. All she had was Reginald, and he was not a replacement for a best friend. She could not imagine discussing flirting with Colin with Reginald. It was a ridiculous notion.

She shook off the troubling thoughts, preferring to dwell instead on Colin and his surprise. But what else could it be if not flowers? Her stomach danced, making the tea slosh from side to side. What if he'd composed a poem for her? She let out a quiet giggle. Or even better . . . a poem *about* her. What would he write? Would he mention her sun-kissed blonde hair? Compare her eyes to amber or her skin to porcelain. She cringed slightly, hoping he had more originality than that.

She was not usually fond of poems. She'd read the work of Coleridge and Wordsworth, but if she was being honest, she did not fully understand them.

However, if the poem were from Colin, she would surely love it. How could she not? She sank down onto the cushion and leaned back against the window cove. Staring out at the street and then back at the clock, she watched as each second slowly ticked by. Gracious, could the morning last any longer? Did the clock not understand she had an appointment with destiny?

Mariah walked as quickly as was proper to the park, but it proved rather difficult as her excitement drove her feet to move faster.

Miriam hurried along behind, trying to keep up. "Must we walk with such haste, my lady?" She puffed out a breath.

Mariah hadn't told her maid why they were going to the

park—only that she was feeling restless and needed to take a turn. She could hardly tell her maid that her restlessness had a schedule to keep. And they were much too early for the fashionable hour at Hyde Park.

She pulled to a stop and placed a hand on her hip. "I read in the *Lady's Companion* that brisk walking is good for the heart," she justified.

"I think my heart is already spent, my lady." Miriam placed a hand on her chest.

"You are simply being dramatic, Miriam," Mariah chided and resumed her quick pace. "You may rest once we reach the park."

The park came into view and Mariah pulled up, slowing her pace to a more sedate speed. It would not do to have Colin there early and have him witness her obvious excitement.

Miriam, obviously not paying heed, bumped into Mariah's back. "Oof. Begging your pardon, my lady."

Mariah released a deep sigh and placed her hands on her hips again. But she tamped down her frustration with the girl and refrained from lecturing her. Miriam was new to the position and there were obviously some areas in which she still needed training. "Not to worry, Miriam. It was an accident."

The girl dipped her head. "Thank you, my lady."

"Why do you not rest on that bench over there?" She motioned to a bench just far enough away that Miriam could see Mariah, but far enough as to hinder any eavesdropping.

Miriam nodded and walked over to the bench, sinking down with a heavy sigh.

Mariah glanced over at her maid. Once she was sure the girl was situated and unable to hear a conversation, Mariah casually strolled over to where she'd met Colin the other day. She glanced around. They were alone in this part of the park. A man with his back to her bent over, picking something up off the ground, farther up the path. But he was the only other person in sight.

While it was not the prettiest part of the park, it was *their spot*. Which meant it was now Mariah's favorite location.

She clasped her hands in front of her lips. *They had a spot.* This surely meant something! She held back the squeal hovering in her throat and bit her cheek. One didn't think about a location in such a way if it did not mean something—if they didn't mean to talk about it with their children and perhaps even grandchildren. She closed her eyes for a moment, envisioning what their children would look like.

"Are you too tired to continue with our walk, my lady?" Miriam asked, dread in her voice.

Mariah pulled herself out of her dreams and looked around the area. "Are you ready to return home already? I thought you were still resting." But Mariah did not hear Miriam's answer as the man turned around and her breath caught in her throat.

It was Colin.

He was not in precisely *their spot*, but Mariah was not about to trifle with the details.

She let out a slow, breathy sigh. His hair was perfectly imperfect, in the way it swept off his brow, creating a small little hair wave. And his eyes? She could not actually see his eyes, as he was not looking at her and he was not close enough. But she knew they were clear and beautiful, just as they always were.

He stood off to the side, petting a small white and black dog tethered to the leg of a nearby bench.

Mariah raised her brows.

He had already discovered a dog? Where was the dog's owner? She had thought they were going to be alone, but she did not see anyone else. Maybe the owner was hidden from view by a bush or a large tree.

She returned her gaze to Colin. Just how long had he been

waiting for her? The thought that he might wait for her brought a chill to her skin, even in the repressive heat. Men did not wait for ladies they did not care about, did they?

Colin played with the dog—it chased him in one direction and then the other. Gads, he certainly liked dogs. Although he seemed a sensible man in all other respects. She stayed still, watching him for a moment. While she had no affinity for the animals, the way Colin played with the mongrel brought Mariah's thoughts back to their imaginary children. Surely a man who was so kind and gentle with a dog would also be a kind and gentle father, would he not?

She took a step forward, and he looked up.

He smiled, but it differed from what it had been the last time. Perhaps it was the smile of desire? She shook that thought from her head. She was being ridiculous. Perhaps Sarah had a point about Mariah's lack of decorum. She smirked. Certainly not.

"Lady Mariah." He sounded happy to see her.

She studied him. Did he look as if he'd written her a poem?

"Thank you for meeting me. I know it was most improper of me to ask you to come and likely even more improper that I purchased a surprise for you. But the moment I saw it, I knew you must have it. And I could not let another day pass without presenting it to you."

He had purchased her a gift, then? The surprise seemed unlikely to be a poem. But what could it be? A cameo? Perhaps a comb?

Mariah batted her lashes. "Lord Heatherton, you're too kind. I can hardly imagine what this surprise could be. But I would be lying."

Did he just cringe? Why would he cringe when she was expressing her excitement?

She brushed it away as her imagination.

"I must say, I am pleased to hear you have been thinking

of me." Was she too untoward? Perhaps. Which seemed to be further proof that Sarah was not so far off. Drat it all.

He flicked up a grin, and Mariah's toes curled. Lawks, she could look on that smile forever.

"Close your eyes, my lady, and I'll fetch the surprise."

Mariah pinched her eyes shut, then opened them only slightly as she could not stop herself.

"No peeking." His voice was stern but held a playful note. He could be playful with her. How delightful!

She squeezed her eyes tightly, not wishing for him to change his mind because she could not follow directions. Her stomach was a mess of flutters and twists, and she thanked the stars that she had not agreed to return to the country with Sarah.

A cool strip lay across her hand, and Mariah closed her fingers around it. What was it? It felt as if it were leather or some other stiff material. It was not a cameo or even a comb. What could Colin have bought her? She was at a loss.

"There you are, my lady. You may open your eyes now." There was humor in his voice.

Mariah grinned as she opened her eyes and looked at her hand. A red leash sat tucked within her fist. Her gaze followed it down to the collar. A collar that fit snuggly around the neck…of a dog.

Mariah gasped.

*A dog*? Who gave a lady a dog?

She looked up at him, her brow knit with confusion. "It's a dog."

He grinned, but it held a slightly wicked edge to it. "Indeed. You seemed so saddened by the loss of your dear Lady G, I could not stop myself from finding you a replacement. Someone with such love for an animal should not have to be deprived of the company for a whole fortnight. But now, you shall have your own. A dog you may keep with you always."

Mariah's mouth dropped open. He'd bought her a dog to replace Lady G? Was this some kind of joke? "I, uh…that is —" She didn't know what to say. What did one say to the gift of a dog?

The animal sniffed at Mariah's hem before jumping up on her legs and sniffing the hand hanging down at her side.

She pushed the furry pest back to the ground and noted with irritation the paw prints on her gown. What in the name of all that was holy was happening?

She swallowed. "My lord." She licked her lips as her dreams came crashing down around her. Compared to this, flowers seemed the most proper gift there was. "You're too kind, but I'm afraid I can't accept such a gift. It's too. . .extravagant."

He shook his head, his lovely blue gray eyes dancing bright with excitement. How could she not love the gift when he was so happy to buy it for her? "Indeed, you can. Just seeing the happiness on your face makes any cost worthwhile."

She put a hand to her forehead. What was she to do with a dog? Had she not just congratulated herself on the removal of Lady G? She'd had barely any peace, and now another beast was nipping at her ankles.

The leash tugged, and Mariah tightened her grasp as the dog moved toward a tree, barking at an innocent squirrel.

What could Colin be thinking? Who gave a flea-ridden animal as a gift?

Mariah bit at her lip. Oh, goodness. It was her own fault, was it not?

He thought he was being kind because she lied to him and made him believe she liked these mongrels. The gesture only made her love him more. But how . . .? What . . .? Indeed, she was truly at a loss. It seemed she could only hope to convince Colin to keep the animal for himself.

"My lord. I can't accept." She took a step forward with the leash outstretched.

He shook his head at her. "I must insist you do." He raised a brow. "Come. I cannot allow you to be so downhearted after losing such a dear friend." He bent and lifted the dog into his arms, scratching it beneath the chin. The dog's tail beat frantically against his belly. "And look at the rascal. Is he not the most handsome dog you've seen?" He leaned forward and placed the dog in her arms. "He isn't a pug, but I thought him even better. He is a fox terrier."

Mariah put her hands around the dog's middle and held his squirming body away from her. His head moved from side to side as he tried to lick at her fingers and hands. "A fox terrier?" She knew not what to do with a pug. A fox terrier was no different.

"A wire fox terrier, to be precise. He will make a very fine pet but will also prove quite capable as a hunting dog. It's why I chose him for you."

"You believe I enjoy hunting?" How had he come to that idea?

The little dog was mostly white, with a large black band around his middle and light brown patches on his ears and over one eye. His hair felt softer than Lady G's and had a bit of a wave to it. If she were a dog-loving sort of person, she might think the animal rather agreeable. Even without being such a person, she could concede to a certain handsomeness. Still, she could do little more than scrunch up her nose. She could not keep this thing—*would not* keep it. But how was she to be rid of it?

She pouted. "I'm afraid Reginald won't look favorably on me bringing home a dog. He isn't overly fond of Lady G, and I believe he was looking forward to the peace that comes with her absence."

Colin stepped forward, petting the dog on the head and pushing him lightly toward her. "I'll be more than happy to speak to Stoke. He is fond of you, and I'm sure he won't begrudge you your dog."

Mariah gritted her teeth. Why was he not understanding?

She held the dog in her arms, leaning her head back as far as she could to avoid his incessant licking. "He is terribly busy, my lord. I do not wish to bother him."

Colin grasped her elbow and moved her toward the entrance to the park. "I'm certain Stoke will make time for you, my lady. Come along, we will seek him out now."

Mariah allowed him to lead her from the park, certain she liked the feel of his hand on her arm but uncertain of the circumstances under which it was happening.

# Chapter Nine

Lady Mariah stumbled along the walking path next to Colin. He grinned to himself. Her response had been just what he had hoped. Indeed, he suspected he would have several good laughs whenever he thought on her face when she opened her eyes and saw the dog at the end of the leash. He had never quite seen such an expression of horror followed by feigned delight.

He chuckled as he held onto her elbow and led her toward Berkeley Square.

She looked up at him. "What are you laughing at?" She eyed him with suspicion.

He grinned down at her and then motioned to the dog, sniffing at everything they passed. "He is just such a curious animal. I was merely laughing at him."

She stared hard at him for a moment longer and then glanced down at the dog. "Yes, he is rather like Lady G in that regard."

"Well now, that is an unexpected advantage, is it not? Will that not make your separation from Lady G that much easier if you can find commonalities between the two animals?"

Lady Mariah's nose flared ever so slightly and Colin bit his cheek to hold back the laughter.

She stopped abruptly with a sigh as the dog pulled the leash taut, sniffing the closest tree.

Colin's chest collided with her arm.

She glanced up at him and he cleared his throat. Why did she have to look so handsome? It made it more difficult to relish her discomfort. He glanced away, determined not to feel any guilt for what he had done. She deserved every minute of disapprobation.

Lady Mariah tugged on the leash. "Come on—" She glanced over at Colin. "What is his name?"

Colin shrugged and gave her a wide smile. "That's for you to decide. He is your dog." Again he bit his cheek to stop the laugh yearning to come out.

"Come along . . . dog." Lady Mariah sounded even more irritated than she had been the first time he had seen her with Lady G and the dog had run into the bush.

It was perhaps the longest walk he had ever endured from Hyde Park back to Berkeley Square. But also, quite possibly, the most enjoyable one.

He said very little, preferring to watch as Lady Mariah tried to act the part of a caring dog owner, while completely perplexed by the animal.

After stopping by at least a dozen bushes and barking at anyone who passed, they stopped in front of Reginald's London Townhouse. Colin stopped just behind her. He placed his hand on the small of her back, convinced that if he did not, she would likely bolt like a skittish horse. And he intended to see this through. She would either admit her lie, or be forced to accept the care of the dog.

And it rather intrigued him to see what Reginald would say. Would he tell his sister of Colin's ploy to get even with her? Or would he go along with the ruse?

Lady Mariah thrust the leash at him. "You may as well

hold this. I'll need to remove my spencer. And since it's unlikely the animal will stay for long, I think it best that you keep him with you."

Colin shrugged and grasped hold of the leash before picking up the dog and placing him under his arm. He held out his hand and motioned Mariah to the front door.

"Good afternoon, Robert." She addressed the footman at the door. Pulling at the tips of her gloves, she yanked them from her hands.

She glanced at him from under her lashes and Colin looked away, focusing on the "gift" in his arms instead. The little dog licked at his chin and Colin chuckled. His laugh grew when he saw Lady Mariah's face. She looked as if she might turn out her breakfast upon the carpets.

Although, when her gaze shifted from the dog's licks and found Colin's, he leaned back slightly at the look of adoration he saw on her face. His stomach rippled in a most unwelcome way.

Colin placed the dog on the floor, and it ran around his legs, barking and nipping.

"What the devil is all that noise?" Reginald appeared on the upper floor landing. His mouth dropped open when he saw the dog jumping up on Colin's legs. But then his lips turned up into a grin. "Colin." His voice held a hint of censure. "What have you there?" Colin could hear the sarcasm in his friend's voice. Did it mean his ruse was up? Was Reginald going to put a stop to it?

Colin ran his tongue over his lips and took a step forward, lifting his chin. "When I saw how downtrodden Lady Mariah had become over the removal of Lady G, I knew I must remedy the situation at once." He glanced down at the dog, still running in circles around his and Lady Mariah's legs, the leash trailing along behind him. "I hope you do not mind, Reg. But I bought her a dog of her own." He glanced over at Lady Mariah and winked. He was uncertain where the wink had come from. But he could not regret it. It felt right for the situation.

Reginald's brow rose high, and he sucked his bottom lip between his teeth. "Remedy the situation? By purchasing her a dog?"

Colin squared his shoulders and nodded, glancing at Lady Mariah from the corner of his eye.

She sent a pleading look at her brother. Was she willing him with her thoughts to say no to the gift?

Colin raised his own brow and looked at Reginald. "Indeed."

Reginald moved slowly down the staircase, his face a mask. Colin had known Reginald long enough to know that was his thinking face. But what was there to think about? He came even with Colin and paused. "Well played, Colin," he murmured.

Did that mean the ruse was up? Was Reginald going to expose Colin?

Reginald looked from Lady Mariah to Colin and then at the dog. Both Colin and Lady Mariah stood still, as if waiting for a judge to deliver his verdict.

Colin stepped forward, not wishing to leave his fate in Reginald's hands. "Come now, Stoke. You can't disappoint Lady Mariah. Please, I beg of you, *as a friend,* to allow her to keep him."

The dog barked and wagged his tail as if he were giving his approval to the plan.

Reginald sucked in a deep breath, apparently ready to give his decree. Who did he think he was? Caesar? "I'm amiable to you keeping the dog, Mar."

Colin grinned wider.

Lady Mariah's eyes widened. "But Regi—" She looked as though she were about to lunge at him—to force him to change his mind.

"However," Reginald paused rather dramatically and then

turned to Colin. "It may only stay if it receives proper training." Reginald turned his attention to Colin. "And as you're the one to give the gift, I think it only right that you help Mar with the task."

The grin fell away from Colin's face. What did Reginald mean by that? Surely he did not mean for Colin to train the dog. He stepped forward. "Come now, Reg. I do not have time for such things."

"Nor do I, Colin." Reginald narrowed his eyes. "Are you implying that you do not wish to spend time with my sister?"

Colin hesitated. How was he to answer such a question without causing offense to both Reginald and Lady Mariah, but still excuse himself from training the animal?

Colin sighed deeply. There was nothing for it. He was trapped.

He clamped his mouth shut, his jaw tightening. "Very well. I'll help train the dog." He bent over and plucked up the leash off the floor. Holding it out to Lady Mariah, he took a step back. "I will send you word when we shall begin." He raised a brow. "I hope by then you will have given him a proper name."

Lady Mariah's brow creased, but it smoothed out and she smiled, her lashes fluttering again. Lud, what had he just agreed to?

"It sounds very diverting, my lord. What shall we teach him first?"

"Put an end to his incessant barking." Reginald clasped his hands behind his back and turned on his heel. "I will be in my study, Mar. I'll meet you here at seven to go to the Bambroughs' card party."

Mariah nodded. Once her brother left the entryway, she turned to Colin. "It looks as though we shall spend much more time together."

He sighed. "Indeed."

She frowned and his stomach twisted. He should not

completely blame Lady Mariah for his displeasure. After all, it was not her idea for Colin to train the animal.

The dog barked, and Lady Mariah looked down. "Hush now. . .dog."

Colin shook his head. Was it safe for him to leave her alone with the animal? Would she mistreat it? He sighed, hoping that her desire for his good opinion would keep the dog safe—at least until she admitted her lies. Besides, he had never seen Lady Mariah lift a hand to anyone or anything. And he knew Reginald would not allow her to mistreat the animal. He dipped his head and turned toward the door, confident that the dog would be safe. "Good day, Lady Mariah."

As he left Stoke's townhouse, Colin shook his head. He looked up at his driver. "To Brooks's."

He settled onto the bench as the carriage lurched forward. What would the gents think of his predicament? And what would they think of Reginald's part in it all?

# Chapter Ten

Mariah watched Colin's back until the door closed behind him. Once he was out of sight, she clapped her hands together, dropped her head back, and laughed as she turned in a circle. While it may have been a dog, Colin had given her a gift. A gift he had purchased with only her in mind. And a gift that ensured they would be together—at least for the short term.

She intended to make that short-term count. By the end of this mongrel's training, Colin would be deeply in love with her. She would brook no opposition. It was just the opportunity she'd been waiting for.

She practically glided across the floor and slid the leash into the footman's hand. "Robert, please do something with him."

She turned toward the steps but stopped when she saw Reginald leaning against the corridor wall, watching her.

"Do not think you're going to foist the care of that dog onto one of the servants. He is yours, and you will take care of him."

She placed her hands on her hips and pouted. "But Regi, I

don't even want it. Why did you not tell Lord Heatherton that I could not keep him? This is all your fault."

Reginald pushed off the wall. He extended a hand toward Robert. The footman scurried over and relinquished the leash, disappearing back into the cloakroom. Reginald stood in front of Mariah and handed the leash to her. "Do not blame your troubles on me. I'm not the one who lied about my love of Lady G."

"I didn't think he would—" She paused. "Wait a moment. How did you know I pretended to love Lady G?"

"Colin's comments seemed to indicate that you had discussed it at some length." He tilted his head to the side, his shoulders dropping. "And yesterday while the gents were here, he may have mentioned how sad you were that Sarah took Lady G back to Staffordshire." He raised a brow. "Imagine my surprise when you have done nothing but complain about the animal."

Mariah's eyes widened. "Did you tell him it was not true?"

Reginald shrugged. "Of course I did. I didn't realize until it was too late that it was part of your plan to trap him into matrimony."

"Did you tell him that was my plan?" Mariah's voice squeaked and her skin heated.

Reginald shook his head. "I was uncertain that was the case until just now."

Mariah's shoulders fell. Colin knew she had lied? But if he knew, why had he given—her eyes widened, and her hands shook at her side.

He'd done it on purpose.

She stared down at the little devil at her feet. This was a spite dog. A gift simply to vex her.

She fisted her hands and put them back on her hips. "I want nothing to do with the mangy cur. Heatherton did not intend him as a kind gift, but as a punishment." Her head shook, even as tears filled her lids. How could he be so cruel as to make her believe he thought her something special when all it was to him was a joke? Could she enjoy their forced time together, knowing he had not even meant the dog as a kind act? "I'll not stand for it." Her voice quivered, which only proved to increase her anger.

Reginald tsked. "It's not the dog's fault the two of you have started some sort of war."

Mariah paused. She and Colin were at war? How had that happened? She had started off the day with thoughts of poems and love. And now she was at war. She didn't like it. It left her feeling shaky and somewhat nauseous.

She stared down at the dog, unclenching her hands. What was she to do with him? If she got rid of the dog, she would miss out on her chance to spend time with Colin. But keeping the dog would be a constant reminder that she was nothing special in his eyes. Indeed, she was worse than that. She was an object of contempt.

Reginald stepped closer to her. "Perhaps if instead of ridding yourself of the dog, you learned to like him—even love him…" He paused. "Would that not be the best punishment for Colin? If his gift—which he intended to vex you—actually became a gift you loved and treasured?" Reginald shrugged. "Indeed, that would be the best revenge."

Mariah's shoulders sagged. "But how can I, Regi? They are such vile creatures." The dog seemed to have spent all its energy and now lay on the ground at her feet. Mariah stared at him. Perhaps he was not as terrible as she thought. He did look rather sweet with his eyes closed.

"He seems to me to be a good sort of fellow. He simply has some rough edges. But with a little training, I believe you could smooth him out and grow to love him." He dropped his gaze to the floor but then looked up at her through his lashes. "He sounds a bit like someone else in this house."

Mariah glared at her brother. Was he inferring she had rough edges or that she was a dog? Neither scenario pleased her. How dare he.

Besides, what did he know about dogs? Or her, for that matter. She was not rough around the edges. She was the daughter of an earl. Besides, it was not as if his great wisdom had changed Lady G.

She sighed. But what choice did she have?

She kneeled in front of the dog, and he sat up, obviously anticipating a scratch or something else endearing. His tail thumped against the carpet, and his eyes held a hopefulness she'd never seen in Lady G's. That was a point in his favor.

Was Reginald right? If properly trained, might she come to like him? It seemed rather far-fetched.

The dog held her gaze, and his head tilted to the side. Curses. Why must he look at her that way? Her heart softened and she almost believed it might be possible to tolerate him.

"Very well. I'll try." She still glared, not wishing for Reginald to think he had won. "It would serve Lord Heatherton right." If she were truly evil—which she had not fully discounted—she would also circulate word of Colin's gift around the *ton*. In the eyes of most, such a gift would be an announcement of his intentions. It was tantamount to offering for her hand.

She grinned. If it would not ruin her far more than it did him, she would surely spread the rumors as fast as she could walk Rotten Row. But alas, she would have to be denied that pleasure.

She stood and tugged on the leash. "Come along . . . dog."

Reginald grunted. "Lud, Mar. He needs a name."

"A proper name takes time." Mariah squinted down at the dog. What should she call him? It must be perfect if she were to come to love him, as Reginald had said. There was no way she could fall in love with a stupidly named dog. She looked at him, sitting on his haunches and staring back at her.

Still, nothing came to mind.

A maid scurried past, and Reginald called out. "Penny, please have tea sent to the parlor." He looked at Mariah. "Do you wish to join me?"

Mariah nodded. "I shall be in shortly, but I wish to take the dog outside first. Mrs. Church will surely have apoplexy if he should soil the carpets in the parlor."

"A wise decision." Reginald grinned. "I knew you were up to the task, Mar."

A soft smile turned Mariah's lips. He thought her capable of something? She stood a little taller. It had been some time since anyone had thought her capable. Even if it was only to take care of a dog. "Thank you, Regi." She tipped her head at her brother as she passed him on her way to the terrace. "Come along, you mangy cur."

She paused at the doorway. "What shall I call you?" The dog tugged toward the doors and she followed along behind.

Slowly she walked around the gardens as he sniffed out each flower, bush, and tree. "How do you feel about the name Bob?" The dog moved along to the next bush without even looking up at her. "You disapprove of that name, then? Yes, I think it rather stupid as well." She shook her head in bewilderment. What was she doing speaking to a dog as if he understood her?

What did one name a dog, anyway? Lady Guinevere was a completely ridiculous name. But then, Lady G was a ridiculous dog. So she supposed it fit. But this dog in front of her was not ridiculous. He deserved to have a distinguished name. Or at the very least, something appropriate.

"What about Hero? Do you believe you will do anything heroic?" The dog continued to ignore her as he smelled out his new home. Looking at him, she didn't see him as the heroic type.

Mariah grinned. "What about Spite?" It certainly fit the situation. Spite might have been why Colin gave her the dog, but any ill will she had felt toward him was slipping away. Even after such a terrible present, she couldn't think of him as wholly bad.

Perhaps it was because she'd loved him for so long. Or perhaps it was because she thought him so handsome. Or perhaps—she sighed. Perhaps it was because she hoped he'd not done it completely out of spite. She wanted to believe that deep down, he hoped to convince her that not all dogs were deplorable so that perhaps she might also like his pointers.

Or that was the version she preferred. Because it gave her hope that perhaps he might love—or come to love—her.

The doors to the terrace opened, and a maid stepped out. "Tea is served, my lady," she called.

Mariah waved her hand to let the maid know she'd heard the message. Jiggling the leash, she prodded the dog. "Come on, now. Finish your business so we might go in for tea."

The dog finally obliged, then continued to sniff the next patch of flowers.

Mariah tugged him toward the terrace. "You need not sniff at every flower and bush today. You'll have plenty of opportunities."

Once inside, she settled on the couch opposite Reginald and the dog lay down at her feet.

The tea chest sat on the tray next to the steaming pot of water.

Mariah dropped the leash to the floor. It was close enough at hand that should a problem arise, she could handle it promptly. She withdrew the key from under her fichu, unlocked the tea box, then set about preparing their cups.

A plate of biscuits sat on the tray also, and Mariah leaned over, placing one on Reginald's plate. "Why did you ask for biscuits?"

He leaned back against the chair and took a sip. When he pulled the cup away from his lips, he smiled. "I spoke with Mr. Bambrough at the club this morning, and he said they'll not serve dinner until ten. I thought we could both use something to hold us over until then."

Mariah poured out her own tea and took a biscuit, nibbling on the end. "Perhaps you should have asked for more than just biscuits." She motioned to the single remaining biscuit on the plate. "Or perhaps more of them if we are to eat nothing else until ten."

She sat back, and in a flash, the dog lurched forward and claimed the lone biscuit.

"Mar! Your dog." Reginald sat forward, frowning disapprovingly.

"My dog? What about my biscuit?" She glared at the dog. "Perhaps you should tell Lord Heatherton you've changed your mind about keeping the little demon." Her earlier feelings of goodwill toward the dog waned.

Reginald leaned back and shook his head. "No. I think this is a good lesson for you on the evils of lying." He gave her a smug look.

Mariah sat back and stared at him. She wanted to refute what he said, but what could she say? It *was* her fault she was in this muddle.

She looked back at the empty biscuit plate and a smile came to her face. "I believe I have the perfect name for him." It was not the first time someone had stolen a biscuit from right beneath Mariah's nose.

*Mariah sat on the sofa, clutching her teacup, but her gaze stayed focused on the one remaining biscuit on the plate.*

*She wanted that biscuit.*

*She would have simply reached out and grabbed it, but her mother would object. It was the first time Mariah had been allowed to take tea with adults, even if the adults were only Regi and his friend, Lord Heatherton. Still, she didn't dare take the biscuit. At least not yet. If she did, it would certainly send her back to the nursery. And Mariah could not allow that to happen.*

*But if it was still there when Regi and his friend left, then surely her mother would not object.*

*She stared at the biscuit, willing it to remain. Glancing up at Regi and his friend, she sent silent warnings for them to leave it be.*

*The men—that was what her mother called them, but Mariah didn't believe she could ever think of Regi as a man—stood up to leave, and Mariah felt her chance coming closer.*

*"Thank you for your hospitality, Lady Stoke." Lord Heatherton bowed toward Mariah's mother, who dipped her head in silent acknowledgment.*

*The men turned to leave, and Mariah scooted to the edge of the sofa.*

*But just then, Lord Heatherton turned and plucked the biscuit off the table, eating the whole thing in a single bite.*

*Mariah's mouth dropped open, and a shocked squeak sounded. He had eaten her biscuit! How dare he steal it from right beneath her nose!*

*She glared at his back, hoping he felt her ire. He was no gentleman. He was nothing more than a . . .than a biscuit thief!*

Mariah dropped her head to the side, smiling. She hadn't thought of Colin as a biscuit thief—or "Biscuit" as the years went by—in a long time. She had only called him such in her mind or muttered it under her breath when he displeased her, which had been oft in her younger years.

Mariah looked down at her dog. Perhaps Colin and his spite gift had something in common.

"Well, what is this perfect name? I am all a flutter in anticipation." Reginald's lips twitched.

Mariah sat up straight and lifted her chin along with a single brow. "I believe I shall call him Biscuit."

Reginald looked at her as if she'd gone mad. "Biscuit? That's quite possibly the most idiotic name I have ever heard. Unless, of course, you're six years old."

Mariah grinned and patted the dog on the head. "I do not care what you say. He is my dog, and I have decided he shall be called Biscuit." She clucked her tongue as she stood.

"Come along, Biscuit. Let us see if Mrs. Leach has any other food to sustain us until supper." The dog stood and followed her several paces.

She glanced over her shoulder. "You see? He likes the name."

# Chapter Eleven

*How had this happened?*

When Colin purchased the dog for Lady Mariah, he'd done it as retribution for her deception. She'd been the one in the wrong, yet he was being forced to help her train the animal. Had she even named it yet?

He lifted the knocker and took a step back. Pulling his watch from his pocket, he checked the time. How long would it take before he could make his excuses and be on his way? The Season was winding down and Colin did not wish to be engaged in this task for the rest of his time in London.

But it was too late to cry off now. Or was it? They had not begun their training. Perhaps he could speak to Reginald and be on his way to Brooks's before eleven.

The butler appeared in the doorway. "Good day, my lord."

"Is Lord Stoke at home? I wish to speak to him."

The butler opened the door wide. "I was told you were coming to see Lady Mariah, my lord."

Colin rubbed his thumb along the side of his finger, soothing his frustrations. "I'm helping Lady Mariah after speaking to Lord Stoke." Unless he could convince Reginald that this plan was ill-conceived.

The butler nodded. "I shall see if his lordship is at home."

"You need not ask, Maxwell. I shall take Lord Heatherton to my study." Reginald leaned against the wall of the entryway, his arms folded across his chest, and his brow arched.

"Very good, my lord." Maxwell bowed and moved toward the cloakroom.

"I thought you were here to help Mariah train that beast you bought her."

Colin bristled at the inference that perhaps he would not keep his word, even though that was precisely what he wished to do. "I am, but I wished to speak with you first." He followed his friend down the corridor. Although, could he really consider Reginald a friend any longer? Friends did not trick you into training a dog.

He motioned Colin inside his study. "Come in and sit down." Reginald settled himself behind his desk and leaned back. "What did you wish to speak to me about?"

Colin narrowed his eyes. "As if you don't know."

Reginald shrugged innocently. "I can't imagine."

"Do not play with me, Reg. You know I had no intention of helping your sister train that dog. She played me for a fool, and I was giving her what she deserved."

"And you wish to punish the dog for Mariah's folly?" Reginald steepled his fingers in front of him.

"Your superior looks do not work on me, Reg. I will not be cowed." He narrowed his eyes, giving his own equally quelling look.

Reginald sighed. "Why do you think she misled you, Colin?"

"To make me look the fool. I already told you that."

Reginald released a heavy breath. "I think you are mistaken. She might scowl at anyone who looks at her wrong, but that is about the extent of her malice." He shrugged. "Except, perhaps, for Lady G. She truly loathes that dog. Although, I believe it may have more to do with my wife than with the dog itself." He waved a hand in front of his face. "But that's neither here nor there."

"Then why did she mislead me? What could be the point of it?"

Reginald leaned forward. "I believe Mariah may have a small tendré for you, Colin."

Colin rocked back. Lady Mariah had done nothing to indicate she was in love with him. "You're daft. She does not think herself in love with me."

"I did not say she loved you. I said she had an affection for you." Reginald tilted his head to the side. It was the look he gave those of lesser intellect. A look Colin didn't appreciate receiving.

"She has confided this to you?" Colin moved to the front of his seat and clasped his hands, letting them dangle between his knees. Lady Mariah had an affection for him? What did that mean, exactly? He knew she had flirted with him on occasion, but did not all ladies flirt with men? It meant nothing.

He sank back into his chair, absorbing the information Reginald had just given him. He was not certain what to think. He was surely not looking to leg shackle himself to anyone. Let alone a spoiled, giggling girl who had a propensity for lying to get what she wanted.

Reginald cleared his throat. "Not in so many words."

Colin threw his hands up and grunted. "Then you can't be certain. Perhaps there is no truth to it at all and you are simply trying to help her out of the briars she has landed herself in."

Reginald shook his head. "I know Mar, Colin. She has been trying to catch your attention since her come out three years ago but to no avail. I'm certain she thought you would pay her mind if you had something in common."

She had been seeking his attention for years? He had never noticed it. How had Reginald? Had his new marriage made him more aware of all women's ploys?

Colin cringed at the thought.

But even if he recognized it, he would never have pursued it for several reasons. Namely, he was not looking for a wife. He was perfectly happy with his life and could not conceive of a woman changing that. But additionally, Lady Mariah was Reginald's sister. Stoke would never allow the alliance, would he?

Colin rested his elbows on the chair's arms and steepled his fingers. Placing them to his lips, he speared his friend with a narrow-eyed gaze. "Surely you do not look favorably on the match?"

Reginald reared back slightly. "Why should I object? You're my dearest friend. And she is my sister. Why should I not desire a match between you? I already think of you as a brother. A marriage would simply make it legal." He smiled almost sentimentally—which was far more disconcerting than his arrogant looks. "How could I look down upon that proposition?"

A heaviness settled on Colin's shoulders. Reginald was his dearest friend. What if Colin decided there was no partiality on his part toward Lady Mariah? What would it do to their friendship?

"When she brought home that ridiculous animal, I thought perhaps this might be an opportunity for you to become better acquainted with her." Reginald sighed. "But if I did wrong by you, then I'm sorry. I only wish to see her happy. And by all accounts, you make her happy." A grin spread over Reginald's face. "Except perhaps when you gave her that dog. She was not so very happy then."

Colin remained quiet. Reginald and he could be brothers. That would not be so terrible. Indeed, Colin would like it very much. But it came with a catch. Lady Mariah. Was becoming Reginald's brother worth being married to her?

"But you do not even know that it is true. You are only guessing at her feelings."

Reginald steepled his fingers and pushed out his lips. "Perhaps. But I know for certain she did not do any of it out of spite." He leveled his gaze at Colin. "Which I cannot say for you. What were you thinking?"

"I thought if she pretended to miss the dog so much, then I should give her a dog. She would either confess her lies to me and I could take the dog back. Or if she insisted on continuing with them, then she deserved the animal."

"Again, why must you punish the dog for her wrongs?"

Colin furrowed his brow. "She would not hurt him, would she?"

Reginald lifted a shoulder. "No. But you did not know that. You took a risk."

Colin leaned back. He had not meant to put the dog in danger. "I knew you would not allow anything to happen to it. You are too good of a man."

"I am not always with her." Reginald released a long, slow sigh. "But I think your risk paid off. From what I have seen, the only danger the dog faces is a ridiculous name."

"She has picked a name? What is it?"

Reginald shook his head. "You may ask her when you meet her for the training."

"Then you have not changed your mind? You are intent on making me help her?" Colin's stomach twisted. He was in a no-win situation. He did not feel he could challenge Reginald. If he were being truthful, he would do almost anything for his friend. Even if that meant training a dog with his sister. But he might have to put his foot down at marriage.

"It was a bacon-brained idea, and you shall feel the sting of it. Perhaps while you are training the dog, you might see what I have always seen—Mariah is delightful. She has many great qualities. She is rather charming when you come to know her. And perhaps you might just change her mind about dogs."

Colin grinned as he recalled the look on her face when she

opened her eyes to find the dog at her feet. But it faded as quickly as it came. He swallowed, sweat breaking out on his brow. What if this training didn't end as Reginald supposed? What if Lady Mariah did not end up appreciating the dog? And what if *he* did not end up appreciating Lady Mariah? What would come of his friendship with Reginald if Colin found he could not tolerate his sister?

She was handsome, so at least he would not have to endure an ugly woman. But as he thought about it, he thought he might just prefer that to the irritating giggles and eyelash fluttering he would surely endure for days on end. Ugh, days on end. Could it be any worse?

He placed his palms together and rested them on his lips, his thumbs beneath his chin. He hadn't disliked all their time together. Indeed, he reflected on their time in the park often. Could he hope the giggles would decrease as they spent more time together?

He rolled his eyes, already regretting his decision. "Very well, I will help her. But will you not assist as well?"

Reginald barked out a laugh. "Oh, no, my friend. I shall enjoy this show from a distance."

Colin glared at Reginald. "You might just be the worst friend ever."

"Perhaps," Reginald grinned broadly. "But I believe in time you will come to change your tune."

"Mariah is waiting for you in the gardens." Reginald led the way out of his study and down the corridor. They moved into the room next to Colin's office, the music room if Colin remembered correctly, and then through the terrace doors.

Lady Mariah walked around the gardens as the dog scurried around her, sniffing and barking at every bush and butterfly it saw.

The dog neared the path to the mews, and Lady Mariah patted her hands on her thighs, saying something he could not hear. But from the look on her face, she was giving the terrier a slight scolding.

The dog stopped for a moment and looked back at her, but then promptly went back to sniffing.

Lady Mariah's shoulders and face sagged in what was surely frustration.

As the doors of the terrace swung shut, both Lady Mariah and the dog turned toward Reginald and Colin. A smile spread across her face. Was she even now plotting out her next lie to him?

The dog turned from his course and bounded toward the house.

Colin glanced over at Reginald and grunted at the large smile on his face. He truly was a terrible friend. Perhaps Colin should reconsider Rags as a best friend.

He glanced back to Lady Mariah, his own smile tight and forced. Why did he have to be there?

Lady Mariah frowned at the ground. Lud, now he had made her unhappy. This was sure to be a very long morning.

She reached the brick terrace and dipped into a curtsy, smiling more pleasantly at the men. "Good day, Lord Heatherton."

He nodded. "And to you, Lady Mariah." His voice sounded dull, but he could not muster any enthusiasm. He bent forward and plucked the dog off the ground, scratching it under the chin and nuzzling his face into its neck. "And good day to you, sir."

Once he finished greeting the dog, he felt better about the situation. The dog seemed an amiable creature. If nothing else came of his time there, at least he could enjoy his time with the terrier.

He moved the dog's body under his arm and continued to run his hand from its head to its back. "Have you decided on a name?"

Lady Mariah focused on the little dog, her brow knit

tightly. She looked up into Colin's face. "Indeed, I came up with the perfect name." She grinned, and Colin wondered if Reginald was not correct about it being ridiculous. "I have named him Biscuit."

Colin's mouth dropped open. "Biscuit?"

"Did I not tell you it was ridiculous?" Reginald clucked his tongue.

"It's not a very dignified name for a hunter." Colin looked from Lady Mariah to the dog. What an indignity for such a fine and noble creature.

Lady Mariah tilted her head to the side. "I considered naming him Spite." She looked to be waiting for a reaction from him, but he did not give her the satisfaction. "Or perhaps even Bob. But Biscuit seemed far more dignified than either of those."

Colin's face heated to the tips of his ears. "I have a pointer named Bob."

"Oh . . ." She stammered.

"Are you implying Bob isn't a dignified dog? Because I can assure you that's not the case." He could not rightly decide if he found the whole situation vexing or humorous.

"I mean, Bob is a fine name." Her eyes widened, and her face pinked rather pleasantly.

Colin smoothed the scowl from his face and shook his head. How could she have known he'd named his dog Bob? It was not as if they'd discussed it.

"I'm certain the name fits your pointer very well, my lord. Biscuit simply didn't seem to like it. For himself. I'm certain he would think it appropriate for your pointer." She stared at the ground with her hands clasped behind her back.

Lady Mariah sucked in a deep breath, twisting at the tips of her short gloves. "Thank you for coming to help train Biscuit. I'm at a loss where to even begin."

Colin put the dog back on the ground and gave her another tight smile at the mention of the training and the assumption that he had willingly agreed to it. "You are welcome. I'm happy to help." His voice dripped with sarcasm.

Reginald thumped him on the back. "I will be in my study. Just shout if you encounter a problem." He chuckled as he turned on his heel and closed the terrace doors behind him.

The louse.

"What shall we do first?" Her voice was unusually high-pitched.

"I think the basic commands should be our first order of business." It seemed common sense to start there. "But as I have never trained a dog, I am not an expert."

Lady Mariah's brow furrowed. "You have never done this before? Then why did Reginald insist you help?"

Colin lifted his hand up in confusion. "I have no notion."

She looked at the dog and then at Colin. "Then I suppose we shall learn together." Again she smiled at him, but it looked more tentative.

"We should begin immediately. I'm certain you have other plans this afternoon. I know I do."

Lady Mariah frowned. Had she expected him to stay all day? He had no intention of staying any longer than necessary.

Her shoulders drooped, and she sighed. "Miriam, stay here and serve as chaperone while Lord Heatherton and I train Biscuit."

Miriam nodded. "Yes, my lady."

Colin raised a brow, and he tossed a grin at the young lady. "Thank you, Miriam." He tipped his head toward a chair. "Perhaps if you pull that chair into the shade, you will still be able to see us but not be in the heat."

Lady Mariah scoffed. "She will be fine. Will you not, Miriam?"

The maid nodded, but Colin noted she glanced at the chair.

He paused and turned back toward the terrace. In four quick steps, he grabbed the back of the chair and pulled it over to the shaded area. "There you are."

The maid kept her face turned down, but he noticed a quick curtsy. "Thank you, my lord."

Colin nodded and hurried back to Lady Mariah's side. This is what Reginald wished Colin for a wife? "I brought some mutton strips. I thought they may prove useful in training...*Biscuit.*" He said the name with only partial derision. If only he could train Lady Mariah on how to treat people with a few bits of meat. Not that it would change his mind about marriage to her. But perhaps it would make their time together bearable.

# Chapter Twelve

Mariah walked toward the music room. She was feeling restless after her less-than-fruitful training session with Biscuit. Indeed, nothing had come from the time spent with Colin. For either the dog or Mariah.

Biscuit was just as ill-mannered as he was when she awakened this morning. And Mariah had not noticed any change in Colin.

Indeed, if anything, he had only grown more quiet and reserved. What was she doing wrong? She had felt certain that they need only spend time together for him to take notice of her. But she had spent more time with him in the last week than she had in the whole of her life combined. And he seemed no more inclined toward a proposal than he had when he returned from the continent.

She released a frustrated sigh. She needed something to occupy her thoughts until it was time to ready for Mr. Cleverly's ball. Perhaps she should practice her harp. Nothing helped to calm her better. Lord Perryweather's musicale was the following evening, and she wished to sound her best when she performed. Reginald had said Colin was attending the musicale also. And what better way to earn his attention than through a lovely piece of music? Training Biscuit certainly wasn't helping.

She passed Reginald's study on her way to the music room but stopped just past the door. Was Reginald at home or at his club? Perhaps she should speak with him about freeing Colin from his forced helping. If their time together did nothing to draw his attention to her, was there any point?

She sighed. Except that it would end her time with him. And even if he did not enjoy spending time with her, she enjoyed his company. Perhaps not as much as if they both took pleasure in it. But she would take what she could.

She raised her hand to knock on the partially open door, but paused when she heard several male voices. She frowned. It seemed his friends were meeting at Berkeley Square rather than at Brooks's.

Mariah leaned in closer, wondering what they spoke about. She glanced over her shoulder down the corridor. The last thing she needed was to be caught eavesdropping by one of the servants. That would be lowering.

A low growl sounded, and Mariah scooped up Biscuit. Without thinking, she ran her hand down his neck and back, as she peered into the room to see if the occupants had heard the noise.

No one looked toward the door.

Mariah frowned down at the dog. "Quiet, Biscuit," she hissed as she continued to pet the dog's back.

"How was your training session, Colin?" Lord Montcort's voice sounded through the cracked door. Mariah did not know him any better than she knew Reginald's other friends. But even she could hear the laughter in his tone. Did they all know of the trick he played on her?

"How do you think it went? It was excruciating, and the longest hour of my life." Colin's irritated voice sounded through the crack.

Mariah's throat tightened.

"Come now, Colin. It could not have been as bad as all that." Reginald grinned at his friend.

"Why are you making him help, Reg? Is it truly necessary or are you just trying to play matchmaker for your sister?" Lord Berwick's voice sounded, but she could not see him.

Mariah placed a hand on her chest, slowly rubbing at the tightness there.

A chair squeaked as if someone shifted. "If Colin isn't interested in my sister, I know of several gentlemen about London who would be very happy to ask for her hand."

Someone scoffed, and Mariah wondered if it might not be Colin. "And yet, Colin is the one helping her train the dog." She couldn't see Lord Ponsonby, but she recognized his voice.

"Colin was the one who gave her the dog. Why should he not help her?" Reginald sounded indignant.

"You could do it." Mr. Bancroft spoke up.

"That dog is not my problem. I have plenty of business that needs my attention. Colin made this muddle; he can be the one to fix it."

"Why do you feel the need to foist Lady Mariah upon us whenever there is something you do not wish to happen—to save her from this gentleman or that? Now you are making poor Colin train her dog?" Lord Ragsdale grumbled. "I'm thinking your friendship may come at too steep a price."

Mariah put a hand to her mouth to cover the intake of breath. Did they all feel as Lord Ragsdale? Did Colin look at her as someone that was simply another problem that he must help Reginald solve?

"I have to wonder if there is not more to it than that." Lord Montcort spoke up. "I wonder if Ben doesn't have the right of it. Perhaps you are regretting being the only one of us with a wife and wish to see the rest of us in a similar situation."

"I regret nothing about my marriage to Sarah. I am happier than I have ever been." As much as she wished to hear it, Mariah heard no doubt or hesitation in her brother's voice. He truly was happy that he had married Sarah. Even though it meant he had drifted apart from Mariah.

She pursed her lips. That was rather disappointing.

"Just because you decided to marry, does not mean the rest of us are in want of it." Lord Ragsdale grumbled from across the room.

"It is not as if I was looking for it, but when I discovered the perfect lady right in front of me, it was difficult to enjoy my days as a bachelor any longer." There was a grumble of dissent from the others in the room. "Trust me, gents, there will come a time when each of you will capitulate to the parson's mousetrap."

"Perhaps you are right. But I just have yet to discover a lady that does not send me scurrying to the club to hide." Several chortles sounded at Colin's remark. "And I am certain I won't discover her anytime soon."

Mariah's eyes burned. After all she had done—after all the work she had put forth trying to have him take notice of her, it was all for nothing. He saw her as a chore.

Biscuit let out a yelp and Mariah loosened her hold on him, petting him more softly, hoping he had not given her away. But the conversation within continued.

"I do not believe you would know the right lady if she came and landed you a facer." Laughter rang in Reginald's voice. "It is good that I am around to help you see what I am certain you would miss otherwise."

A door shut somewhere down the corridor and Mariah jerked around, placing her hand around Biscuit's mouth. But no one seemed to be there.

She placed her hand to her heart. She really should move on to the music room before someone caught her listening at the door. But her feet seemed disinclined to move. What if Colin mentioned her again? Could he possibly have found something amiable about her?

She leaned in, nearly resting her ear on the wood, hoping she had not missed anything that would aid her in her quest to earn Colin's attention.

"There's just so little to like in the ladies of the *ton*. Let alone love about them." Colin's voice held a note of frustration.

"Oh? And what is it you are looking for in a lady, Colin?" Lord Berwick snickered.

"Several are pretty enough, like Charlie's sister. Or even yours, Reg. But a pretty face does not negate other less desirable characteristics."

Mariah sucked in a calming breath. Colin thought her handsome! That was something, was it not?

"And just what are our sisters lacking?" Mr. Bancroft asked, sounding affronted on his sister's behalf.

Mariah placed a hand on the door frame as she leaned even closer and peered through the crack. She had to admit she wondered the same thing.

"It's not that I think your sister is lacking, Charlie. But she is not even out. Therefore, she can hardly be considered a match this Season. And…" Colin's silence stretched on. What did he think of her? What was wrong with her that he could not consider her as a suitable match?

Her heartbeat hammered in her neck and chest. Was it possible it did not matter what she did to draw his attention because he could not find anything in her character to like? Would nothing she did matter?

"I did not miss your incomplete assessment of Mariah, Colin." There was a touch of defensiveness in Reginald's voice. At least Mariah could take solace in that. Since he married Sarah, she had wondered if he even cared about her anymore.

"Now Reg, do not feign indignation. You have said yourself that your sister can be rather vexing."

Mariah's skin went cold. Knowing he thought her pretty

was delightful. But what was he not saying? There was more to her than her beauty. Surely he had seen it. But why was he not mentioning it? What did he not like about her that outweighed the rest of her good qualities?

"I am her brother. It is her duty to vex me."

"The chit is completely improper. Surely you have seen that." Lord Ragsdale grunted.

"That is what you find lacking in her? Propriety?" Reginald's voice rose in pitch and volume.

"Perhaps on occasion. But that is not what concerns me." Mariah saw him wave a hand toward Reginald.

"Then what is it? I should like to know."

One of Colin's shoulders dropped. She could not see the other one through the slim crack. "Have you not noticed her incessant giggling? What of her constant pouting when she does not get her way? And let us not forget her tendency to lie."

Reginald rolled his eyes.

"And while those things are annoying, it is her treatment of servants and those who are beneath her that makes me certain I could never form an attachment to her."

"What do you mean, the way she treats those beneath her?"

"She can be rather unkind." Colin pushed back into his chair as if he were trying to put a greater distance between Reginald and him.

The room filled with silence.

Indeed, Mariah could scarcely take a breath. That is what he thought of her? How was one to overcome such an opinion? He thought her unkind? She treated servants as everyone else of her status did, yet he believed her unkind?

She clenched her fist at her side, hugging Biscuit a little tighter to her. Perhaps listening at the door had been unwise.

Or perhaps it was for the best. Lord Heatherton was not the man she thought him to be. For years she had put him on a sort of dais, thinking him perfect in nearly every way. But he was not perfect. He was mean and uncaring.

She looked down the corridor, expelling her breath slowly and evenly. If she had thought she needed to play her harp before, it was nothing to what she felt now. Indeed, she hoped the strings survived the treatment they were likely to receive.

She only barely kept herself from stomping the rest of the way to the music room. How could Colin say such things about her? And why had Reginald not refuted them? What kind of brother allowed a man to belittle his sister in such a way with nary a comment of objection?

She placed Biscuit on the floor beside her and sat down at her harp. Her mind was a jumble of questions and emotions. Pulling the instrument onto her shoulder, she placed her fingers on the strings, not even bothering to withdraw a piece of music from the music stand. For the moment she just needed to play—to clear her mind of everything swirling about inside.

As the music filled the room, little tendrils of frustration fell away, until finally, she could think beyond just her hurt and anger.

Could what Lord Heatherton—she was not certain she could think of him as Colin anymore—said be true? Was she unkind to those she thought beneath her?

One thing was obvious. Her means of flirting was not working. He found the giggling annoying. Perhaps it was not that Sarah had done it wrong after all. Or perhaps Miss Ashdown was the only lady who did it well. Or perhaps it simply did not work on the kind of gentleman that Mariah wished to attract. At least that was something she could change. She need not giggle at what he said. But that was not enough. Indeed, he said her unkindness was what had decided him against her. When had she been unkind?

Reginald's words from months before about her treatment of Sarah came back to her. But she had apologized for those.

And Colin had not even been in London during that time. He could not be recalling those interactions.

Her fingers stilled on the strings as she recalled Lord Heatherton's words from their walk in Berkeley Square. He may not have heard her earlier interactions with Sarah, but she had not kept her disdain for her sister-in-law to herself in recent months. She had said many things about Sarah that might not have been considered kind.

But Colin did not know their history. He was wrong to make assumptions when he did not know the whole of the story.

Mariah plucked at the strings, frowning as she played a rather soulful tune. She had not been helpful to Sarah in securing her footing among the *ton*. Even though Mariah knew Sarah was anxious about being accepted.

She pulled her hands away from the strings again. Why had she not been helpful? Was it just because of Sarah's interference at Vauxhall? Or was there more to it?

She swallowed painfully past the lump growing in her throat. Had it been because she viewed Sarah as inferior? She remembered her words to Reginald at the Peerless Pool, pointing out that Sarah's family had been the ones to rent a house in Cheapside. It was no wonder Reginald had said she thought only of herself. A sick feeling settled in her stomach.

"Why did you stop playing?" Reginald stood just inside the doorway, with his friends peering in behind him.

Mariah jerked her head up, looking at her brother and his friends. Had they been listening? Her face heated at the thought that Colin—perhaps she was not completely ready to dismiss using his Christian name—had been listening as well. Had he liked what he heard? Although, did it really matter? He found her character lacking, and it seemed unlikely that some prettily played notes would change his opinion.

"I am to perform at Lord Perryweather's musicale

tomorrow evening. I thought it best if I practiced as much as possible. I should not like to embarrass myself."

"I have heard you play many times, my lady. And I have never once thought you had had any reason to be embarrassed. Indeed, I have rarely heard anything so lovely." Lord Ponsonby gave her a lopsided smile.

She tried not to stare at Colin, trying to interpret what he thought of her by the look on his face. But it was all for not, as he gave nothing away. Indeed, it seemed likely he thought of her just as he had in Reginald's study.

"I hope you play that second piece you practiced tomorrow evening. It is one of my favorites." Reginald smiled at her. It was a smile she had not seen from him of late. And she had not realized how much she had missed it.

"If that is what you wish me to play, I suppose I should practice it more."

Reginald tipped his head to the side, studying her as if he saw something he had not seen before. "Do you wish to join us for tea? The gents will be leaving soon so we might all prepare for the ball tonight."

Mariah shook her head and tilted the harp upright. "I appreciate the offer, but I believe I will practice a while longer and take tea in my chambers. I should not like to keep you waiting this evening."

Reginald nodded slowly. "If that is what you wish, you need not bother Miriam. I will let the kitchens know where to send your tray."

Mariah smiled tightly and nodded. "Thank you, Regi."

As a group, the men turned from the music room and disappeared into the corridor.

Mariah did not move for several minutes as she stared at the door where the men had just disappeared. Could she trust what Colin had said about her? And if what he said was true, what could she do about it? Was it just Sarah she had treated badly?

She thought back on her interactions with the servants over the past few days. The examination did not leave her feeling vindicated in the least. While she did not like to admit it, she had to concede that she could show more kindness to those beneath her.

Indeed, one thing—although there were many—that vexed Mariah so much in the last few months was the way Sarah always thanked Maxwell and Mills, her lady's maid.

Mariah had thought it rather lowering of her to do it. She had even wondered if Sarah did it to earn the servant's loyalty over Mariah. But perhaps it was Mariah who had been wrong.

Was there something she could learn from Sarah? Her first impulse was to push the thought away. But instead, she let it settle in her mind. Was it possible for Mariah to change? And if she did, would Colin even notice? Had her feelings for him changed after his unkind words?

Her stomach fluttered in response.

Perhaps it wouldn't be amiss if she showed a little more kindness. Might Colin then see that she was worthy of him?

# Chapter Thirteen

MARIAH SAT IN A CHAIR, WAITING FOR THE NEXT SET TO begin.

Reginald moved in behind her, his arms folded almost as tightly as his pursed lips.

She sighed. As much as she disliked Sarah of late, it was times such as these that Mariah missed her former friend. Since their marriage, Reginald had allowed them to stay together in the ballroom, while he excused himself to the cardroom—which was a far better use of his time, in Mariah's opinion. Perhaps she should just be grateful that he had not seen it necessary to have his friends step in as her dance partners tonight. Although the night was still young, and it was possible Reginald might still discover an objectionable gentleman to save her from.

Now that she knew the opinions her brother's friends held for her, she did not know if she could even look them in the eye long enough to dance a set with them.

Especially Colin.

Mariah pulled her bottom lip in between her teeth to staunch any tears that threatened to fall. Although, she did not think it likely he would ask for a set of his own accord. The evening, it seemed, would be rather dull.

Mariah glanced up at Reginald over her shoulder. "I do not understand why you do not leave me and move into the cardroom. We both know that is where you would prefer to be."

Reginald cleared his throat. "Now that Sarah is not here to accompany you, it would be improper for me to leave you unattended."

"You have already taken a measure of every man in the room. I will be safe enough." She glanced around. "Look, there is Miss Thornton. I will go sit next to her. Surely you cannot object to that."

"Oh, but I do. Miss Thornton has not a brain in her head. I am not leaving you, Mar, and I will brook no more opposition." Reginald shifted from one foot to the other.

"Are you just to stand here, even while I dance? Have you asked any lady to dance?" She looked straight ahead. "Mr. Cleverly asked for my next set."

Reginald shrugged. "I have not yet decided. You know I am not fond of dancing."

Mariah chuckled. "Perhaps if you had paid more attention to the dancing master, you would not feel so inadequate in a ballroom."

Reginald tugged at his collar. He had always complained that he did not enjoy the ballroom because of the calculating gazes of the mothers in attendance. But Mariah knew that was not the only reason. It had as much to do with Reginald's rather clumsy attempts at dancing. Although, it was curious. He had never seemed so very clumsy when he danced with Sarah.

"It is not as if you have to worry about the machinations of the mothers in the room now that you are a married man."

Reginald growled. "I care little for dancing, Mariah. And that is that."

Mariah grinned to herself. "Then why can you not see it would be better if you simply went to the cardroom?"

"I am not leaving you unattended and that is the last I will say on the subject."

She released a sigh and turned her lips down into a pout. But then Colin's words from earlier came unbidden to her mind. She pulled her lips upwards into what must have been a very awkward-looking smile.

"I do not suppose any of your friends will join you this evening?" Mariah did not care if any of Reginald's friends joined them. Indeed, if any of them should ask her for a set, she had a mind to decline. Even if Colin was the one asking. She cast a hopeful glance toward the doorway, knowing fully if he asked her to dance, she would readily accept.

"I cannot imagine they will. They have nothing to protect them from fortune and title hunters. I am certain they will stay safely hidden in the cardroom."

Mariah's shoulders slumped.

Reginald was surely correct. He knew his friends better than Mariah did. What cause did they have to enter the ballroom?

Why were the fates making her match with Colin so difficult? Surely other ladies in the *ton* did not have so much trouble in securing the affections of the gentlemen they sought.

The orchestra held the last strains of the song before putting their instruments down. The set was over, and it was time for her to dance with Mr. Cleverly.

Mariah watched as he made his way across the room. He may not be as handsome as Colin, but Mr. Cleverly was a decent enough sort. Even if his eyes were a rather dull brown and his hair a rather limp and dirty looking blonde. His jaw was rather weak, but his character was impeccable, making him a desirable gentleman for many of the ladies in the room. Many among the *ton* might not agree with the assessment, but as far as those in attendance, he was a rather fine catch.

"Lady Mariah, I believe this is our set." He bowed before her but looked up at her from beneath his lashes. It really was not his fault that Mariah had no inclination toward him. Indeed, no gentleman could compare to Colin.

*Oh, Colin.*

Since overhearing Colin's opinion of her earlier, Mariah had thought of little else. While originally she had thought the obstacles impossible to overcome, she now thought them not so insurmountable. If a lack of kindness and some pouting was all that kept Colin from forming an attachment with her, she could change. She *would* change. She would become the sort of lady he desired. How hard could it be? She need only say a few pleases and thank yous to a few servants and cease pouting—that one seemed the most difficult—when Colin was around, and it would be done. He would finally see her as the perfect wife for him.

Mr. Cleverly led her out to the dance floor and deposited her in the line before taking the spot opposite her. Mariah smiled widely at him, hoping he thought her amiable. Colin was not around to see it. But hopefully word of her amiableness would spread and reach those in the cardroom. It still counted even if she did not feel amiable, did it not?

She moved about the dance floor, making certain she smiled at Mr. Cleverly whenever he looked at her. When he turned to her, however, she looked toward the doorway, almost willing Colin to enter.

As if she had summoned him with her mind, midway through the first set, Mariah's eyes widened.

Colin stood beside Reginald. He had come to the ballroom after all? But why? The sound of blood rushed through her ears, drowning out the music and the sound of everyone around her. Would he ask her to dance?

Mariah shook her fist at her side. Drat it all. She had not a set available until after supper. Would he return to the card-room once he discovered she was not available?

A sick feeling settled in her stomach. What if he had come in search of another lady?

That could not be, could it? Would not Reginald have told her if Colin had set his sights on someone else? Reginald knew of Mariah's feelings for Colin. Surely he would have warned her about such a thing.

She tried her best to keep her attention trained on Mr. Cleverly. But her eyes seemed to move of their own accord to Colin.

He still stood beside Reginald. Perhaps he simply needed to discuss something with her brother. But would he not have had his say and left already? Or was he waiting for a lady already occupied?

Mariah looked down the row of dancers, trying to discern which lady might have captured Colin's attention. While there were several pretty young ladies in attendance, none were of prominent social standing. Indeed, their small group was the highest-ranking members of society in attendance.

If it were Lord Ragsdale she was worried about, Mariah knew for certain he would have no interest in any lady in attendance. However, Colin was not so high in the instep. She could easily see him doing as Reginald had and marrying far below him simply because he fell in love.

*Fell in love*? Colin had fallen in love? But with whom? He had only returned from the continent two months ago.

Thought after thought tumbled about in her head. What was she to do? In the back of her mind, she had known it was possible Colin might marry another. But she had not really believed it would happen. She had always believed he would come around and offer for her in the end. They were meant to be together. How did Colin not understand that?

The line of dancers shifted. Mariah stumbled, knocking into the gentleman beside her. He gave her a little shove away from him, and she fell into the man on her other side. Knocking him to the ground, she tripped over him and landed in a heap on top of him.

Mariah let out a gasp, but she did not know if it was from embarrassment or pain.

Mr. Cleverly looked down at her in surprise, and then with concern. He reached out for her. "Lady Mariah, are you injured?"

Humiliation flooded over her, and her face burned as she hurried to her feet. But it only took the slightest pressure on her foot for her to realize she had injured herself. She stood on one foot, trying to balance, but the shuffle of people around her nearly made her topple over again.

Mr. Cleverly reached out to her, putting a hand on her arm to study her. "My dear lady, you are injured."

Mariah nodded her head sheepishly, carefully keeping her foot elevated off the floor. "I am afraid I have twisted my ankle. I do not think I shall be able to continue with our set."

He smiled down at her kindly and again guilt wormed around in her stomach. Why could she not desire the man's affections? He seemed genuinely concerned for her. He sought her out at any event they both attended. But it was for naught. Even as he held onto her arm, Mariah's gaze slid over to Colin.

"Do not worry yourself over it. No one will fault you. Now, let me see you over to your brother." Mr. Cleverly slid a hand around her back to give her support as she hopped off the dance floor. His hand felt hot and damp even through her gown and his gloves.

They barely made it off the dance floor when Reginald stopped them, his eyes wide. "Let me help you to the chair." Reginald's hand replaced Mr. Cleverly's around her waist, and she could not admit disappointment. The three of them hobbled toward the chairs where Colin still stood sentry.

Once he had her settled on the chair, Reginald looked down at her. "Mariah, what happened?"

"I am afraid I tripped on my own feet." She flicked her glance at Colin, wondering if he would laugh at her. But her skin warmed when she saw the look of concern flit across his face.

Mr. Cleverly turned to Reginald. "I shall leave her with you, my lord." He glanced at Mariah. "While it pains me to say it, I understand if you must return home early."

Reginald bowed slightly. "Thank you, Cleverly. I believe I will give her a few moments and see how she recovers before I decide."

Mr. Cleverly smiled at Mariah. "I shall cross my fingers in hopes that you recover quickly. But if you must leave, perhaps you will save a set at Lord Trenton's ball for me? I should not like to end the Season without dancing another set with you."

Mariah smiled up at him, even as her ankle throbbed. "Indeed, I shall."

With one last smile at her, Mr. Cleverly turned and disappeared into the crowd of dancers.

Mariah sighed and looked up at Reginald. "I suppose I should not have said those things about your dancing when it is I who looked like a drunken giraffe."

One side of Reginald's lips lifted. "Perhaps we both inherited the trait." He moved around the chairs and kneeled in front of her. Gingerly, he picked up her foot and she winced. He raised a brow as he looked at one side and then the other. "The bruise is already showing, Mar. I think it best if we return home."

"Are you certain?" Mariah glanced up at Colin. He could not ask her to dance, nor could she discover the lady he was interested in if they left. How would she know which scenario was correct?

Reginald lifted her foot slightly and looked at Colin. "What is your opinion?"

Mariah sucked in a breath as her heart pounded against her ribs. Would Colin touch her ankle? It felt very intimate, but she would not object. At least not strenuously. "Regi, that is most improper."

Reginald rolled his eyes. "He is only looking at your ankle, Mariah. I believe your reputation will remain intact."

Colin did not touch her ankle. Nor did he even move around the chairs, only glancing at her foot from behind.

Mariah sunk down into the chair.

"I can see the discoloration from here. I believe you may be right, Reg. It is probably best if you return home."

Mariah released a frustrated sigh. Why did it feel as though she made progress, only to be pulled back to the beginning again? There was only one more ball before the close of the Season. Then she would return to the country. How was she to accomplish an entire Season's worth of work in only one ball? Especially now that there may be competition.

As far as she knew, Colin would be in London next Season. But much could happen over the summer. She needed every moment that remained in the Season.

The pain in her ankle increased, and, to her disappointment, she realized that there was no way she could dance with Colin tonight, even if he asked her. "If we are to leave, I see no reason to stay a moment longer. We may as well depart now." She sounded like a petulant child, she knew. And it would likely only add to Colin's dislike of her. But she could not seem to help it. Her hopes and dreams were crashing down around her and there was nothing she could do about it.

"I agree." Reginald nodded and helped her to her feet. He glanced over at Colin. "I need your help to see her to the carriage."

Colin stayed still for a moment. But finally, he shrugged and rounded the chairs, presenting his arm for Mariah to hold.

Reginald slid a hand around her waist, but she leaned into Colin, clinging to his arm as if it were her only lifeline. He had not given her much opportunity this Season. She planned to make the best of every opportunity presented to her.

Colin glanced down at her hands wrapped tightly around his upper arm. For a moment, she thought he might shake her off. But when he simply looked ahead, she allowed a small smile to form.

Reginald helped Mariah onto a bench in the entryway, where she grudgingly released Colin's arm. He would surely leave now that he had done his duty.

"Sit there until the carriage comes, Mar." He turned and grabbed Colin by the arm before he could move away. "Why do you not go fetch the gents from the cardroom and come over? I'm sure we would far prefer one another's company to anyone here. Unless there is someone in the ballroom one of you wishes to spend time with." Reginald looked sideways at Colin.

Mariah perked up, leaning slightly forward to hear Colin's response.

"People will notice if we leave before supper. But I can see no reason why we couldn't join you after." He dipped his head to the side, a half smile on his face. "Although you may not wish to invite anyone on a winning streak. You have paid out a fair amount of money in lost wages this Season."

Reginald chuckled. "You have my permission to leave anyone behind who does not wish to leave the table. I have paid those men far more than they deserve."

Colin raised an eyebrow. "They have saved your sister from the likes of Lord Muckrake. I believe they earned every shilling."

Reginald lifted his shoulder. "Perhaps you are correct."

"I am certain you could entice them with a few of Mrs. Leach's tea cakes." Colin waggled his eyebrows.

Reginald laughed. "I know not if there are any tea cakes left."

"As I have tasted nothing unfitting from Mrs. Leach, I should think about anything she has on hand would entice the gents from the cardroom."

Reginald nodded. "I shall see Mariah settled and call the doctor. By that time, you all should be able to leave without causing offense." He clapped Colin on the back. "See you soon."

Colin grinned at Reginald, then glanced at Mariah. "I hope you are well soon, my lady."

Mariah smiled widely. "Thank you, my lord. I am certain I will be well by morning. Shall we continue Biscuit's training?"

His shoulders dropped, and her hopes with them. "I will send word after you in the morning and make my decision." He dipped his head. "Good night." He turned and disappeared down a corridor.

He obviously still saw her as a chore—still wished to be released from his obligation to her. "How long does it take to summon a carriage?" She growled, feeling very out of sorts.

"It will be here soon." Reginald glanced down at her. "Are you more hurt or angry?"

"What have I to be angry about?"

Reginald sat down on the bench beside her. "You are trying too hard, Mariah."

"What?" she snapped.

"Give Colin time and please, whatever you do, stop trying to flirt with him. You do it very ill."

Mariah folded her arms across her chest. "What would you know about flirting?"

Reginald grinned. "Oh, I know a great deal. Perhaps one day you could ask Sarah about it."

Mariah opened her mouth to question him, but a footman stepped forward. "Your carriage is waiting, my lord."

# Chapter Fourteen

Mariah cracked open an eye, peering into the line of sunlight streaming through the crack in her bed curtains. She had not felt so rested in months.

She lifted her arms above her head, stretching out her back and her shoulders, moving down to her legs and her feet. But the stretch did not last long as a sharp pain shot up her leg.

She frowned, pushing back the counterpane on her bed, remembering the embarrassing incident from the evening before. A puffy blue and purple-colored ankle greeted her.

She sucked in a breath. What had happened? She had been certain she had only twisted her ankle. But never had she seen a twisted ankle look like this.

The door to her bed chambers opened, and Miriam came in carrying a tray with her breakfast. "Good morning, my lady." Miriam placed the tray on the bedside table. "I did not think you would be up to eating in the breakfast room."

Mariah looked at the tray. It held breakfast meats, eggs, and several slices of bread. But there were also two small bouquets. She leaned over and grabbed the card from the first bouquet, smiling when she opened it and saw it was from Mr. Cleverly.

*Lady Mariah,*

*Words cannot express my disappointment over the abrupt end of our evening. I hope you will be well soon, and we might complete our set after all.*

*Yours,*

*Henry Cleverly*

Mariah read the card again, smiling. Mr. Cleverly really was a gentleman. In another time and perhaps another place —a place without Colin—Mariah might be inclined to accept Mr. Cleverly's attentions.

However, Colin *was* in this place. And as long as he remained a bachelor, Mariah did not know how anyone else could satisfy her.

She tossed Mr. Cleverly's card to the side and retrieved the card from the second bouquet. She had not expected many bouquets this morning, as her injury had taken them from the ball before it had barely begun.

She turned the card over, and her heart thumped erratically when she saw the signature at the bottom. Colin had sent her flowers. She had not even danced with him, and still, he sent her a bouquet. He could not be so opposed to her if he was sending her flowers, could he?

Pulling her gaze away from his signature, she allowed herself to read the card slowly. Enjoying each word.

*Dear Lady Mariah,*

*I hope you recover quickly. I will await your word to resume our training of Biscuit. Perhaps in the meantime, you might reconsider his name?*

*Yours,*

*Heatherton.*

Mariah clutched the card to her chest. It had to mean something that he sent her flowers. Could he only have said those mean things about her for his friends' benefit? Had he really not meant them? The bouquet and card made her question her earlier beliefs.

Did he mean the flowers to tell her something? He had not danced with her, so he was not fulfilling an obligation. He sent them simply because he had been thinking of her.

She pulled the bouquet closer, looking at and smelling every flower and herb he had included. Had he picked each one himself? Were they from the hothouse, or had he picked them himself in his own gardens? Had he requested specific flowers or had he allowed the flower girl to put the bouquet together?

Some ladies might not care about such details, but to Mariah, it mattered. She had heard or read somewhere that certain flowers held special meaning. And while she did not know what those meanings were, she liked the idea that Colin might have picked each plant in the bouquet as a way of telling her something. It was not unlike her flirting with her fan.

Miriam brought the tray and the tea box over and sat it on the bed next to Mariah. Mariah pulled her chain off the table and unlocked the box before handing it over to Miriam. "Please be so kind as to pour out the tea, Miriam."

Her maid simply nodded and set to work.

Mariah slathered butter on a slice of bread and brought it to her lips, but before she could take a bite, she paused and glanced over at her maid. "Thank you for bringing my tray to my room, Miriam. You always seem to know what I need. I do not tell you enough, but I appreciate your service."

Miriam paused halfway through pouring and looked up at Mariah. What was that look in her eye? Did she not believe Mariah was in earnest?

The maid recovered her senses and finished preparing the tea, handing it over to Mariah. "It is my pleasure to serve you, my lady." She ducked her head and hurried to the far side of the room.

Mariah shrugged. While she had not received the reaction she had hoped for, she had to admit she felt pleased. She picked at her food, not eating much more than a slice of bread and some cheese.

She threw back the covers again. "Miriam, will you please help me dress? I am to perform at Lord Perryweather's musicale tonight and I do not yet feel prepared. I should like more practice."

Miriam paused and looked at Mariah. "Are you certain, my lady?" She glanced down at the discolored ankle. "Lord Stoke did not seem to think you would be attending. He sent your regrets this morning."

Mariah let out a huff of indignation. "What does Reginald know? I simply twisted my ankle. I need only to walk on it a bit, and it will be fine. It is simply stiff."

Lord Heatherton was to be at the musicale. Showing him her skills on the harp seemed of vital importance. Especially since he had singled her out by sending her flowers. But she could not show him her talent if she were not in attendance.

"I only need your help in walking the first few steps—just until my ankle is not stiff anymore."

Miriam looked at Mariah and then looked at her ankle peeking out beneath her nightgown. Uncertainty filled her eyes. "If you are certain, my lady."

Mariah gave a firm nod. "I am." She swung her legs over the side of the bed and carefully slipped to the floor, placing most of her weight on her uninjured foot. She stood up tentatively, offering Miriam a triumphant smile. "You see? I am perfectly able." She took a step and crumbled quickly to the floor.

Miriam dropped the clothes in her arms and rushed to Mariah's side. "My lady, let me help you back into bed."

Mariah grunted in frustration but allowed the help. Beads of perspiration dotted her brow as pain pulsed up her leg. This was not what she had planned. If she could not even stand, there was no chance Regi would allow her to go to the musicale. But if she could not go, how would her new plans to draw Colin's attention happen? Was she to be forced to sit by and do nothing?

She pulled the covers over her with a huff. Why could nothing go as she planned?

She leaned her head back against the headboard and closed her eyes, frustration lacing its way through her. Why had this had to happen? And why now, when her time was so limited?

Tears pooled in the bottom of her lids and she pinched her eyes shut against them.

A bark sounded next to her bed and Mariah opened her eyes. Biscuit stood on his hind legs, his front paws perched on the edge of her bed. His whole body shook as his tail wagged from side to side.

Miriam hurried over to the bed. "Shoo, now." She waved her hand at the dog. "Her ladyship does not need you on the bed."

Mariah lifted a hand and patted the counterpane. "Actually, I do not mind, Miriam." She smiled and patted the bed again. "Come on, Biscuit."

The dog dropped his paws to the floor and sat back on his haunches. Then, quicker than Mariah had thought possible, he launched upwards, landing on the bed with a thump.

"My lady, your ankle." Miriam put her hands out as if the action would stop what had already happened.

"I am well, Miriam. He did not step on it." She ran her hand down the dog's back. "I'm happy to see you, Biscuit, but I do not believe we shall have training today."

Biscuit looked at her with sad eyes.

"I know. I am disappointed as well."

Miriam eyed the dog and then Mariah. "I will remove the dog if he is bothering you, my lady. Your brother cannot possibly expect you to care for it in your condition."

Mariah grinned, scratching Biscuit under the chin and around his ears. "He is fine to stay here for now." She looked at her maid. "Thank you, Miriam."

A knock sounded at her door.

Both Mariah and Biscuit looked up just as Reginald poked his head in. "I am glad to see you are awake." He took a step inside the room, followed by the doctor. "Dr. Canton stopped by to look at your ankle this morning."

Mariah looked at her brother with exasperation. "I simply twisted it, Regi. You need not fuss so much." Although she would never admit it aloud, she liked that Reginald was fussing over her. It had been far too long since he had paid her any mind outside of lecturing her. His focus had been too much on Sarah of late.

The doctor moved over toward the bed. Mariah lifted the sheets so Dr. Canton might more easily see her ankle. He tilted his head from one side to the other but did not touch her.

Biscuit moved slightly forward, placing himself next to Mariah's ankle. He bared his teeth, a little growl sounding deep in his throat.

Mariah leaned forward and pulled the dog to her, scratching at the top of his head. "There, there, Biscuit. You need not protect me from Dr. Canton." Even though she knew she was in no danger, Mariah could not help but appreciate Biscuit's desire to protect her. She looked down at him.

Could she have been wrong about him? Was there more to him than those qualities that annoyed her most? She would admit, she had grown slightly fond of him, but that was only because he had an adorable face. Could there be more to him than that?

Her fingers stopped scratching. Could it be that she and Biscuit had more in common than she thought? Had she misjudged her dog, just as Colin continued to misjudge her?

The doctor continued to stare at Mariah's foot. What could he find so interesting after all this time?

Mariah glanced at Reginald, and he lifted a shoulder.

How could the doctor determine the extent of her injury if he did not even touch her? Did not he need to feel to determine if the bone was intact?

Dr. Canton looked at Reginald and raised an eyebrow. "Did you feel to ascertain if the bone had broken?"

Reginald frowned. "It was already very swollen when I felt it. I do not pretend to know what a broken bone should feel like."

The doctor shrugged. "You would surely know." He glanced at Mariah and then back to Reginald. "It appears to be a sprain. She should stay off her feet and rest for at least a fortnight."

Mariah sucked in a breath. "A fortnight? But I will miss the rest of the Season."

The doctor barely spared her a glance. He turned to Reginald. "I should think in four or five days, she might walk a bit with the help of a cane. But only for short distances and short periods of time. After which she will need to rest."

Mariah dropped her hands onto the mattress. The man was paying her no mind at all. It was quite vexing.

Reginald nodded. "I will see that she rests."

The doctor thrust a bottle at him. "Here is some laudanum. You may send to the apothecary if you need more. Only one small spoonful if the pain is severe." He then turned and left the room without a backward glance at Mariah.

Reginald glanced at the door, then at Mariah. "I will see to the doctor, but I want you to do as he instructed, Mariah. Stay in bed, and let your ankle heal."

Mariah grunted. "But Regi, I have practiced and practiced for the musicale tonight. And now I cannot go? It is not right."

"It will not be right if I should have to carry you to the

front of the room to perform, either." Reginald gave her a look that said he would not brook any opposition.

She pulled her copy of *The Lady's Magazine* off her side table, flipping the pages with more force than was necessary. But she could not help it. Frustration surged through her. Colin had shown an interest in her by sending her flowers, and now there was nothing she could do to reciprocate.

Her ankle throbbed painfully.

Biscuit stood on the edge of the bed, staring toward the door Reginald and Dr. Canton had just stepped through. As if satisfied the danger was not returning, Biscuit walked to the center of the bed. He turned in two circles and then lay down, curling up beside Mariah's legs.

She smiled over the top of the magazine and patted him on the head. He would not carry on a conversation with her, but that did not mean she was not happy for his company.

# Chapter Fifteen

COLIN STOOD IN THE BACK OF LORD PERRYWEATHER'S SALON, looking among the crowd for the faces of his friends. They had all said they would be there, even Reginald. Although, that was before his sister had twisted her ankle the previous evening.

Colin looked to the front, noting the absence of a harp. It seemed Lady Mariah would not be performing after all. But was she simply not able to perform, or would she be absent completely?

His lips turned down in a frown, and his brow furrowed. He had rather been looking forward to listening to Lady Mariah play. While there were things about her he was not fond of, her musicale ability was not one of them. Indeed, he had heard nothing so lovely as hearing her practice her harp. If it would not have drawn unwanted attention, Colin might have stayed longer to listen to her the other day.

He sucked in a deep breath. It seemed the evening was to be filled with only music from the pianoforte, and the voices of those young ladies who thought themselves rather talented at singing.

Not that he did not enjoy a pleasant performance by

someone proficient. It was simply that all the performances were so much the same. Each musicale he had attended, each piece that was performed, sounded precisely like the one before it. Except, perhaps, for the times when Lady Mariah played. Indeed, when he had children of his own, he would insist that his daughters learn several musical instruments. It was his gift to all those who would attend musicales in the future.

He smiled, feeling both magnanimous and ridiculous about his decision. It would be years before he married. And even longer before he had any daughters.

"Colin, there you are." Montcort sauntered towards him, a drink in his hand. Reginald and Bancroft followed close behind.

"You took your time in arriving," Reginald thumped him on the back. "I wondered if you had changed your mind."

"I had wondered the same of you," Colin nodded his head toward the front. "Since your sister cannot attend, I thought you might cry off." He grimaced. "I certainly would have used the excuse to my advantage."

Reginald released a dramatic sigh. "I was tempted. I will not lie. But when I sent word that Mariah could not attend, Lady Perryweather practically begged me not to stay away."

Charlie laughed. "Oh, yes, everyone desires the company of the great Earl of Stoke at their parties."

Reginald shrugged dramatically. "It is a trying burden I must bear."

"Have you seen anyone even worth listening to?" Ragsdale came up behind Bancroft and patted him on the shoulder. "I am wondering if anyone with any talent is even in London. With every party, it seems less of the *ton* is in attendance."

"It is no wonder. There is hardly anything worth discussing in Parliament. We have settled everything of consequence." Berwick looked bored.

Montcort looked over his shoulder. "Miss Martin is not without talent. Nor is Lady Jane."

"Yes, but we have heard them half a dozen times already this Season. And Lady Patricia is certainly lacking," Berwick lowered his voice and grimaced.

Bancroft clapped Reginald on the back. "There are only a few days left, and then we can leave for the country. We are looking forward to visiting Staffordshire next month."

"Is your sister to meet you there?" Reginald asked.

"No. I will return home and travel with her. I do not feel comfortable having her travel without some protection." He grinned at Reginald. "Madi was quite excited about the invitation. Thank you for including her. Even though she had a brief experience with the Season this year, I still believe she is rather anxious about her come out in the autumn."

Reginald nodded. "Both Sarah and Mariah grew quite fond of your sister." He glanced at the other men. "Although I confess, the invitation was not completely selfless. I did it as much for me as anyone. I thought it might help if there were another lady there, as Sarah and Mariah rarely stay in the same room together."

Ponsonby stepped into the group. "What is the matter, Reg? You look positively bereft." His nose curled up. "This isn't because your wife has gone, is it?"

"Reg was simply bemoaning the fact that his wife and sister are at odds. Something he could've avoided if he had not betrayed us and taken a wife to begin with." Ragsdale threw back the rest of his drink and set his glass on the tray of a passing servant.

A clap sounded from the front of the room, and the men all turned and looked at Lady Perryweather.

"Ladies and gentlemen, we are about to begin this evening's entertainment. If you would please find a seat, we will begin momentarily with Lady Jane Curtis."

Ragsdale let out a grunt. "I suppose the fun is about to begin." His tone said nothing of impending fun.

"Good evening, gentlemen." Lord Muckrake stepped up beside Reginald. He looked at all the men, and then out at the crush of people. "Stoke, I was hoping to see your sister this evening. But I have not seen her. Where are you hiding her?"

Reginald narrowed his eyes at the man. "I thought you were to attend a different party tonight."

"Yes, I had thought to attend Warrington's party this evening, but I found myself wishing to see your sister again." His eyes glinted with malevolence.

Colin's jaw tightened, as did all of Colin's friends'.

Reginald, however, smiled widely. "I am afraid my sister was not able to attend with me tonight."

Lord Muckrake's smile dropped slightly. "Oh? Has she returned to the country?"

Reginald narrowed his eyes again. He was not to give Muckrake more information, was he? A man like Muckrake would not allow a simple sprained ankle to deter him. Indeed, he would use it to his advantage—sending flowers and other such tokens to gain Lady Mariah's affections.

However, Colin also knew that Reginald was not inclined to lie. Even if it was for the best. Perhaps Colin needed to step in and do what Reginald could not.

"Indeed, she left for the country just yesterday." Colin folded his arms across his chest.

Reginald jerked his gaze over, but Colin ignored him. "You missed your chance with her, Muckrake. Perhaps you'll have better luck next Season." He lifted his chin. "Unless, of course, she does not return to London for next Season."

Lord Muckrake glowered at him before dipping his head to the group. "It seems Lady Jane is already at the pianoforte. We should take our seats." He strode away and found a seat next to Miss Glover.

Colin pulled his gaze away from Muckrake's back and

grinned as he looked around at his group of friends. But the faces that looked back surprised him. They were not laughing or grinning. Rather, they looked at him in confusion.

"Why did you tell Muckrake Mariah had left for the country?" Reginald's brow pulled low.

"And why should I not? You do not wish him with her." Colin lifted his chin as if readying himself for a debate.

Reginald shook his head and mimicked Colin's stance. "Of course, I do not desire him to be with her. But with her sprained ankle, she is safe."

Colin let out a rueful laugh. "If you think a sprained ankle will keep Muckrake away, you are daft." He shifted back onto his heels, leaning slightly away from the group. "Only instead of pursuing her in other people's parlors he will pursue her in yours. I was doing you and her a favor."

Montcort narrowed his eyes. "Are you certain it was only Reg and Lady Mariah you were thinking of?"

Colin gave him a bland look. "I would do the same for your sister if you had one. Do not suppose you are uncovering some great mystery. I was only being a friend."

The men moved as one toward a row of chairs at the back of the hall. They had discovered it was best to stay behind the crowds as much as possible. They each had stories of being cornered by well-meaning mothers searching for a match for their daughters.

Colin leaned back in the chair and crossed one leg over the other, lacing his fingers together around his knee.

Lady Jane placed her hands on the keys, and the room fell silent. Unlike others to perform, Lady Jane was a true proficient. However, Colin still could not say that he enjoyed the performance. While it was technically flawless, it lacked any warmth or emotion. It was nothing to listening to the harp, which tones were so much softer, especially under the touch of Lady Mariah.

Lady Jane finished and moved back to her seat, followed by a lengthy applause.

A procession of young ladies made their way to the front of the room, one after the other, blending one performance into the next. By the time intermission came, Colin was exhausted.

"I've had enough." He looked at the others, wondering if they felt the same. Surely he could count on Rags to offer a dissenting opinion on the evening. He always wished to leave an event early.

"You've had enough of what?" Cort looked longingly toward the refreshment table at the far end of the hall.

"I've had enough of the performances. They all sound the same. Why can no one do something other than play the piano or sing? Does no lady play anything else? Indeed, I should even be content with a tambourine, if the player should have even a modicum of talent." He glanced over at Reginald. "Your sister and her harp are much missed this evening. She seems to be the only lady in society with some imagination."

Ponsonby stared at Colin for a moment. "There are many among the *ton* who consider the harp out of fashion." He flicked his eyes to Reginald, as if trying to decipher if he had offended both his friends.

"Indeed, it is deuced inconvenient to train a lady up in the ways of the harp only to have it go out of style, just as she comes of age." Reginald shrugged. "But Mariah does not seem to care. She loves the harp. And I, for one, am glad for it. I enjoy listening to her play."

"The harp is out of fashion? The guitar is in fashion, but I saw nothing of it tonight. Or even a loot? I am not so very picky. I am just deuced tired of only hearing the pianoforte." Colin scrubbed a hand over his face.

The men all looked at each other.

"There are only a few days left in the Season. I'm certain

you can endure the dreaded piano a few times more. I am certain you will hear the harp often enough when you come to visit Oakdale next month. Mariah plays often when we are in the country. And by then her ankle should be healed." Reginald grinned wickedly. "Perhaps you can resume your training of her dog."

Colin glowered.

Cort chuckled. "Do you think, Reg, that she might perform on a loot? I should hate for our friend to grow tired of the harp, as well."

Colin sighed loudly. "I do not see why it is asking too much for society's ladies to have varied interests. I know there are ladies who play the violin or the guitar. But where are they? Why are they never at the musicales I attend? Perhaps next Season I shall host one and I will limit the attendance to only those who do not play the pianoforte." He nodded his head as if he had just made a life-changing decision. "Yes, that's what I shall do. I believe all of London will thank me for it."

"I am certain it will be a vast success." Reginald rolled his eyes as he motioned to their seats at the back of the room. "It looks as though the musicale is about to resume. Are we to take our seats?"

Colin shook his head. "I was serious before. I cannot take another song. I am done for the evening."

"But it is not yet even eleven," Rags lamented. "I cannot return home before midnight. I am certain my butler is spying on me for my father. I do not wish to give him anything to report."

"You are welcome to join me at my house." Colin looked toward the door.

Reginald shook his head. "If I am to leave early, I should check on Mariah." He looked at the other men. "But if you should like to come around to my place, we could have drinks there."

Would Mariah still be awake? Would she come down and join them? He shook his head. It seemed most unlikely. Drinks with the gentlemen was no place for a lady.

"I'll have my beaver momentarily, and shall likely arrive before you," Rags said as he turned on his heel and headed toward the door.

Colin grinned. "It is rare I find myself in agreement with Rags, but I believe he might just have the right of it." He moved out around the group. "I will see you at your place, Reg. Please, do not keep us waiting."

# Chapter Sixteen

It had been two days since Mariah had left her room. Indeed, she had never been so hardily sick of looking at the same four walls.

When she was well, she had a right mind to order new wallpapers and paint for her bedroom. Simply so she might stand the sight of it when she returned next Season.

The clock on her mantle chimed eleven. Reginald had gone to a card party without her. He attended everything without her, saying he had already sent his acceptance, and it would be improper if he did not at least make an appearance.

She released a sigh. Most evenings he at least returned before the events ended. But he had not yet returned that evening, and Miriam had long since gone to bed.

Mariah tossed her book to the side, unable to concentrate on it a moment longer. She stared at the drab, ugly draperies hanging from her bedposts. How was she to stay abed for another week? She could not do it. At least not without going completely mad.

Biscuit shifted on the bed next to her. Even he no longer brought her out of her doldrums.

Her eyes landed on her walking stick propped up against

her side table. Reginald had brought it in just that afternoon, telling her that perhaps in a few days' time, she might be ready to use it.

Mariah threw back the covers. She had no intention of waiting a few days' time. She was ready to leave her room and couldn't wait a moment longer.

Quietly she lowered her feet to the floor. Grasping hold of the cane, she pulled it to her. She did not know where she was going to go, only that she was going to escape the prison she'd been confined to for days.

She leaned heavily on the cane, gently and slowly testing out the strength of her injured ankle. It had been two days since her accident. Surely it had healed at least a little bit. Pain shot up her leg, but she pushed it aside. She could handle the pain if it meant she could breathe in fresh air. Or at least different air than that of her bed chambers.

Taking small hobbling steps and biting the inside of her cheek against the pain, Mariah moved toward the door. Her stomach let out an angry whine, and she remembered how little she had eaten at dinner. It seemed her pale yellow walls had done little to boost her appetite. Even then, the thought of rich gravy and heavy soups did not appeal to her. But a thick slice of bread with butter would not go amiss.

Mariah moved out of her room, looking in both directions. Her shoulders dropped as she looked down the long corridor toward the main staircase. How had she never realized how far away it was from her bedroom door? Now, with her foot already throbbing, it felt as if those stairs were in another country.

She looked in the opposite direction. The servant's staircase was much closer. While she was not in the habit of taking those stairs, she could not find a good reason not to.

With a pronounced limp, she hobbled down the corridor. The first stair she managed, but when she stepped down onto her injured ankle, her knee buckled, and she sat down in a heavy heap.

Perspiration covered her skin and ran down her brow and spine. How had she never realized what a blessing the mere act of walking was?

Mariah stared down the flight of stairs. Was it worth seeking something in the kitchen? It was such a long way away. And for what? She did not even know if Mrs. Leach had any food from dinner remaining. What if she went downstairs and discovered nothing there? Her effort would be in vain.

Her stomach let out another groan. Why did she not just summon a servant to fetch her something to eat?

She looked back toward her bedroom door and shook her head. She could not go back there. At least, not yet. She simply needed to find a way to make it down the stairs. Staying in her seated position, Mariah scooted from one stair to the next, one stair at a time, until she made it to the kitchen.

Using the walking stick for support, Mariah pulled herself to standing. She bit her cheek, waiting for the pain in her leg to subside enough for her to walk the rest of the way to the kitchen.

Her shift wet from perspiration, she lifted a hand to push inside the kitchen. But she paused when she heard a noise inside and she waited to see if it sounded again.

A stuttering breath echoed through the quiet rooms. Someone was crying. But who?

Softly, Mariah pushed into the kitchen. Peeking her head around the door, she spotted Mrs. Leach hunched over the baking table, her shoulders shaking gently.

Mariah's first instinct was to back away and leave the woman to herself. But something made her stay.

Mrs. Leach was obviously in despair. Could not Mariah offer some sort of consolation? She had never done something so personal before. Indeed, she did not even know how to go about it. But hearing the older woman's sobs made Mariah's chest ache.

Hobbling as quietly as possible with her cane and injured ankle, Mariah moved into the kitchen. But she was not quiet enough, and Mrs. Leach looked up, hastily wiping the back of her hand across her face. "Lady Mariah, I did not see you there."

Mariah moved slowly forward. Was she doing the right thing? It seemed rather intrusive. Yet she could not seem to put it from her mind, nor make herself retreat. "Mrs. Leach, you seem distraught. Is there anything I can do?"

The cook looked at Mariah oddly, as if truly seeing her for the first time. She shook her head. "No, my lady, it is nothing you need to concern yourself with."

Mariah paused. Should she press further? Or should she just allow Mrs. Leach her privacy? What was the proper thing to do? She bit her lower lip. What would Sarah do?

She looked at the older woman, holding her gaze. Never had Mariah seen anyone looking so miserable, except for Reginald, when their parents had died.

Mariah's throat tightened. Could that be what was wrong with Mrs. Leach? In truth, Mariah knew very little about Mrs. Leach's family. She had no notion whether the cook's parents were still alive or not.

Was it even proper for her to seek more information?

Sarah would surely know. She took an interest in all of the servants. And if Sarah did so, would it not be acceptable for Mariah to do so as well?

She prayed she was not about to make things worse. What if Mrs. Leach took offense and left their employ? Then what would they do? Mrs. Leach was one of the best cooks in Staffordshire. But she could not worry about that now.

Mariah placed a hand on Mrs. Leach's shoulder. "It is no bother, Mrs. Leach. If there is something troubling you, I should like to help if I can."

As surprised as Mariah was about the sincerity in her voice, she was even more surprised to realize she meant it. Why had she thought it beneath her to take an interest in those who lived in their house and served them?

Mrs. Leach sniffed and stared at Mariah as if she had never seen her before.

Was it so hard for everyone to believe that Mariah could be kind? An uneasy knot formed in her stomach. But then, why should they believe her to be? She had done nothing to give them the idea that she was. But was it too late to start? Had everyone already formed their opinion of her?

Mrs. Leach held Mariah's gaze until she seemed to realize Mariah was not leaving. "It is nothing you need to worry about, my lady."

"But I should like to help."

Mrs. Leach sucked in a jerky breath. "It is my sister. She has taken ill, and I fear the worst."

Mariah's eyes widened. Mrs. Leach had a sister? And she feared she would die? Mariah's shoulders slumped and shame heated her face. But Mrs. Leach did not feel Mariah needed to be troubled.

Colin had been more correct than Mariah wished to acknowledge, and it seemed the staff shared his opinion if they believed her so unfeeling as to care nothing about their families.

Feeling quite uncomfortable, Mariah pushed away the urge to run from the kitchen and return to her prison cell. Instead, she pulled a stool from under the table and gingerly sat down. She tugged at the stool next to her, carefully lifting her foot up and placing it on top.

Mrs. Leach jumped to her feet. "Oh, mercy, my lady. I'm sorry I did not think about your ankle sooner. Let me fetch you a cold cloth."

Mariah lifted her hand. "Please, Mrs. Leach. You need not worry over me. My ankle will be well now that it is up." She knew it was likely an untruth, but it was a justified one, was it not?

Mrs. Leach paused mid-stride. "What may I make for you? You hardly ate a thing from your dinner tray. You must be near starved."

Mariah smiled. "You always know when we need food, Mrs. Leach." She leaned her elbows on the table and dropped her chin into her hands. "But I do not wish for you to go to any trouble."

Mrs. Leach waved a hand at her. "Nonsense, my lady. There is not much. But I am certain I can find you some bread, cheese, and meat, at least."

Mariah grudgingly nodded. "Thank you, Mrs. Leach."

The cook paused and stared at her again, but then scurried about the kitchen, collecting food on a plate. She placed it on the table in front of Mariah.

Mariah stared down at the plate wondering what she was to do now. It did not seem right for her to just sit there and eat. Not when Mrs. Leach's sister was in such a condition.

Mariah chewed thoughtfully at the bread in her mouth. When she swallowed, she looked up at the woman still sitting across from her. "Mrs. Leach, has your sister seen a doctor?"

Mrs. Leach pulled her bottom lip between her teeth and shook her head. "I sent for the apothecary, but he would not see my sister until I had paid his fee."

Mariah dropped her hand to the table and stared at the woman. Her sister was in this condition because she could not afford the apothecary?

Mariah pushed a slice of cheese around her plate with her finger. What should she do? Should she offer to give Mrs. Leach the money? Or would she be too proud to accept the offer? Was it even proper?

She chewed slowly, hoping the answer would come to her. How did Sarah know what to say? Had it been part of her training? If so, why had not Mariah's mother taught her what to do?

Again, she thought about Sarah. Would she be worried about offending, or would she simply do what needed to be done?

Not for the first time, Mariah wondered if she might not have been unfair in her treatment of her friend. While she and Sarah had not spoken more than biting words—and that was more Mariah than Sarah in past months—Mariah had known Sarah her whole life. And she knew what Sarah would do. Sarah would help.

"Mrs. Leach?" Mariah sounded tentative. "We are to return to Staffordshire soon. What will your sister do when you are gone?"

Mrs. Leach's eyes filled with tears again. "I don't know. She has no husband and no children to look after her. Only me."

Mariah pondered this. Was it enough to pay for the doctor? What did she need beyond that? What was her occupation? If she had been ill for some time, she may have lost her position. Mariah took a deep breath and plunged ahead.

"Mrs. Leach, send for the apothecary again. Have him send the bill to me. And if a doctor is needed, send his bill to me as well. I will see they are paid."

Mrs. Leach shook her head. "I could not ask that of you, my lady."

Mariah reached across the table and patted the woman's hand. "You did not ask, Mrs. Leach."

The cook wiped at her eyes with the corner of her apron. "I don't know what to say. It is too much."

Mariah shook her head. "You have taken care of us for as long as I can remember. I'm sorry we did not help you sooner."

Mrs. Leach lifted a hand in protest. "Lord Stoke and you

have been very good to me, my lady. I have nothing to complain about."

Mariah took a bite of her bread. It felt good to help, but she was not completely satisfied. She had helped with the woman's current needs. But what of her future? "What does your sister do for work?"

Mrs. Leach looked down at her hands. "She worked as a cook in a large house, just as I do. But she was relieved of her position when she became ill."

Mariah nodded. It seemed logical both women should know how to cook. Although she could imagine no one cooked as well as Mrs. Leach. "And she had no promise to be rehired once she is well?"

Mrs. Leach twisted at the corner of her apron. "No, ma'am. Though I don't blame her employer. They couldn't go without food simply because she had taken ill."

"No, I suppose they could not. But that does not seem to be of any consolation to your sister." Mariah tapped her finger against her chin. "Why do you not bring your sister to Oakdale? She may recover fully there, and once she is well, she may work in the kitchen with you until we can find her a permanent position."

Mrs. Leach shook her head. "I know I should reject your offer, my lady. It is not proper of me to accept. But I cannot decline it. You are an answer to my prayers. I did not know what I was going to do about my sister when we left London. And I feared what would happen to her when I left." Again, her eyes filled with tears. "I do not know how to thank you."

Mariah smiled for a moment, allowing herself to feel pleased. Not in a proud and haughty sort of way. She was simply grateful to be of use—to have a purpose.

She pushed her plate away from her, suddenly too tired and in too much pain to eat anymore. Her ankle throbbed with every beat of her heart. Perhaps Dr. Canton had been right in ordering her to bed for a fortnight. It had only been a few days, but the pain was not much better than it had been the morning after it had happened.

With a sigh, she pushed away from the table and stood up, using her cane for support. She took a few hobbling steps toward the kitchen door before Mrs. Leach's arm curved around her waist. "Let me help you to your chambers, my lady. The pale look on your face makes me think you might not make it on your own."

Mariah tried to shake her off. "I will be fine, Mrs. Leach. You have enough to worry about without concerning yourself with me."

Mrs. Leach shook her head. "If I am to accept your help, my lady, it is only proper for you to accept mine."

Mariah nodded. "I suppose you are helping Miriam, too. It is late, and I do not wish to wake her."

Mrs. Leach tipped her head to the side. "Please, forgive me if I am overstepping and sound impertinent, but I have watched you grow for many years, my lady. I am pleased with what I see. And I'm certain your parents would be, as well."

Mariah ducked her head. "Thank you, Mrs. Leach." While she would never say it aloud, it was something Mariah questioned often. She spent many days in front of the portraits of her mother and father, wondering if they might be proud of her. She could not say she believed the answer to be yes. At least, not of late. But perhaps if it was not too late for her to think beyond herself, it was not too late to make her parents proud. The thought made her chest tighten.

They stopped at Mariah's bedroom door. Mrs. Leach studied her closely for a moment. "If I might say one more thing, my lady."

Mariah nodded, even though she was physically exhausted.

"I believe there are times in our lives when we don't live up to our potential. The true test of a person is when they discover their potential and decide to do what they must to become what they were destined to be."

Mariah looked over at the cook she had known for the whole of her life.

Mrs. Leach patted Mariah's hand. "I believe you have discovered your potential. And I believe you will do great things with it."

Mariah's throat thickened. Her character had taken several hits lately. She had heard few compliments but many reprimands. It was refreshing to hear something she could be proud of. But perhaps that was because she had finally done something to be proud of.

# Chapter Seventeen

Colin stepped from his carriage and looked up at the front of Reginald's London townhome. It had only been a week since he came to the ball hosted by Reginald and his wife, yet it felt much longer.

In that short time, so much had happened. He had learned Lady Mariah admired dogs as much as he did, only to discover she disdained them, and it had all been a lie in order to…what? Gain his approval? He had purchased her a dog as revenge, only to be coerced into helping train the dog. Additionally, Lady Mariah had injured herself, putting a stop to the training after only one attempt.

He shook his head. *One week.* Who would have guessed so much could happen? And in London?

A smile turned up the corners of his lips as he remembered Mariah from the day at the park. With her hair sticking this way and that—twigs and leaves sticking out all over her head and her dress stained with dirt and grass. Even after a week, it was still a picture he found himself thinking about more often than not.

He had not seen her in days. Which felt rather odd when he thought about it. He and his friends naturally attended the same events in Town. They had been doing it for most of their adult lives. If they had to endure society's events, they all agreed it was best if they did it together. And this year, with Lady Mariah having her come out, where Reginald went, Lady Mariah went too. It meant Colin had seen her nearly every night since he'd arrived in London. And sometimes he even saw her during the day, as they had taken to meeting in Reginald's study rather than at Brooks's.

Indeed, he had noticed Mariah's absence the last week. And while he did not like to admit it, he missed seeing her—which he could not understand why. There were more things than not that he disliked about her, such as her ridiculous pouting and rather selfish behavior.

However, there were a few things he found tolerable. She was quick-witted, and he could not deny he found her quite the most handsome woman in London. But still, those were nothing to justify his constant thinking about her. It was rather maddening.

Over the last few days, he had oft wondered what was becoming of her relationship with Biscuit—he shook his head. It was truly a dreadful name. While he had bought the animal as a sort of joke, if he were being truthful, he hoped perhaps Mariah would come to like the animal, eventually.

The door opened without Colin ever pulling on the doorbell. "Good evening, my lord." Maxwell motioned Colin inside. "Lord Stoke and the rest of his guests are in the Green Salon. If you will follow me—"

Colin held up his hand. "Do not trouble yourself, Maxwell. I know the way."

Reginald meant the evening to be an informal event with only close friends in attendance.

He had not said he had invited anyone other than their small group of friends. And while it would make the seating at dinner rather awkward—as Lady Mariah would likely be the only female there—Colin did not care. He was not in the mood for a crowd of people he did not care about. And he did not wish to make small talk with those of no consequence.

He stepped into the room and was happy to see Cort, Ponsy, and Charlie already seated near the fireplace. Along with Charlie's sister, Miss Bancroft, and Ponsy's mother. But his lips did not turn up until he saw Mariah sitting on the opposite couch. When had he begun to think of her in such informal terms? He had to admit he liked the thought of it.

She looked lovely with her blonde hair gathered up in a knot at the back of her head. Unlike at the ball, she did not have pearls or rose buds dotting her braids. But it mattered not because Colin thought she looked just as lovely as she had at the ball. Although he missed the sticks and leaves.

Everyone turned when they heard him enter the room.

"Colin, you have arrived at last." Reginald stood from his seat and motioned Colin forward.

"I am not the last to arrive, am I? I do not see Ben and Rags here."

"Ben is here, but he received a message that demanded an immediate reply. He is in my study." Reginald stood until Colin rounded the couch.

Several seats sat open. One between Ponsy and Cort—which would put the men shoulder to shoulder. Colin had no desire for that. There was also a seat next to Mariah and one next to Charlie.

Colin hesitated, looking between the two spaces. While he preferred to sit next to Mariah, he did not wish to explain his choice or see the looks he would surely get. However, sitting next to Charlie held no appeal.

Without thinking more about it, he dropped onto the seat next to Mariah, scooting himself closer to the arm of the couch to put as much space between them as possible. Perhaps if it did not look as though that was his preference, he would avoid the raised brows. Cort and Ben seemed to raise their brows at him far too often of late.

Mariah sat with her hands clasped in her lap. Her foot sat propped up on a pillow on the low table in front of them. A delicate slipper clad her foot, along with a thick fabric wrapping.

She looked over at him from the corner of her eye and smiled. Lud, why did that make his heart quicken? Why was he having such a reaction to her when he barely even tolerated her? "Good evening, Lord Heatherton."

He smiled back at her. "And good evening to you, my lady." He motioned to her foot. "I had hoped you would feel better by now."

"Oh, I am." She glanced down and frowned.

"Yes, her ankle is so much recovered that I had to carry her from her chambers so she might join us tonight." Reginald sounded irritated, but Colin could see the sparkle in his eye. He was happy to have his sister joining them at last.

Mariah frowned. "Come now, Regi. It is better than it was the morning after the ball."

Reginald tilted his head to the side, a look of incredulity on his face. "Is it really, Mar?"

She opened her mouth the speak, but Reginald cut her off.

"Although, I assume the reason for your increased pain might have something to do with the little jaunt you took to the kitchens last night."

Mariah's eyes widened. "How did you know about that?"

Colin grinned and leaned slightly toward her. "I believe you have been caught, my lady." A light floral scent tickled his nostrils.

"I have spies everywhere, Mar. When will you realize that?" Reginald grinned mischievously at her.

Mariah folded her arms across her chest and her lips turned down in a pout. But before Colin could even roll his eyes, the pout was gone. Instead, Mariah lifted her brows and pursed her lips at her brother. "I suppose if you did not leave me here alone for hours on end, you may not need all those spies."

"Ah, Reg, I think she might have you there." Colin leaned back in his seat. But then he frowned. "How did you make it all the way to the kitchen with your ankle?"

Mariah shrugged. "I used the walking stick Reginald gave me." She looked down at her hands as if she could not look them in the eye.

"And…" Reginald pressed.

Mariah looked up at him. "I do not believe your friends are interested in the details of my trip to the kitchen, my lord." She snapped.

Reginald grinned even wider. "As Jones tells it, you had to sit and scoot your way down the stairs."

Colin looked from Reginald to Mariah. She had scooted all the way down the stairs because she could not stand? "Why did Jones not assist her? She was obviously in need of help." Indignation welled up inside him.

The smile fell from Reginald's lips. "He did not think it proper. And by the time he fetched a maid, she had already made it to the kitchen." He cleared his throat and looked at his sister. "I'm sorry, Mar. I should have been here for you. I will not leave you again."

"Have I not been trying to rid myself of you for the whole of the Season?" Mariah ducked her head. "Really, Regi. I am fine on my own." While her voice said she did not need him to watch over her, her face held relief.

Colin leaned over toward Mariah. "Your injury appears to be worse than you thought after the accident."

Mariah shrugged. "The doctor says it is a sprain and that I shall have to stay off it for the rest of the Season."

Miss Bancroft sucked in a breath. "But you will miss Lord Trenton's ball." She looked at Mariah with pity in her eyes.

Mariah's shoulders fell. "Indeed. It is the thing I regret the most." She glanced at Reginald and then back at everyone else. But her gaze rested on Colin. "But I am very grateful to Regi for allowing you all to come for dinner tonight. I have been dreadfully lonely this past week."

Colin glanced down as she shifted her fan from her right hand to her left.

She looked from the fan resting in her lap to him. Her head tipped to the side, and she pulled her lip between her teeth.

Colin's brow furrowed, and her face pinked slightly.

What was she embarrassed about? Was it her admission that she was lonely? He supposed the comment exposed a vulnerability. And the Mariah he knew would never show a vulnerability—unless perhaps it would give her what she wanted. Was this all a ruse so Reginald would stay at home with her? Or did she wish for Colin to pity her?

He shifted in his seat.

Reginald had already told her he would stay home, so Colin's assessment did not feel accurate. Could it be he did not know Mariah as well as he supposed?

She caught his gaze as she lifted her closed fan and slowly drew it across her face. Her lashes fluttered and her face turned nearly crimson.

Colin stared at her in confusion.

"Oh, dash it all, Mariah!" Reginald rolled his eyes at his sister. "Stop it this instant. It will not work."

Mariah jerked her gaze to her brother and her face reddened even more.

Colin's attention pulled away from Mariah and her fan as he darted his gaze between brother and sister. What the devil was going on between them?

"I've had a break in a pasture wall at my estate." Ben's voice sounded from the doorway, drawing everyone's attention away from Reginald and Mariah. "I need to travel to Berwick and see to it before I can come to Staffordshire."

He rounded the couch and dropped into the seat next to Charlie.

Colin glanced over at Mariah from the corner of his eyes. She kept her gaze down, but he did not miss the look of relief.

"You have a month. That should be enough time, should it not?" Reginald asked with a furrowed brow.

"I am certain my bailiff can handle mending the wall and relocating the sheep while the fence is broken. However, my sheep have made a few enemies among my neighbors, and I must speak with them to make amends. Once I have finished my business, I shall come forthwith to Staffordshire." He stretched out his legs and crossed his feet at the ankles.

"Are you traveling with Lord Minton and his daughter?" Cort asked. He glanced at Reginald. "They were invited?"

Ben looked to Cort. "Have they sent their acceptance? Lady Amelia is not usually inclined to accept invitations to house parties. She rather prefers to stay close to home."

"I have not yet heard from them. Although, it is possible they sent their reply on to Oakdale." Reginald lifted a shoulder.

"She is one of your dearest friends, is she not?" Charlie asked. "Surely you could convince her to come."

"Indeed, she is. Which is how I know she will not be moved. If her father should exert his influence, I fear no one will be safe from her temper."

"That certainly gives me something to look forward to," Rags grumbled from the doorway. "Why did you invite someone who is so grumpy?"

"Come now, Rags. You can't be the only curmudgeon in attendance." Reginald glanced over his shoulder. "Besides, I thought it might give you someone to talk to. Someone who might share in your disdain for just about everything."

Rags smirked at them. "I am not grumpy. I'm just particular."

Charlie dropped his head back and laughed. "I shall keep that in mind the next time we attend the theater."

Colin looked over at Mariah. Her eyes bounced from one gentleman to the next as she listened to their conversation. It gave him a chance to watch her without her notice. She seemed quieter than normal. Or perhaps it was just that she was still in pain from her ankle. Or perhaps she was taking laudanum, and it was making her drowsy.

He leaned slightly closer to her, taking a more thorough look at her. She did not appear to be drowsy. He tilted his head slightly downward so he might see her face more clearly.

"Is something the matter, my lord?" She did not speak loudly, but it still caused him to jerk upright.

Lud, she had caught him staring at her.

"No, not at all." He knew he should come up with an excuse for why he was staring at her, but he could think of none. Instead, he looked away.

Thankfully, Maxwell entered the room and announced dinner.

Colin stood and extended his hand to help Mariah stand.

She stared at it for a minute but did not move to take it.

Finally, she shifted and pushed herself to the edge of the couch. Pushing up on the cushions, she stood up on one foot. Gingerly, she set her other foot on the floor, reaching for his arm to support her.

Colin's whole body warmed the moment her fingers wrapped around his arm.

What was happening? His first impulse was to shake her hand off, but he refrained. Why was his skin tingling and his heartbeat pounding in his ears? He lightly touched his hand to his brow, wondering for a moment if he might be starting with an illness. It was the only explanation that made any sense.

Reginald pushed past him. "Excuse me, Colin." He stooped slightly, placing one hand around her back and the other beneath her knees. Then he swept her up into his arms and moved around the couch.

Colin watched after them with his mouth turned down in a frown.

The group moved into the small private dining room and Reginald placed Mariah in the seat next to him.

Colin held back, waiting to see where everyone else would sit. He did not wish to look overly anxious about sitting next to Mariah. Especially not after he had sat next to her in the salon.

But when Cort moved toward the seat next to her, Colin stepped forward and grabbed hold of the back of the chair, pulling it out and dropping down hard into it.

Cort raised his brow—something Colin was becoming rather tired of—but then chose the next seat.

Quiet conversations hummed through the room as everyone settled in and waited for the footman to serve the first dish. Colin, however, remained quiet. He had nothing he wished to say to Cort, and he could think of nothing to say to Mariah.

When had he ever had trouble carrying on a simple conversation?

The footmen entered, giving him time to think of something to discuss with her.

He cleared his throat as he picked up his spoon and dipped it into his soup. "Lady Mariah, have you done much training with Biscuit since your injury?" He did not look at her, keeping his gaze on his bowl.

She shifted closer to him, and his hand stilled with his spoon halfway to his mouth.

"I have not. Regi has not allowed me to leave my chambers until tonight. Indeed, he has hardly let me leave my bed."

He cautioned a glance at her. "Thus, your need to sneak out when he is away?"

She tilted her head to the side and smiled.

His stomach flopped as if he were about to jump his horse over the fence.

"I was not sneaking," she pursed her lips together and Colin's eyes dropped for a moment. "Even if it felt as though I were a prisoner. I simply needed to look at something other than the dreadful pale yellow wallpaper decorating my chambers."

Colin grinned down at the table. He did not know why he should have thought that a sprained ankle would keep Mariah confined anywhere she did not wish to be. From what he had seen, if she wanted something, she obtained it by whatever means necessary. Even if it meant feigning fondness for a dog. Odd how that thought no longer made his fist clench or his stomach sour.

"I do not suppose while in the kitchens you decided upon a more dignified name for Biscuit?" He glanced over at her with a hopeful look.

She raised a brow at him, but her lips were upturned so he did not think her very offended. "I have no intention of changing his name, my lord. His name has great significance."

"Oh? And just what is it?"

Mariah shook her head. "Perhaps I shall tell you someday. But not now."

Colin pushed out his lips and grunted. "Very well."

She scooted closer and the floral smell overtook that of the white soup. "While I have not been able to properly train him, that does not mean we have not spent time together. Biscuit has been my only company these past few days. Except for Miriam, of course."

"Oh? Pray tell." Colin was perfectly content to allow her to control the conversation, as he had thought of little else to contribute.

She let out a quiet laugh. Not a giggle as she used to do, but something more soft and reserved. It had a decidedly opposite effect on him than her giggles. "Although I cannot condone his behavior, he found his way onto my bed the morning after my accident, and I was at a loss to force him from it. Now it seems he has made it his duty to wake me each morning."

A footman leaned in with a plate of greens and a plate of pheasant.

Mariah smiled. "Thank you, Henry."

Colin stared at her. Had he just heard her thank a servant? He dished his food onto his plate and thanked the footman.

"I am happy to hear you and Biscuit are getting along so well."

"As am I. After Lady G, I did not think I should ever enjoy the company of a dog." Her brow furrowed. "Although, my newfound affection for Biscuit has had me question several other judgments I had made. It is possible Lady G was not as disagreeable as I believed. Perhaps when I return to Staffordshire, I can find something pleasing about her as well."

Colin abandoned his fork and sat back for a moment, watching Mariah. He never would have thought she would admit she might have misjudged someone. It was a dog, but even so, was that not a sign of change? He knew the notion deserved more of his attention, but he could not think about it just then. But he *would* think about it. Just as he would think about what it all meant.

He placed his knife and fork on his plate and met her gaze. "I wonder, my lady, if we might continue the training lessons before you return to the country? He won't be completely trained, at least until you can walk, but I think there are some things we might start on that will make things easier for you. Things that we can teach him in the house."

Mariah pulled her bottom lip between her teeth, and Colin's gaze dropped again. Had she always done that?

"That would be wonderful, my lord. And I am certain Reginald would appreciate it." Her lashes fluttered, but it did not seem to bother him as much as it had previously.

Colin sat up straighter in his chair. "Capital. I shall come around tomorrow morning if that is agreeable."

Mariah nodded as she lifted her fork to her lips.

Lud, she had fine lips. Curious he had not noticed them before.

# Chapter Eighteen

Reginald excused himself and carried Mariah into the drawing room, depositing her on the couch in front of the fireplace. Lady Ponsonby and Miss Bancroft followed in behind her.

Lady Ponsonby pulled a stitchery from the basket she had brought with her and quietly set to work unknotting and straightening her threads.

Reginald bowed to them. "Ladies, I will return with the gentlemen after they have finished their port."

Mariah nodded and smiled up at him, trying to hide how badly her ankle hurt. If he knew, he would surely take her back to her chambers and she would miss out on the rest of the evening.

She noticed Miss Bancroft eye the pianoforte. "Miss Bancroft, you're more than welcome to play, if that is what you wish."

The girl shook her head. "I am certain you are far more proficient than I."

Mariah waved her words away. "Oh, pish. I have practiced far more on the harp. And I am certain my playing would not measure up. Besides, my ankle is paining me. I should like to keep it up on the cushion for a bit." She motioned with her head toward the instrument in the corner. "I am certain Lady Ponsonby and I would both enjoy some music."

Lady Ponsonby looked up and smiled. "Oh, yes, dear. Do play for us."

Miss Bancroft ducked her head but moved quickly over to the piano. Without even looking at the sheet music, the girl played a lovely piece.

Mariah plucked a pillow from the corner, placing it on the low table in front of her. Taking care, she gently placed her foot on the cushion and released a sigh.

Lady Ponsonby glanced up from her stitchery. "Are you certain you should be about on that ankle so soon?"

Mariah lifted a shoulder. "It has been nearly four days. I could not stand my room a moment longer." She sucked in a long breath. "I will take it easy tomorrow. But for now, I am going to enjoy the company."

The other woman looked at her just long enough for Mariah to smile, then she dropped her gaze back to the stitchery in her lap.

Mariah settled back against the seat cushion. Her stitchery was still in her room, as was the book she was reading. There was little else for her to do but sit and think, which seemed a futile endeavor. Her thoughts seemed to always be about the same person. And she never seemed to come up with any ideas that changed the way things with him went.

Voices sounded down the hall, and Mariah released a sigh of relief. The men were already coming, thus saving her from her repetitive thoughts.

She slipped the string of her fan around her wrist, wanting it at the ready should she need it. While her flirting with the fan had vexed Reginald overly much, she had thought it had shown promise. Colin had seemed to pay her more mind that evening.

The men entered the room laughing and smiling.

The small creases at the sides of Colin's eyes that always made her sigh, deepened as he caught her gaze and his smile widened. Had the joke been about her, or was he simply happy to see her?

She closed her eyes, offering a quiet prayer that it was the latter.

Miss Bancroft stopped her playing, her eyes darting between her brother and the other men.

"Do not stop on our account, Miss Bancroft. Your playing is lovely." Reginald smiled as he rounded the couch and looked down at Mariah. He glanced at her foot up on the pillow and frowned. "Are you in much pain?" His voice lowered to nearly a whisper.

Mariah shook her head. "No. But I did not wish for it to become unbearable." While that was a complete bouncer, she was not about to share just how much pain she was in. Her room held no appeal for her. Especially not when Colin was still in the house.

"Shall I have Miriam fetch your medicine?"

Mariah shook her head again. "No, I will save it for bed."

"Are you certain?" Reginald's voice held concern.

"Yes, Regi. You need not worry about me. I am well."

Unlike before dinner, Colin chose a seat opposite Mariah. Which left her feeling rather cross. Had she said something that made him unhappy with her? The way he kept glancing at her was concerning. But she could not say exactly why. He was not scowling or glaring. But he did not smile, either. What could she possibly have done? She had not giggled at all.

The men talked about their plans for the last few days of the Season. While there was little to do in the Lords, there were still several prominent events before the *ton* removed themselves from London for the summer.

Mariah leaned into the side of the sofa, putting her elbow up on the arm and resting the side of her head on her hand. She discreetly watched Colin as he spoke with his friends.

While he was not so very different that evening than he was at formal events, she believed him more at ease when he was among his friends. Although, she glanced at him again, he did not appear at ease just then.

A rustle sounded in the corridor and Mariah looked over her shoulder toward the doorway just as Sarah stepped inside the room.

Reginald leapt to his feet and very nearly ran to her.

Mariah tried to frown, but she simply could not. While she was obviously not as glad to see Sarah as Reginald was, Mariah was happy to see her friend. There was much she needed to say. And perhaps Sarah might have some insight into what could be done about Colin.

Mariah twisted nervously at the tip of her glove. The conversation would need to wait until tomorrow, but that did not stop the churning in her stomach.

"Come join us," Reginald tugged on Sarah's hand, pulling her toward the couches.

"I really must change my gown. I have been in a carriage all day." She smiled nervously at the group.

Reginald turned to face his wife. "You need not change. No one at this party will think less of you if you stay in your traveling clothes. You are among friends." His voice was low, but Mariah could still hear what he said, as she was the closest to them.

"They are *your* friends, Reginald." Sarah glanced over his shoulder. "I am uncertain several of them have even forgiven me for marrying you yet."

"Only Rags. But he will come around in time." Reginald lifted her hands and kissed her knuckles. "Please stay, Sarah."

She tilted her head to the side. "You act as if I am leaving for good. I am only going to change my gown. I will return shortly. I promise." She pressed a finger to his lips when he opened his mouth to protest. "I promise." She pulled away from him and disappeared into the corridor.

"That is a surprise, is it not?" Berwick rested his elbows on the arm of the chair and intertwined his fingers.

Reginald grinned so widely his eyes nearly closed. "Indeed, it is." He settled into the couch. "A most pleasant surprise."

Mariah stared at him. Was it possible for her to have such a match? To feel so much love for one person? She glanced over at Colin. Did she love Colin that much or was she simply in love with the thought of him?

Mariah frowned. She did not like the idea that she may have been wishing for the wrong thing for all these years.

Colin glanced over at her, and her heart thumped noisily in her ears. Obviously, not all of her was ready to accept that Colin might not be what she desired. Or perhaps she simply needed to discover if she had been right all along.

Sarah glided into the room and again everyone turned to look at her. Her face pinked, and she moved toward the open seat next to Lord Ragsdale.

Reginald looked at Cort, who sat next to him, and shooed him away. "I should like to sit by my wife. Why do you not take the seat next to Rags."

Cort sulked. "But I don't want to sit next to Rags. He is grumpier than usual tonight."

"I am not, you coward." Rags grumbled under his breath.

Cort stood, but shot Reginald a look of contempt, irritation, and pleading all in one.

"Oh, no, Lord Montcort. You need not move on my account." Sarah moved toward the seat next to Lord Ragsdale. She clasped her hands in front of her. "Lord Ragsdale and I are not enemies." She paused, as if uncertain she wanted to utter her next sentence. "Are we, my lord?"

"I never assumed you were enemies. But I have not seen you in over a week. I wish for you to sit by me." Reginald stood and motioned to the couch. "Lord Montcort does not mind moving. He was simply being theatrical." Reginald eyed Cort.

"Indeed," Cort muttered as he stood up and moved to the next sofa, settling in next to Ragsdale. "And I am not a coward." He folded his arms across his chest.

Miss Bancroft straightened. "Lady Mariah, I would very much enjoy hearing you play. I know you prefer the harp, but I should enjoy hearing you on the pianoforte."

The grunting and grumbling stopped, and everyone looked at Mariah. Including Colin.

"Oh, yes, Mariah. Do play. It has been some time since I heard you play the pianoforte." Sarah offered a tentative smile and Reginald stiffened as if readying himself for an argument.

Mariah shook her head. "I appreciate your confidence in me, but I am certain I will sound dreadful. Miss Bancroft's performance will surely be more enjoyable." If they had been speaking about the harp, Mariah's protests would have been only for attention. But she was not lying when she said she had not practiced the piano often. It was as likely as not that she would make a complete fool of herself.

"I have never heard you play the pianoforte." Colin looked over at her and smiled. "I should very much enjoy hearing you play."

"I thought you were deuced tired of piano performances." Ben said in a voice of feigned innocence.

"I simply said that so we might leave the musicale." Colin flicked a glance at Mariah. "I did not mean it."

Mariah's face warmed. Did he really wish to hear her play? She smiled, and a genuine giggle very nearly escaped. But she caught it just in time. "If you insist. But I am certain it shall disappoint."

She gingerly lifted her foot off the pillow and placed it on the floor in front of her.

"Let me help you over to the pianoforte, Mar." Reginald moved to stand, but Colin stood up and held his hand out.

He cleared his throat. "Let me help you, my lady."

Her stomach erupted in flutters as she had never experienced. Clasping Colin's hand, she glanced at Reginald. He stared at them with narrowed eyes and a furrowed brow.

She looked away, unable to stand the scrutiny. Indeed, the entire room seemed to stare at them as Colin pulled her to her feet or rather her foot. She balanced, trying to put as little pressure on her sore ankle as possible.

At the last moment, she realized her fan sat on the couch, far out of reach. And she could see no reason she would need to take it with her. She did not intend to play anything so strenuous as to make her heated. And it seemed impossible to flirt with it while trying to play. With a backward glance, she reluctantly left it where it was.

Mariah reached for her cane, but Colin pulled her closer to him, snaking his arm around her waist. "You will not need that. I will assist you to your seat."

The flutters moved from her stomach to her chest and ears. Colin's hand rested just above her hip with the slightest pressure. For a moment, Mariah wished he would carry her as Reginald had carried her to the couch. But she shook the thought away. Should she not be grateful for what she had?

Colin led her around the grouping of chairs and toward the pianoforte in the far corner.

Mariah stumble-walked, but only partially because of her injured ankle. It was almost as if her body could only react to Colin's touch. Her hip and side burned with tingles. The fluttering in her ears drowned out any of the conversation taking place behind her.

What were they saying? They could not possibly be as excited as Mariah.

She didn't know what it all meant. But at that moment, she wouldn't allow herself to consider the implications. She was simply going to enjoy it.

Colin helped her onto the stool and stood staring down at her for a moment. "Do you need me to fetch you any music?"

Mariah swallowed and shook her head. "No, I believe I shall just play the songs that I know by memory." If only she had her fan. It seemed the perfect moment to swipe it across her face. Surely he could understand what she meant by it—see how much she adored him.

But if he did, why did he not say anything to her? Could it be he already knew but felt not the same and did not wish to hurt her feelings? She frowned down at the keys, her elation of moments ago gone.

He turned as if he were going to leave her, and she panicked. This was the most private time they'd had together since before she sprained her ankle. And she did not think she could let him go so easily. "Lord Heatherton, do you sing?"

She knew he had a rich baritone voice. She had heard him sing several times when he stayed at their home for Christmas. But if he was anything like Reginald, he would never admit to the talent. Especially not in front of the other men.

He stopped and turned back toward her. "I sing very ill, my lady."

Mariah tipped her head to the side and smiled pertly at him. "Now who is telling the lie, my Lord?"

He took several steps toward her, his brow creased. "And just what do you know of my singing?"

Mariah twisted her hands about in her lap. Perhaps she should abandon her plan—if she could actually call it a plan. Indeed, she was simply making it up as it came out of her mouth. "I've heard you sing at Christmas. And as I recall, it was very pleasing."

"Ah, but that was Christmas. Everyone can sing Christmas songs. I believe it is just the nature of it." He moved a few steps closer.

If she could get him to sing with her, would he pull over a chair and sit next to her? Or would he simply stand beside her? Perhaps it would be best if she convinced him to play the piano along with her.

She bit at the side of her cheek, tapping her finger against her lips.

"I have to disagree with you, my lord. Regi cannot even sing Christmas songs."

Colin let out a chuckle. "Ah, Reginald. I forgot how dreadful he sings."

Mariah grinned. "He manages on *The Twelve Days of Christmas*, but every time he attempts to sing *The First Noel*, the hounds howl just to cover the sound."

Colin chuckled deeper.

"What are you saying about me?" Reginald called from across the room.

Mariah pulled her bottom lip between her teeth as a giggle threatened to come out. "It is nothing, Regi. We were reminiscing about the Christmas we spent together. Do you not recall it?"

Reginald nodded his head thoughtfully. "Indeed, I remember. They are some of my fondest memories."

Colin grinned at her. "I suppose I should be happy to learn that I am not the only one you lie to. Although I suppose I can see the justification for this one."

Mariah's mouth dropped open, and she put a hand on her chest. "I did not lie. Were we not recalling memories of Christmas?"

Colin tipped his head to the side, a playful smile on his lips. "I stand corrected, my lady."

Mariah ran her tongue across her lips. Colin's gaze followed the path, and Mariah's breath caught. She swallowed hard and cleared her throat. "You did not give me a truthful answer to my earlier question. Would you be amiable to singing with me?"

Colin folded his arms across his chest, watching her, as if trying to detect if there was some kind of trick involved. If only he knew that the only tricks she played were because she wished to earn his affection, not his ire.

"What if I do not know any of the songs you have memorized?"

Mariah shrugged. "I am certain you must know the words to something I know how to play." She grimaced. "Although, it has been so long since I played the pianoforte that neither of us might perform to our best. However, you may look through the music, if you wish."

"What songs do you know?"

Mariah put her finger to her lips and raised her gaze to the ceiling. "Do you know *Robin Adair*?"

Colin stared at her for a moment, thinking. Did he not know the song? Or was he simply trying to decide if he should admit to knowing it?

# Chapter Nineteen

THUNDER AND TURF, WHY MUST SHE CONTINUALLY TOUCH OR lick her lips? If she did it again, he may just need to kiss her to stop her from doing it.

He shook his head. Which was exactly why she *must* stop doing it. It made him think things he should not be thinking—that he did not *want* to be thinking. He was quite content with his life, and he did not need complications. And kissing Mariah would surely bring complications.

She tilted her head to the side, and his eyes dropped to the delicate curve between her neck and shoulder. No skin should ever look so enticing.

He shook his head, trying to rid himself of the thoughts. If he did not rein himself in, he may just do something he would regret. Although, could he completely regret one small kiss from Mariah?

She stared intently at him. What had she asked? Oh, yes. Did he know the song? But what song had she asked about? He had no recollection, if he had heard it to begin with.

He cleared his throat. "I know the song, but I am uncertain I know the words well enough to sing along."

Mariah pulled her lip between her teeth again. Lud, he

should say something. But what would he say? *Lady Mariah, please stop touching your lips lest I be forced to kiss you quite thoroughly.* He was an idiot. He could not say such a thing. Reginald would surely have him thrown from the house.

He sighed. Perhaps it would be best if he simply returned to his seat.

She frowned up at him. "If you do not wish to sing, I shall not force you. I simply thought it would be entertaining." She turned her attention to the piano, placing her fingers on the keys. But she did not play. What was she waiting for?

She glanced over at him. "Do you play?"

He shook his head. "My mother taught me the notes, and how to read them so that I might turn her pages. But I never practiced. I cannot play well enough that I should presume to entertain anyone." He dropped his voice to a whisper. "Can you imagine what the gents would say?"

She dipped her head to the side, motioning to a chair sitting against the wall. "Would you mind turning the pages for me?"

He looked at the empty music stand. "I thought you wished to play those you knew by memory."

She fisted her hands and pushed out her lips in a pout. Although it was not her usual sort of pout. This one was not practiced, but rather a look of genuine frustration. Although, what was she frustrated about? Did it frustrate her that he refused her invitation to sing or play?

"All the songs I know are rather mundane. I thought perhaps I should play a few that are a little less…common." She bit her bottom lip again, and Colin lost his focus.

She moved her stool back to the center of the piano. "But if you prefer not to turn pages, then I will abandon the idea completely."

He could not refuse her, could he? It would not be proper to leave her, not when he had said he would assist her. Did that only mean his assistance with the instrument? He could not deny the thought of sitting close to her was appealing. Nor could he deny it made him uneasy.

What would his friends say? What would the ladies say? Would they circulate stories? And what would Mariah think? He glanced down at her through his lashes. If only he could spend time with her, without the fear that she would believe too much of the interactions. Or that his friends would.

Drat it all. She had asked for his help, and, as a gentleman, he had to oblige her.

He released a sigh and grabbed the chair. Placing it next to her stool, he made certain there was a bit of space between them.

Mariah leaned to the side and lifted a basket of sheet music onto her lap. Her fingers walked across the tops of the pages, pushing some to the side while pulling others out. After a few moments, she had a small pile sitting on the top of the pianoforte.

She pulled the music from the top and opened it. Placing it on the small stand, she turned to Colin. "You can follow along enough to turn the pages?"

He nodded. "It has been a few years, but I believe I am still up to the task."

Mariah gave him a brief smile, then turned back toward her music. Placing her fingers on the keys, chords from the piano filled the room.

Colin allowed a small smile. She was much better than she had led them to believe. Indeed, even without her supposed practice, she was even better than Miss Bancroft.

He followed along with the notes, turning the page when she reached the bottom. He noticed with pleasure her quick nod and grin at him. He wondered if perhaps she had thought he was telling her a lie. Was she surprised—perhaps even impressed—that he read music?

The pages were stiff and closed in on themselves. Mariah stumbled as she tried to see the notes as the pages slowly shut.

Colin shifted his chair closer to her and leaned forward, pressing them open before they disrupted her playing any more than they already had. His shoulder brushed against hers, as did his thigh when he reached across the music. Heat seared through his trousers and even through his coat and shirt sleeves.

Lud, it was deuced hot in there. Perhaps they should open a door and allow some fresh air in.

A hint of rosemary, lavender, and vanilla wafted past his nose, and he closed his eyes as the scent filled his nostrils. He sucked in a stuttering breath. Perhaps he should have followed his gut and returned to sit with the men. Even Rags seemed less dangerous than sitting there with Mariah.

She cleared her throat, and Colin realized she was waiting for him to turn the page. Drat. He needed to keep his attention on the notes. But every time she moved forward or backward with a crescendo, the same intoxicating scent filled his nostrils.

How much longer must he sit there and endure the torture? He could hardly think, let alone breathe normally.

And yet Mariah did not seem the least bit affected. It was rather a disaster. He had been concerned that she would interpret their interaction to mean more than he wished. Yet he was the one who could not even focus on the simple task of turning the pages.

Mariah cleared her throat again. Lud, he'd done it again. *Focus, man.*

He watched the notes as she played them, relieved when he turned the next page without her having to clear her throat. He could do it. He could pretend he smelled nothing—pretend there was no attraction to the woman sitting next to him. Gads, he was an idiot.

The song finally ended, and Colin jumped to his feet, anxious to be away from her.

Mariah looked up at him, her brow knit in confusion. "Do

you wish to stop?" There was a hint of disappointment in her voice. Indeed, if he had not just witnessed how completely unaffected she had been, he might have thought she was more than slightly disappointed. But it did not seem possible when she had only missed her notes because he had neglected to turn pages.

"I proved to be a very inept page-turner. I thought…that is, perhaps you might be more successful if you either turn the pages yourself or play those songs which you know from memory."

She pulled her blasted lip between her teeth again, and Colin nearly reached and pulled it back out. She could not possibly expect a man to ignore such an action. Why had Reginald not taught her such a thing?

She looked down at her hands clasped in her lap and nodded her head. "Oh, yes. I understand." She did not look as if she understood in the least. She looked almost hurt. "I'm sorry. I should not have taken you away from your friends. It was selfish of me. You came to visit with them, not turn my pages."

She fumbled around with the music sitting beside the music stand, moving sheets of paper around, only to discard them back into the basket.

Colin stood there for a moment, unsure what he should do. He looked over his shoulder at the men talking by the fire. What were they speaking of? Were they making sport of him? Were they even now believing him besotted?

He grunt-laughed. He was not besotted. He was simply hot. Yes, that was it. He was hot and the smell of Mariah's perfume had befuddled him.

But then he looked at Mariah. Her brow was creased, and she seemed in a sort of tug-of-war with the sheet music in the basket.

He suddenly realized he didn't care what the gents spoke about. Indeed, as much as staying would surely drive him to bedlam, he did not wish to leave. And he thought perhaps she might wish him to stay as well.

Sucking in a deep breath through his nose, Colin slid back into the chair next to Mariah.

As their thighs touched, she glanced over at him. "I thought you finished and wished to return to the conversation with the men."

Colin caught her gaze and held it. "Am I not at liberty to change my mind?"

She ducked her head, and he was certain she was biting her lip again. Thankfully, he could not see it.

He looked at the stack of music and dipped his head. "I do not know how I thought you could play through all of that, with no one to turn your pages."

She looked up at him, and just as he suspected, her lip was caught between her teeth.

Colin lifted a hand and lightly placed his thumb beneath her lower lip. Gently, he tugged it free. "You really should not do that."

Her stuttered breath seemed to match his. "And why not?" He heard a hint of sauciness in her tone.

He leaned in slightly. What would she do if he kissed her right then? Would she slap him? Or would she enjoy it as much as he would?

Mariah stared at him, the tip of her tongue poking slightly out at the corner of her mouth.

That was an invitation, was it not? He leaned in even closer. Their faces were only a breath away from each other. Indeed, with only the slightest movement, his lips could be on hers.

She drew in a long breath but seemed almost to hold it.

"What song are you to play now?" Lady Ponsonby's voice sounded from across the room, and Colin jerked back.

He dropped his hand into his lap and turned his attention to the sheet of music now sitting on the stand. What had he been thinking? They were not alone. He had nearly turned what should have been a private moment into a public spectacle.

He cleared his throat. "This looks to be a challenging piece, but I know you will handle it masterfully. I shall try my best to keep up." He tapped the music on the stand, trying to get his mind off what had almost happened. "I'm here to assist you. Begin when you are ready." Colin stared hard at the papers, reciting each of the notes in his head to help him keep his concentration.

Mariah placed her hands on the keys, leaning forward and then back as the music crescendoed.

Colin held his breath, anticipating the all-too-pleasing scent that would surely waft toward him. He could afford no more distractions.

The song ended and Mariah sat back. She smiled shyly at him. Had he embarrassed her when he nearly kissed her? "I do not think I can play anymore. My ankle needs rest. If you would not mind helping me back to the couch, I would appreciate it."

Perhaps he had been wrong, and she did not desire a kiss as much as he did.

Colin refrained from scrubbing a hand over his face. What had he been thinking? And in the middle of the drawing room for all his friends to see. Curses, he was a nodcock.

He smiled and helped her up from the stool—once again sliding his hand around her waist. Only this time he anticipated the electricity dancing around his fingers and arm and pushed the thoughts from his mind. It would not do for him to get any more ideas in his head about Lady Mariah. Not that he had any ideas beyond kissing her. But he did not believe Reginald would appreciate those ideas. Indeed, *especially* those ideas.

# Chapter Twenty

Mariah sat in her bed, her ankle propped up on a stack of pillows. She shifted restlessly. She had sent Sarah a card, asking her to come to visit at her earliest convenience. But when would that be? What if it was not convenient for her until next Tuesday?

Mariah threw her hands down on the counterpane. Such antics seemed like something Mariah would do. Not Sarah.

Mariah picked up the book off her side table and opened it with the pretense of reading. But she read not a single word. What would she say to Sarah? While she had rehearsed it at least a dozen times in her head since Sarah returned last evening, as the conversation drew closer, Mariah could not think of the proper words.

A knock sounded at her door, and Mariah's heart jumped into her throat. Could she hope it was Reginald coming to check on her?

"Come," Mariah called.

But it was not Reginald's face that appeared in the doorway. It was Sarah.

She looked uneasily at Mariah. "I received your note. If now is not convenient, I can return later."

Mariah lifted her hand and shook her head. "No. Now is perfectly agreeable."

Sarah stood near the door, twisting her hands as they hung in front of her.

Silence filled the air as they both stared at each other.

Mariah motioned to the chair next to her bed. "Would you care to sit down?"

Sarah quietly sat down, but her hands continued to work in her lap. Finally, she nodded at Mariah's foot. "What happened to your ankle?"

Mariah released a heavy sigh and raised an eyebrow. "Would you believe it happened on the very first set I danced at Lord Cleverly's Ball?" She shook her head. "One misstep and I am to miss the rest of the Season."

"How did it happen?" Sarah looked at her sympathetically. "You are not a clumsy dancer." She grinned. "We left that task to Reginald."

Mariah laughed. "Yes. Do you remember the time he tripped over Mr. Paulson, the dancing master, and the two of them fell to the ground?" Mariah shook her head as she grinned. "Mr. Paulson was so angry."

Sarah lifted a shoulder. "It was hard to blame him. Reginald's misstep resulted in Mr. Paulson spraining his ankle. He was unable to work for more than a month."

"Yes, but it was not as if Reginald did it on purpose. Is not a dancing master supposed to anticipate such things? He is there to teach dancing, after all." Mariah still grinned at the memory.

"I suppose he thought his students would have at least a minimal amount of talent."

Mariah rubbed her hand lightly over the bedding. "It seems he thought incorrectly when it came to Reginald." She kept her focus on her lap. "Although I noticed that Reginald's dancing seemed to improve when you were his partner."

"Perhaps that is because, unlike Mr. Paulson, I anticipated

Reginald's ability. After all, I had been his partner in many of those lessons." Sarah turned her gaze back on Mariah's ankle. "You never said how it happened."

Mariah sighed. "My attention was elsewhere, and I did not see the gentleman before I collided with him."

Sarah smiled and opened her mouth, but paused as if she were uncertain she should say what she was thinking.

Mariah's stomach twisted at the realization that their relationship had changed so much. There had been a time when they told each other everything. And now, because of Mariah, Sarah had to think about what she said.

"I am certain you must have already figured out who the object of my attention was." Mariah tipped her head to the side.

A hint of a smile curled Sarah's lips. "I have my suspicions."

Mariah had hoped that perhaps she would not need to apologize. Hoped they could continue as they had before their fight. Hoped that if she simply acted as if nothing was wrong, they would simply pick up where they had left off. But sitting there with Sarah, Mariah knew it could not be. There were things that needed to be said—things *she* needed to say to Sarah.

"I am very glad you came back. I had thought I must wait until we returned to the country."

Sarah folded her arms around her middle, as if bracing for what she knew was certain to come. "What must you wait for?"

Mariah sucked in a deep breath. She still did not know what to say. What if Sarah refused her apology? Could they go on forever despising one another? "I owe you an apology. I have treated you very ill these last few months."

Sarah sat very still. Her eyes held Mariah's, but she remained close-lipped.

Mariah continued. "Someone pointed out to me—" When

Sarah opened her mouth, Mariah hurried on. "It was not Reginald, so you need not chastise him for interfering."

Sarah tipped her head to the side, confusion knitting her brow.

"Someone pointed out to me that I do not always treat people with kindness. Especially those I think beneath me." Why had she started with that? It meant she either had to confess to thinking that Sarah was still beneath her—which was only partially true. Or she would have to confess the real reason for their disagreement. Which she had hoped to avoid.

Sarah's brows rose nearly to her hairline.

"While I do not think it is solely the case with you and me, it has given me something to think about this last week."

"What else is the problem between us, then?" Sarah's voice was quiet.

Mariah sat still, staring at the embroidery on her counterpane. She had not wished to share that part. In all of her practice, she had stated things in a way that did not require her to actually say why she had been so mad at Sarah after Vauxhall. But the conversation was not happening as she had practiced it. It was all confused and disjointed.

"Perhaps it is a small part of the problem."

"A small part? Then you do think me beneath you?" Sarah looked Mariah steadily in the eyes.

Botheration! Now she was going to admit both her problems with Sarah? "Perhaps only a little. But I have recently realized the error in my thinking."

Sarah's head nodded, but she said nothing for a moment. "Then what exactly is the problem, Mariah?"

Mariah looked out the window, unable to stand the probing gaze of her friend. "I was not completely honest with you about Vauxhall." She licked her lips. "I pretended to be mad at you, when in truth I was more mad at myself."

Any understanding that had been in Sarah's eyes vanished and was replaced by confusion.

"I was so relieved when you found me at Vauxhall. Lord Muckrake had led us much farther into the Dark Walk than I wished. But he would not turn back. I began to fear what he might do."

Sarah leaned forward. "Why did you not tell me when I came upon you?"

Mariah closed her eyes and shook her head, unwillingly remembering that night. "I had been so emphatic that Reginald need not be so protective—that I could take care of myself. And then, at the first opportunity, not only did I willingly go with a man I knew had a sullied reputation, but I could not take care of myself as I had insisted. I needed rescuing." She released a breath. "When I saw you, I was relieved. But I was also so very embarrassed. You would never have allowed yourself to be in such a situation. It seemed to prove what you said about me weeks earlier…That I regularly did not act properly."

Sarah perched on the edge of her seat, her lips pinched tightly together.

"Call it pride or superiority or perhaps both. But it seemed easier to place the blame on you rather than on myself. As time went on, the guilt spurred on my anger. Every time you acted properly or pointed out where I did not, it was a reminder of what I nearly allowed to happen to me. It did not take long for your act of salvation to become my source of resentment." Mariah leaned her head back against the headboard. She had not imagined she would feel such relief at ridding herself of those feelings. "If you cannot accept my apology, Sarah, I understand. I acted unpardonably toward you."

Sarah shook her head and placed her hand on top of Mariah's. "I cannot allow you to take full responsibility. I have taken it upon myself to act as your mother. Which I am not. Nor do I wish to be. I think my fears of my own shortcomings led me to advise you in areas that were not mine to advise."

Mariah shook her head fiercely. "No. I will not allow you to take upon yourself any of the responsibility. The fault was mine and mine alone." She twisted her lips to the side. "And you have done nothing a sister would not do. And are we not sisters now?"

Sarah nodded. "Indeed, we are."

Mariah could not yet feel completely relieved. There was still one matter left. "There is something else I must apologize for. You had a great challenge when you married my brother, and I have not helped you. Indeed, I only made it harder. For that, I am sorry. I hope you can forgive me."

Sarah smiled. It was still tenuous and guarded, but it was a smile. "I am certain, in time, we will be as we were before." Sarah patted Mariah's hand awkwardly. But there was a look of relief on her face.

Mariah shook her head. "I do not want us to be as we were before. I wish us to be *better* than before. I'm sorry I did not treat you as a dearest friend, much less a sister. But I intend to change." She lifted a shoulder and picked at a seam on her covers. "I had not realized how truly alone I was until you left me here alone with Reginald." She grinned. "Please, never do that again."

Mariah looked up to see a soft smile on Sarah's lips. It was less tenuous and more the genuine smile Mariah had missed of late.

"I never felt that you thought yourself above me, Mariah. I knew it was just who you are—who your parents raised you to be."

Mariah shook her head. "No. It is who I was. I am determined not to be that girl any longer."

The jingle of a bell sounded only moments before a ball of fur hurled itself up onto Mariah's bed. She smiled as she ran her hand down the dog's back. "Ah, Biscuit. You are late."

Sarah stared down at the dog, her mouth slightly open. "I cannot help but wonder at this dog. Where did he come from?

And why is he on your bed? I thought you were rather opposed to dogs."

Mariah grinned widely. "Oh, Sarah. We have so much to talk about."

She lifted Biscuit onto her lap and lifted his face gently up toward Sarah. "Sarah, this is Biscuit. Biscuit, this is my dearest friend and sister, Sarah." She looked at the dog and made a kissing noise, making certain her face was a safe distance away. While she had grown quite fond of the animal, she still did not wish it to slobber all over her face.

"You did not say where he came from."

Mariah raised a saucy brow. "Would you believe he was a gift from Lord Heatherton?"

Sarah's eyes widened. "No." She pulled the chair closer to Mariah's bed. "I must hear the story, for I am certain it is a good one."

MARIAH LEANED back into her pillows. "And so, while he came to me out of spite, I must admit, Reginald was correct. I quite adore him now."

"Then you are to keep him?" Sarah asked.

Mariah nuzzled her nose into Biscuit's neck. "I cannot imagine parting with him. He has been my only company since I injured my ankle."

Sarah patted Mariah's hand. "That will no longer be the case now that I am back."

Mariah frowned. "Why are you back?" She grimaced at the way her comment sounded. "I am happy for it. But it surprised me to see you."

Sarah leaned back in her chair and pulled her legs up

beneath her skirt. It was so much like the Sarah that Mariah had known since they were children.

"I arrived in Stoke to find my mother completely healed. She was up and visiting with Mrs. Turnbow and had plans to visit the Milliners." Sarah shook her head, but she grinned. "She was quite surprised to see me. It seems they had sent a letter telling me I need not hurry back, but they must have sent it after I already left. My mother insisted I return to London at once. She was quite mortified to think that I would miss Lord Trenton's ball."

"It is such a long way to travel. Especially when we will be returning to Stoke only next week." Mariah could not imagine traveling for nearly a week, simply to attend a ball."

Sarah stretched and yawned. "Yes, it was a rather taxing journey. Although the roads were very dry each way, so we made it in good time."

"You must give me every detail of Lord Trenton's ball so I will not feel my absence so keenly."

"Are you certain you cannot attend?"

Mariah grunted. "Dr. Canton says I cannot walk or stand on it, at least not for any real distance, for a fortnight. I should be able to use a cane once we return to the country. But the ball and all the end-of-Season parties are not a possibility."

"Perhaps Reginald and I will send our regrets and stay home, as well."

Mariah shook her head. "I will not hear of it. You traveled a long distance to attend. I shall not be the reason you miss it. Besides, you are to be my spy at the ball. Did you forget already?"

Sarah smiled, and it almost felt normal. Could it be so easy to become friends again? Mariah was certain they still had some bumps to come, but they were on the right road at last.

Sarah leaned forward, a sly smile and a rather devilish

look on her face. "Now tell me about Lord Heatherton. From what I saw last evening, things have progressed nicely."

Mariah pushed her lips out with a heavy breath. "I do not know what you saw last night, for I saw no progress at all. Nothing I do makes a difference. I do not believe he will ever see me as anything other than Reginald's sister."

Sarah's brow crinkled. "What do you mean you saw no progress? He sat at the pianoforte with you the entire time. And from where I sat, it looked as though he very nearly kissed you."

"You are surely mistaken." Mariah frowned. She had also thought at one point that he might kiss her. But then he had nearly ran from the piano. "Only because I begged him to stay. But he tried to cry off every chance he got." She smiled tenderly. "Although, there was one moment when he pulled my lip from between my teeth with his thumb. I thought for a moment it might mean something. But he was simply warning me against it." She released a frustrated sigh.

"You obviously did not watch him while you were playing. He could barely keep his eyes off you."

Mariah shook her head. "I am certain you are mistaken." She shrugged. "But you were right about the giggling. It does not work. It only made him dislike me more."

Sarah nodded in agreement. "It did not work on Reginald either."

"I believe the fan might hold some potential. Although Reginald did not approve. I am uncertain how he even knew what I was doing."

Sarah grimaced. "He overheard our conversation when you first told me about it. It is one of the reasons he offered to teach me how to flirt." Sarah's face turned a crimson color.

Mariah's brows shot up. Reginald had taught Sarah to flirt? Was that what he had meant when he told her to speak to Sarah about it? But it answered the question of how he knew about the fan.

Biscuit let out a bark, and Mariah pulled her attention away from Sarah momentarily. "Biscuit, you know it is not polite to interrupt. I am speaking with Sarah."

"He likely needs to go outside. I will call for a servant to take him." Reginald stepped into the room and over to the bellpull. Mariah wondered how much of their conversation he had heard.

Mariah looked back at Sarah with widened eyes. "I'm sorry, Regi. I know Biscuit is my dog and I am to take care of him."

"I understand circumstances have changed, Mar." Reginald strode over to the bed, his eyes resting on his wife. He looked at Sarah as if he had never seen anyone so lovely. It made Mariah's chest ache for want of it. Would Colin—or any man—ever look at her in such a way?

"I wondered where you had disappeared to." Reginald flicked his gaze at Mariah. "I am happy to see the two of you talking again."

Mariah smiled and glanced at Sarah. "Yes, we have had a good talk. Have we not, Sarah?"

"Indeed, we have."

Reginald nodded. "Then may I take my wife to the breakfast room? If I promise to return her as soon as we are done?"

"I suppose." Mariah grinned at her brother. It felt good not to be at constant odds with him. Indeed, even her yellow walls did not feel quite so drab.

Sarah stood and leaned over, pulling Mariah into an embrace. She squeezed her tightly, nearly bringing tears to Mariah's eyes. But they were not tears of pain. "Goodness, I have missed you, Mariah."

Mariah embraced Sarah with equal fierceness. "Certainly not as much as I have missed you. I am glad you have returned."

# Chapter Twenty-One

COLIN STOOD OUTSIDE THE DOOR OF REGINALD'S TOWNHOME, his hand poised on the bell ringer. After last evening, would Mariah feel well enough to train Biscuit? Her limp had been very pronounced when he helped her back to the couch.

Perhaps he should've sent a card inquiring after her. But if he had sent a card she may have replied saying she was not well enough. And then he would have no reason to see her.

And for some inexplicable reason, he wanted to see her.

He shook his head. It was simply to make certain last evening's performance had not set back her recovery. He was the one that had encouraged Mariah to play, even when he knew she should not exert herself. He did not want to feel guilty if his request had caused her more pain. And he simply wished to see for himself that she was well. There was nothing more to it.

He reached for the bellpull but held back. He should've sent flowers. Why had he not thought of that sooner? It was completely proper to send the hostess of a dinner party, even if it was among friends, a bouquet as thanks for an enjoyable evening.

He looked down the street, wondering for a moment if he

had time to remedy the error. He had not yet pulled the bell, so perhaps he could make a quick jog down the street and retrieve the flowers. It would surely not be a waste of time.

He found the flower cart just outside Gunter's. Thankfully, it was still early, and the tea shop was not yet bustling. Not like it had been the day he had met Reginald and Mariah in the square. He shook his head, hardly able to believe it had only been a week.

He looked at flowers tucked among buckets on and around the cart. What flowers would Mariah like best? He did not even know. But they were not courting, so he could hardly be expected to know such things. They had never discussed flowers. Although she smelled of lavender and rosemary. Did that mean they were among her favorites? When he had sent the bouquet after the ball, he had simply asked the flower lady to pick an assortment. They had meant nothing. But neither did the bouquet he was choosing now. It was just a thank you sentiment.

The gray-green of the rosemary sprigs contrasted prettily with the deep purple of the lavender. As he lifted the plants from the buckets, their scent wafted up to his nose. His skin heated at the smell. He pulled at his collar.

Perhaps he should have gone with gardenia or honeysuckle.

He pulled a branch of boxwood from a bucket but immediately put it back when he smelled the foul plant. After selecting several Black-Eyed Susans and some white delphiniums and sage, he handed the hastily assembled bouquet to the woman. She rearranged the plants into a more pleasing arrangement and tied a ribbon around their stems.

His bouquet in hand, Colin walked back to Stoke's townhouse and pulled on the doorbell. He bounced his thumb on the side of his leg as worry filled his thoughts. What if she did not like what he had chosen? Or worse, what if she thought he meant something with them? It was simply the proper thing to do.

He let out a growl. He had never worried about the precise flowers he sent any other woman. Why should Mariah be any different?

His breath caught in his throat. Because something about Mariah *was* different. He just could not decide what it was.

The door opened, stopping his thoughts.

"Good afternoon, my lord." Maxwell opened the door wider and motioned Colin inside.

He dipped his head and smiled. "I believe Lady Mariah is expecting me. We are to work on training that dog of hers." Did Maxwell believe that was the only reason Colin was there? Or could he see how much Colin wished to see her?

Maxwell raised his brow. "Many people in the house will be very grateful for that, my lord."

Colin grinned. "I suppose that must be why my ears have burned of late."

Maxwell raised his brow only a fraction. "Indeed, my lord. I have heard your name spoken in vain many times."

Colin laughed. "Then I suppose I have no time to lose. I must make amends as quickly as I can." He looked around the entryway and then up at the landings above, hoping he might see her there. "Is Lady Mariah about?"

"She is in the library, my lord—"

Colin dipped his head. "Thank you, Maxwell. I know the way." He set off down the corridor toward the library.

What color would Mariah be wearing today? If he had his wish, she would be wearing either dark green or bright yellow. While yellow made most people look rather sallow, it was not the case with Mariah. The color only proved to make her brown eyes more prominent.

He pushed open the door and stopped mid-step.

She sat on the couch. The sunshine filtered through the sheer curtains, making her face look radiant.

He stared at her, thinking not for the first time that she looked like an angel.

He shook his head to clear his thoughts. He could not have another experience like last evening. He needed to keep his head. They were training Biscuit, and that was not something to take lightly. What they taught the dog could likely stick with him for the entirety of his life. Which meant there could be no mischief and no distractions.

He released a breath and Mariah turned to look over her shoulder. "Ah, Lord Heatherton. I did not hear you come in."

"I only just arrived." He took a few steps forward and held the flowers out to her. "I wanted to thank you for a lovely evening."

She took the flowers, a grin splitting her face. "They are lovely, my lord. How did you know lavender was my favorite?" She put the bouquet to her nose and inhaled. "Miriam, please ring for a maid to come put these in water. I should not like them to wilt."

Colin took a relieved sigh. He had chosen correctly. Why did that fill him with such a sense of accomplishment? "I am pleased you like them." He clasped his hands behind his back. Now that he no longer held the flowers, he did not know what to do with his hands. "I know we had planned to train Biscuit. But I thought perhaps you may not be up to it. After last evening's exceptional performance, I thought you might be too fatigued."

She drew her fan across her cheek and fluttered her lashes at him. Why did she rub at her face whenever she had the fan in her hand? "I am never too fatigued to spend time with you."

He smiled at her. How had he found her eye fluttering irritating before? Had he not noticed how much it made her eyes sparkle?

She straightened in her seat.

"From Maxwell's remarks when I arrived, I assume that our last lesson did little to help Biscuit."

She shrugged. "He has improved. Unfortunately, it is in ways only I can see."

"Oh, in what ways?" Colin stood at the end of the couch where she sat.

"He is very proficient at jumping up on my bed. And he now barks when he wishes to go outside." She lifted her chin. "I think that is much better than soiling the carpets. But everyone else just seems to grumble about the noise."

Colin nodded. "Perhaps we could work on training Biscuit how to alert you to his need to go outside, without barking." He looked around the room. "That way, most of the training will be in the house where you can sit and rest your ankle."

Mariah nodded. "That sounds diverting." She curled her nose. "And I am certain Mrs. Church will be happy about that."

Colin took several steps toward her, and she tilted her head to the side. "What is that noise? It sounds like a bell."

He grinned and pulled several small bells from his coat pocket. "While I do not know if it is a common practice, the huntsman at Ravencliff used to train my father's dogs like this."

Mariah looked at the bells in his hand with a furrowed brow. "But how does a bell help?"

Colin sat down on the couch next to Mariah but made certain to leave a polite distance between them. He could not have her perfume distracting him again. Because he knew that he would not have been so affected last evening if he had not been constantly smelling the lavender.

Mariah, however, scooted closer to him and peered down at the bells.

So much for keeping a distance. He shifted again on the pretense of facing her so he might show her the bells more fully. "If we can train Biscuit to ring the bell when he needs to go outside, then he will not bark so much."

Mariah looked up at his face, a slight smile causing her eyes to close ever so much. She reached out and put her hand on his arm. "What a clever idea."

Colin jerked at her touch, and she pulled quickly away from him with a frown.

"How does this work, precisely?" She snapped her fingers and Biscuit appeared from behind a chair.

Colin smiled at her. "He comes when you snap? You see? You have done some training on your own."

Mariah shrugged it off. "I am the only one he listens to. If anyone else snaps, he completely ignores them. And he only listens to me when nothing else has his attention."

"It simply means he knows he belongs to you. Do not underestimate what you have done." He looked around the room. "Now, the best places to put the bells are near the doors in the rooms you spend the most time."

She followed his gaze.

"I should think we will want one in here and one in the music room." He twitched his lips to the side. "And I would recommend one in the kitchens. There will always be someone in that room."

Mariah shook her head. "Mrs. Leach does not allow dogs in the kitchen."

"Then perhaps the cloakroom? There is always someone in there."

"Maxwell will be thrilled." She lifted a brow and then looked over her shoulder at her maid sitting on a chair in the corner. She had a basket in her lap and appeared to be sewing. "Miriam, will you please make certain to pick up some bells when next you go to the sundry shop? I should not like to take the bells down before we leave, only to have to rehang them when we return in November. But I do not know if the shop in Stoke will have them."

"Yes, my lady."

Mariah smiled. "Thank you, Miriam." She turned back to Colin. "How do we begin?"

He blinked several times at her. What had happened? Less than a week ago he could not say he had heard a word of thanks leave Mariah's mouth when speaking to a servant. And now she *pleased* and *thank you-ed* every servant she saw. What caused the change? He pushed the question aside. It did nothing to help them in their task. He would have to think about it later.

He looked at the terrace door. "We will need a nail and some string."

Mariah looked over her shoulder, but her maid had already risen from the chair and moved toward the bellpull in the corner.

Colin settled back on the couch, scratching at Biscuit's ears as they waited for the supplies. He glanced at Mariah, uncertain of what he should say. He had never had difficulty speaking with a lady. Why was he now?

She scooted closer to him and joined him in scratching Biscuit.

Colin froze. What was she doing? It was just as he had feared. His actions from last evening had led her to assume he desired something he did not. He was not looking to be in the same situation as Reginald. Lud, why had he not returned to his seat after helping her to the pianoforte? Indeed, why had he not simply allowed Stoke to help his sister?

He cleared his throat. "How is your ankle this morning? I hope playing last evening did not cause you to endure more pain." He would keep to safe topics—topics that would not lead to misunderstandings. If only she would giggle again. That had done plenty to remind him of what he wanted for his life—to remind him he did not want her.

Mariah lifted a delicate shoulder. "I admit it is more

tender than I would have thought. I did not believe I had done so very much yesterday."

"Perhaps I should do the training, so you may sit on the couch and watch." He congratulated himself on his quick thinking. If she stayed on the couch, surely that would keep some distance between them. Colin sucked in a breath and smiled. Yes, that was a fine idea and one he intended to employ often over the next week of training.

# Chapter Twenty-Two

Colin sat in Reginald's study, twisting a glass of claret around on the arm of the chair.

"Colin, what did you teach that dog of Mariah's?" Reginald demanded.

Colin's brow creased. "What do you mean?"

"Every time someone rings a bell, the dog soils the carpets. Maxwell and Mrs. Church are beside themselves."

Ben and Cort laughed loudly while Charlie and Ponsy grimaced. Rags simply looked annoyed.

Colin glanced at the others then stared at Reginald. "That is not what was supposed to happen. He was supposed to ring the bell when he wished to go outside."

Reginald frowned. "He does that too. If only you could untrain him from soiling the carpet."

"I made it very clear I was not proficient in dog training," Colin smirked. "Do not growl at me. This was all your idea."

"It is fast becoming a disaster. Perhaps I should release you from your commitment."

Colin sat up straight in his chair. "Release me?" His voice grew in timber and pitch. He cleared his throat and shrugged, even as his pulse quickened. "Whatever you think best, Reg."

Reginald stared at him, frowning. "I will think about it. But for now, you may continue."

Colin grunted and leaned back in his chair trying for a devil-may-care attitude. "Yes, your highness."

Reginald ignored the comment. "I will see you all at the Kingsleys' tonight?"

"I thought you told Lady Mariah that you would send your regrets for the rest of the parties." Cort crossed one leg over the other and ran a hand down the front of his thigh.

"I did. But when Sarah returned, Mariah insisted that we both attend every party through the end of the Season." He sighed and smiled as if he were a proud father. "She knows it is the reason Sarah returned to London, and she would not hear of us missing even one."

Colin flicked up his brows. That was not the response he would have expected from Mariah. Each time they had spoken, she had seemed rather out of sorts in regard to her sister-in-law.

"Then we will see you in the cardroom." Charlie nodded.

Reginald grimaced. "With Mariah unable to attend, I feel I must stay with my wife. She is still uncertain in large groups. I hoped that you all might consider joining us, rather than hiding out in the cardroom."

"Not likely. I do not plan to make myself available to those young ladies who are hoping to save their Season with a last-minute engagement simply because your wife has problems in society." Rags frowned at Reginald. "I am most disappointed in the turn of this Season."

"Yes, Rags. You have told us as much every time we are together." Ben flicked a glance at Cort and Charlie. "But nothing is going to change what has happened. You may as well put it behind you."

Rags narrowed his eyes at everyone. "Which one of you is next? I feel a change in the group."

Colin rolled his eyes. "Rein in your feelings. No one else is getting married, Rags. Stop your sulking."

"I'm not sulking." He stood up and placed his glass on the table. "I need to leave. My father has requested my presence at Grosvenor and His Grace does not like to wait." His nose curled as he stalked out of the room.

Colin watched Rags' back until he disappeared around the doorframe. He turned his attention back to Reginald.

While Colin could understand Ragsdale's frustration and irritation with Reginald's marriage—they all felt slightly betrayed—Colin could not ignore the notion that Reginald seemed altogether happier since he married.

Their league of friends was the best a man could find. But Colin could not help but wonder if Reginald had found more. He had someone to spend his time with when they left the London parties, or even London itself.

But what did Colin have? He had his mother back at Ravencliff. But it was not the same. He did not confide in her. Indeed, most days they did not even eat at the same table. They were not at odds with each other, they simply did not have any commonalities. Would a sister make a difference? He supposed he would never know. But a sister had not been enough to keep Reginald from marrying.

Colin swirled the claret in his glass as he watched the men conversing around him, but his attention settled on Reginald.

While Colin would never admit it aloud, he was lonely. He had known it for some time. But he had not realized just how lonely he'd been until he returned from the continent and watched Reginald and Sarah together. Now it was so glaringly obvious. But what was he to do about it?

Colin turned a second time as he paced in front of the fireplace. Mariah had said she wished to begin their lessons at one that afternoon. They had not worked with Biscuit the day before so Mariah's ankle could heal a little more and so she could work with him on the bell ringing before they introduced a new skill.

But she had been most adamant that she did not wish to wait any longer for their next lesson. Colin checked his watch. She was now ten minutes late. Was something wrong? Should he leave or should he go in search of her?

Perhaps she did not know he was waiting for her. Colin had arrived early to spend time with the gents. He'd been grateful for their presence because the more time he spent with Mariah, the more awkward his time with Reginald became. He hardly knew what to say to his friend anymore. He could not talk to him about Mariah, nor did he feel comfortable speaking of any other woman.

In truth, he was looking forward to quitting London and returning to Shropshire. His awkward conversations with Reginald would come to an end, and he would no longer be required to help Mariah with Biscuit. His chest tightened, but he willed it away. It was for the best. And by the time he and his mother joined Reginald and the other gents for the house party at Oakdale, Mariah's ankle would be fully healed. Colin would not have to help her anywhere, nor would he be affected by her perfume. They could all go on as they had before.

Zounds, where was she?

Colin moved toward the door, determined to locate Mariah quickly or leave and return another time.

He checked the music room first. There was no sound drifting down the corridor, so he doubted she was there. Maxwell would surely know where she was. He would speak to the butler, and then he would know if he should stay or go.

He stepped from the corridor into the entryway and

looked around. No one was about. He peeked into the cloakroom, but it was empty as well.

Colin stood outside the cloakroom door, his arms folded, and frowned. He did not have all day to wait around for *Lady Mariah*. Did she think them friendly enough that Colin would wait around until she graced him with her presence?

A sniffle echoed around the entryway and Colin turned, looking up the staircase. His mouth dropped open slightly at the same time his stomach dropped. Mariah sat on the third stair from the top, her cane several stairs farther down. She had her arms wrapped around her legs and her head rested on her knees as her shoulders shook. Lud, she was crying.

Colin's mind raced to remember if he had muttered any of his irritations aloud. Could that be why she was crying?

He quietly walked up the stairs and sat down next to her.

She turned her head enough to likely see him but not enough for him to see her fully. He could only see one tear-streaked cheek.

"What is the matter? Are you hurt?" He knew she might simply be sad, but he did not feel prepared to deal with that eventuality.

She sucked in a quivering breath. "I think I am mostly frustrated."

"Frustrated? That is why you are crying on the stairs?" How did crying on the stairs help anything? He would never understand women.

"Perhaps not the only one, but it is the primary reason. My ankle is still too weak to do the simplest tasks, like walking down the stairs. How am I to do anything? Even a child can walk down the stairs." Her voice took on a wail as she finished. "I am completely worthless."

Colin clasped his hands in front of him. What was he to do? What should he say to make her feel better? "I'm certain no one blames you for being worthless. You cannot help that your ankle is injured."

She lifted her head and looked at him as large, fat tears rolled down her cheeks. Lud, was there any instance in which she was not beautiful?

"Then you think I am worthless also?" Her lip quivered.

Wait, that was not what he had said, was it? "No, no. I did not say you were—" He paused. Actually, he had said those exact words. "That is to say, I did not mean to say it that way. What I meant was, you are not worthless. You are injured. They are two different things. As soon as your ankle heals, I am sure there are many things you will do again. No one will think you worthless."

Mariah shook her head and laid her head back on her knees. "Everyone thought me worthless before my ankle injury. The only thing they thought me capable of was walking a dog." She let out a sob. "And now I can't even do that."

Colin lifted his hand and awkwardly patted her on the back.

She leaned into his side and buried her face in his shoulder, moisture immediately seeping through his coats.

That was not what he had planned when he reached out to touch her, but he could not say he was unhappy with the change in plans.

"I am certain no one thought you could only walk a dog. You are capable of many things." He softened his voice, talking to her in much the same way he spoke to his horse when it was spooked.

She looked up at him. "Oh? In what ways do you think me capable?" Her gaze held such hope that Colin searched his brain for something to say. What was she capable of? "You play the harp most proficiently."

Her face fell.

"And the pianoforte. Indeed, even without practice, you played it better than anyone I have heard at a musicale this Season."

She closed her eyes. "That is nothing special. Nor does it show capability. It will not prove useful. It will not improve or save anyone's life."

Improving or saving lives? That was the only trait she deemed as capable? He let out an uneasy chuckle. "By your definition, I am rather useless too." It was not the first time he had thought it. His father had been dead barely a year and still Colin did not believe he lived up to his father's expectations. Indeed, he did not know if he ever would.

She shook her head. "No, you are not. You are very capable."

He nudged her shoulder and leaned in close. Drat that lavender and rosemary. "I have never once saved a life." He whispered in her ear.

She turned her head, and he pulled back quickly as their noses nearly touched. "That is not true. You provide a living to all your tenants and servants. You improve their lives. Indeed, without you, it is possible many of them may not still be alive."

Colin raised a brow. "I believe you are placing too much credit at my hands. Without me, they would simply find farms and employment elsewhere."

She shook her head. "It is not so straightforward, and you know it. Employment and farms are not so easily found. You need only walk down the streets of London to discover that."

He shrugged. "I am only carrying on that which my father and grandfather started. I cannot take the credit." His grandfather had made Ravencliff into a great estate, and his father had built upon that. Colin did not see that he had anything he could add to the estate that was not already there.

"You are wise with your money, my lord, which gives you the means to carry on. There are many among the *ton* who cannot boast such a quality." She gave him a quivering smile. "And do not forget, you are able to go down the stairs. In my eyes, you are very capable." Her voice lowered and she looked at her hands.

"I shall remember to list the stairs among my qualities the next time I am asked." Colin winked, and she grinned again.

She had grinned. Perhaps she was not completely inconsolable.

"What if I helped you down the stairs?"

She stared at him, and he felt as if she might be seeing those things he did not show the world. Could she see his uncertainty? Or his fears and his hopes. He did not share those things with anyone. Not even Reginald. "Helping me might ease my frustration about the stairs momentarily. But it would not solve the bigger problem."

He shrugged. "Why do we not solve one problem at a time? After all, are you changing anything by crying on the stairs?"

Her face pinked, and the last tear that had been hanging onto her lashes fell onto her cheek.

Colin reached out and dried it with his thumb. "I am certain Biscuit finds you very capable."

"I don't believe his opinion matters." A hint of a smile appeared on her face.

"You might have difficulty convincing Biscuit of that." He straightened out, stretching his legs down the stairs. "But I have to wonder if we should postpone our training."

Mariah shook her head fiercely. "No, please don't go. I simply need help down the stairs. I am doing better at walking."

He pulled his legs up onto the step and put his elbows on his knees, his hands dangling in front of him. "But I worry it will only hurt your ankle more."

"It is just the stairs. My ankle isn't strong enough to support all my weight. If you could help me down, I know I will walk fine with my cane."

Colin watched his hands for a moment. Was she telling

him the truth? What if she was lying to him again because she thought it was what he wanted to hear, or she thought it would give her what she wanted? If Mariah injured herself more, would Reginald blame Colin?

He shrugged. "Regardless, we cannot leave you here on the stairs. Let me help you."

She smiled the first genuinely happy smile he had seen since he found her. "Thank you, my lord."

Colin leaned forward and collected her cane. Putting out his hand, she grasped hold and pulled herself to standing. He lifted his arm, but she wrapped her hands around his upper arm, clinging tightly.

"Are you ready?" Colin looked at her from the corner of his eye.

She nodded.

They both stepped down together, and when she let out a gasp, Colin jerked his head around to look at her. "I thought you said you were ready."

She bit her lip and nodded. "I am."

Colin sighed. She was *not* ready. How had she thought she could manage the stairs on her own? She could not even do it with help. He pulled his arm from her grasp and pushed the cane into her hands. "But—," she started.

Leaning forward, Colin slid one arm around her back and the other beneath her knees. In one fluid motion, he stood up, taking her up into his arms. "I will try not to jostle you too much." He walked down the stairs, lavender teasing his nostrils and his heart pounding in his chest.

He had never carried a woman in his arms. But he could not imagine anyone fitting there as perfectly as Mariah.

She leaned against him, her arms encircling his neck.

Colin glanced down at her, and his thoughts turned back to kissing her. Why did he keep thinking about that? And how could he make it stop? It wasn't that he didn't want to kiss her. His constant thinking about it made it abundantly clear that was not true. But it was the complications that would follow that he did not want.

*No complications*. He repeated it several times as he made his way down the staircase. When his Hessians settled on the entryway floor, Colin paused before putting Mariah down. If he was to kiss her, it was his chance. They were alone and their lips were within kissing distance.

*No complications.* The warning sounded in his head. Colin closed his eyes and breathed in deeply. Gently, he set Mariah's feet on the floor.

A throat cleared and Colin's eyes flew open. Reginald, Ben, Cort, and Charlie all stood, arms folded, their gazes darting from Colin to Mariah and back at Colin again. Deuce take it. How much had they seen?

# Chapter Twenty-Three

Biscuit shot past Mariah and raced off the terrace like a shot.

"Oh, dear." Mariah crossed an arm across her middle. "I wonder what helpless animal he is after now." She looked warily after the dog, leaning heavily on her walking stick.

"Not to worry. I believe it was simply a butterfly. It should stay just out of Biscuit's reach." Colin rubbed at his earlobes as he glanced at her sidelong. "Are you certain you are up for this, my lady? We could try again in the morning. I believe your attempt at the stairs has left you fatigued."

Indeed, it was not wholly the stairs that left her spent, but what had happened on them. Colin had been so kind and caring. But there had also been a vulnerability that she had never seen. Could it be that they had more in common than just Biscuit?

But their moment had not lasted long. Especially once Colin noticed Reginald and his friends standing in the entryway watching them.

Mariah had felt a slight embarrassment at being caught in Colin's arms. But her sheer delight overshadowed any feelings of regret or mortification.

Colin had distanced himself immediately, stumbling out excuses and passing the situation off as inconsequential. There were only four days left until Lord Trenton's ball. She did not have time for inconsequential interactions. Although, if she were being honest, her reasons for securing an arrangement with Colin had changed. He no longer felt like the prize at the end of a competition. No, that was not true. He was still a much-desired prize. But not simply for the sake of winning him. The stakes were higher. If she lost him now, she was uncertain if she would walk away whole.

She sighed as she watched Biscuit sniff his way around the kitchen garden. She must spend the next hour or two with Colin, and it would be rather vexing if she did not control her emotions.

She straightened, putting her cane in front of her and resting both hands on the rounded glass top. "My ankle is doing much better. If I am not required to chase after him, I am certain I will be well." She lifted her face to the sunlight, allowing the heat to melt away the doubts that clouded her mind.

Colin cleared his throat, and Mariah turned to face him. "Why do we not stop in the kitchen first? Biscuit seems to learn faster if we reward him with a snack."

Mariah nodded. Who was she to disagree with him? She had no notion of how to train a dog. Indeed, she was mostly there for Colin, not Biscuit. "It seems a sound idea."

They stepped onto the lawn, and Lady Mariah snapped her fingers and called out. "Come, Biscuit."

Miriam stayed a dozen steps behind them—keeping always in view but staying far enough back to give them privacy. Not that Mariah believed they would discuss anything that a servant could not hear. Colin seemed rather formal since the incident in the entryway.

Before they had walked ten paces on the grass, the doors opened, and Reginald stepped outside. He grinned as he strode toward them. "Ah, Colin. There you are." Reginald clasped his hands behind his back.

Colin raised a brow. "I was not hiding. You knew Lady Mariah and I were training Biscuit today." He tipped his head to the side and pushed his lips out. "Reg, are you here to help with Biscuit's training?"

Reginald flicked his brows upwards. "Ah, no. I have far more important things to occupy my time than training an ill-mannered dog." He smirked. "Although, if you are successful with Biscuit, perhaps I can employ you to train Lady G as well."

Mariah gasped. "Lady G is your problem. You will not foist her upon Lord Heatherton, just as you didn't allow me to foist Biscuit on a servant."

"I suppose you are correct. But perhaps you could give me some tips?" He shrugged. "I was not keeping an eye on you. I was simply making certain Mariah was well. But I see she is walking well enough. I shall leave you to your task." He clasped his hands behind his back. Turning, he strode through the terrace doors.

Mariah stopped and put a hand on her hip. "Why do you let him speak to you in such a way? I should not stand for it if I were you." Indeed, she had a mind to march—or hobble—into his study as soon as Colin left and say her piece.

Colin shrugged. "I know he does not mean it." He leaned in slightly and Mariah sucked in a slow breath. "I believe he thinks to scare me."

"Scare you? Why should he wish to scare you?"

Colin lifted his shoulders quickly. "He tries to scare anyone who pays you attention. But I do not find him frightening because I know him too well."

Mariah harrumphed. "He thinks himself my protector. But I don't—" She paused, catching the lie she had told herself and others for months. "Wish for it. At some point, I need to learn to take care of myself." She scoffed. "And it's not as if I have anything to fear from you. You've known me since I was a little girl." She pulled her lip in between her teeth. She made it sound as if she thought of him as a brother. Which was something she had not felt for years.

"But you are not a little girl anymore." Colin rubbed at his ear again and his face pinked. "Your brother is just trying to protect you," he added.

"There is no Lord Muckrake here. I do not need protection in my garden."

"If I had a handsome younger sister, I can only assume I would be as protective as Reginald is. I mean…" He stuttered. "Look at Charlie and his sister."

Mariah lifted her hand to her neck and fingered the cross at her throat. Was he saying he thought Miss Bancroft handsome? Did he prefer her to Mariah? She dropped her hand and came to a stop. Her pulse quickened, and she smiled. "Lord Heatherton, you think me handsome?"

He took several steps back, his head shaking. "It doesn't matter what I think, my lady. It is rather a fact. One would have to be blind not to see your beauty. Surely you've noticed you're never left in want of a partner at balls or card parties." He cleared his throat. "Or did you believe it was because of your skills at both dancing and cards?" He glanced down at her foot and grinned. "We both know that is not the case."

Her eyes widened, and she pursed her lips. But she could not look stern for long before her lips twitched with laughter. "Point taken, my lord."

She sobered. "I rather thought it my dowry that made me desirable. It has nothing to do with me." She licked her lips, trying to eliminate her suddenly dry mouth.

"I can assure you, my lady, it is not simply your dowry that makes you desirable." His voice lowered, and he looked at her intently before glancing away.

The rest of their walk to the kitchen was silent, which

Mariah did not mind. It gave her a chance to think about what he had said.

He thought her pretty, but she had already known that. She had overheard him say it in Reginald's study. But this declaration felt different. Perhaps it was because she had not felt a list of deficiencies would follow. Was that because they were not there anymore? Or was it simply because he was too much of a gentleman to mention them?

Mariah fisted her hand at her side. She was understanding why some ladies wished for spinsterhood. Marrying for love was not for the weak of heart. Indeed, she would be lucky if she escaped London with her heart intact.

They arrived at the kitchen door, and Mariah knocked, grateful for the respite in her thoughts. A scullery maid peeked out. She glanced at Mariah and opened the door wider. "M'lady." She dipped a curtsy.

Biscuit ran between their legs, scurrying around the long prep table in the center of the room.

Mrs. Leach let out a surprised cry. "Remove this fleabag from my kitchen at once!"

Mariah let out a squeal as she shuffled inside and snatched up the dog. "He isn't a fleabag, Mrs. Leach. I'll have you know, I bathed him only this morning."

Colin flicked his eyebrows upward. Did he not believe she was capable of even that? Or did he think it was beneath her to do such a task?

Mrs. Leach put her hands on her hips. "I don't care if you bathed him three times today. I do not want him in my kitchen." She sighed and her face softened. "I am sorry, my lady. How may I help you?"

Colin stepped forward. "May we have a few strips of dried meat?"

Mrs. Leach looked at Colin and then at Lady Mariah and nodded. "Betty, go fetch some meat from the larder."

Mariah shifted Biscuit onto her hip and leaned in toward

the cook. "How is your sister, Mrs. Leach?" She lowered her voice so as not to share the conversation with the whole kitchen. "Did the medicines help? Is she able to travel yet?"

Colin stared with far too much interest at the herbs hanging from the drying rack.

Mrs. Leach shook her head. "But she is doing better, my lady. I hope that by the time we quit London, she will be well enough to travel with me."

"I am so happy to hear it." Mariah placed a hand on the woman's arm. "Is she receiving enough food? You may take what you need from the larder."

"Oh, I could not, my lady. That food is for the household." Mrs. Leach put a hand to her chest.

"We have plenty. And if we fall short, we will order more. But there is no need to leave food to waste when we leave for Staffordshire." Mariah took several steps back and scratched at Biscuit's ears. "I will brook no opposition, Mrs. Leach." She raised her voice and smiled.

"Yes, my lady." Mrs. Leach smiled back, moisture glistening in her eyes.

Mariah looked away.

Biscuit squirmed in her arms, and she moved to shift him to her other hip. But as she moved her cane into her other hand, Biscuit dropped to the floor at her feet. Before Mariah could react, he set out at a run across the stone floor. "Biscuit!" Mariah called out.

As the animal ran past, Colin bent and plucked him up into his arms.

Mrs. Leach shook her head. "That is precisely why I do not want him inside. Animals should not be in the kitchens."

Mariah looked innocently at her. "I shall keep him out of the kitchen from now on. You have my word." She gave the cook a side look. "Especially if you gave us a few pasties to take with us?"

Mrs. Leach clucked her tongue. "You're as much of a

scamp as that dog of yours." She may have said she disapproved, but the twinkle in her eye and the smile on her lips said otherwise as she wrapped four pasties in a napkin. "There are two venison and two apple." She handed the parcel over. "The apple pasties have an *A* browned on the top."

Mariah lifted a corner of the napkin and breathed in deeply. "I am indebted to you, Mrs. Leach."

Betty appeared from the larder and handed the dried meat strips to Colin. He dipped his head and muttered a low thank you.

"Thank you, Mrs. Leach." Mariah leaned in to embrace the cook. "Please, let me know if your sister's condition does not continue to improve," she whispered.

Biscuit barked and wriggled in Colin's arms.

"Come now, Biscuit. I was just singing your praises. Do not prove me a liar."

Colin coughed on a laugh. "Indeed, you would not want to be known as a liar."

Mariah lifted her chin high and fixed Colin with a scolding look. But it did not have the desired effect. He only continued to laugh as they exited the kitchen.

# Chapter Twenty-Four

Mariah kept a firm hold on the pasties. She'd witnessed Colin's sneaky nature before. Especially with food, such as biscuits. She suspected pasties would be no different.

It didn't matter how much she adored him. She was not about to give up her part of the snack. Her mouth watered at the thought of eating one of the apple pasties.

"We have the meat strips. Now, what are we to do?" She looked over at Colin expectantly.

"We'll find a spot and teach Biscuit simpler commands such as sit and come." He sighed. "And hopefully not to soil the carpets," he muttered under his breath.

Mariah nodded. It seemed Colin had been made aware of the latest irritation Reginald had with her dog. She gave a small shrug. What did she care? He had had his chance to rid them of the dog and he passed it up. As far as she was concerned, he was just as at fault for it as Biscuit was.

"Are you prepared for this, Biscuit?" Colin crooned at the dog.

She had noticed his voice did not hold the same disapproval when he said Biscuit's name. Perhaps he no longer thought it ridiculous. Indeed, he might even wish to reconsider Bob's name.

"Does that entail teaching him not to chase poor unsuspecting park animals? I cannot seem to keep him from that." She sighed.

Colin nodded. "In theory, once we are finished, he should come whenever he is called. But I have been wrong about my theories before."

Mariah tilted her head. Hmm. Was it possible to train a man in such a way? She would not mind having Colin stop whatever he was doing and come to her when she called his name.

She glanced down at the napkin in her hands. Just what would Colin do for a pasty? Perhaps she could train two beasts in one day. Although it seemed unlikely Colin would give up bachelorhood just for a pasty. Mrs. Leach's pasties were delicious, but could they secure a marriage proposal?

"How do we begin?"

"Much as we did with the bells. We will give Biscuit the command, and then show him what he is to do. Then we will give him a bit of meat as a reward. Eventually, we should not have to show him." Colin motioned to a spot in the back corner of the garden. "Let's go over there. You can sit on the grass and rest your ankle, but still be shaded by the tree."

They stopped under a large willow tree. The gardener had trimmed the front side high, making it a lovely spot to look out over the rest of the gardens.

Colin put Biscuit down and allowed him to sniff around the grass.

She glanced over her shoulder as she placed the napkin bundle in the joint of a branch, far out of Biscuit's reach, but unfortunately still within Colin's. Experience told her it was a risk, but she took it anyway.

Tucking her gown around her, she carefully situated

herself on the grass and looked up at Colin. He moved next to her but didn't sit down. That was disappointing.

He dropped to his haunches, and Mariah grinned. *Much better.* She would surely have a crick in her neck if she had to look up at him standing beside her all afternoon. Besides, he was close enough that she could smell the bergamot and clary sage of his soap. It made her stomach feel all tingly.

Colin ripped off a small piece of meat and held it out in his hand. "Come, Biscuit," he called to the dog.

Biscuit paid him no mind and continued sniffing at the tree trunk.

Colin frowned. Moving over to the dog, he bent and placed meat under the dog's nose until he had Biscuit's attention. Then he pulled the meat away and walked back to Mariah.

Biscuit watched Colin's every move. So did Mariah, but she was certain it was for an entirely different reason. She had no interest in the *meat.*

Dropping back down to his haunches, Colin held out his hand, the chunk of mutton resting in his palm. "Come, Biscuit."

The dog scurried over, his eyes never leaving the morsel Colin held.

When Biscuit came to Colin, he held the meat between his fingers while Biscuit snatched it with his teeth. "Good dog, Biscuit." Colin scratched him between the ears.

There had been a time, not so long ago, that Mariah would have gagged to see the dog nip and lick at Colin's fingers. She still did not wish for Biscuit to do it to her, but it did not bother her if he did it to others. Indeed, she felt nothing more than a tug of jealousy at the attention Biscuit received from Colin.

He patted the dog on the head before standing up. "I will take Biscuit over there and we will try it again. I think this time you should call him."

Mariah's nose turned up. "But what if he should lick me?"

"Then you will die, of course." Colin stared at her with a bland face before breaking into a grin.

Mariah arched a brow at him. "Now won't you feel terrible if I should really cock up my toes?"

Colin rolled his eyes. "You will be fine, trust me."

"And if I'm not?"

He tilted his head to the side and stared at her earnestly. "Then I shall save you."

A shiver skittered up her spine and neck. Perhaps a little dog licking would not be so terrible after all. "Promise?" She whispered.

He reached forward and grasped her hand, bowing over it gallantly. "You have my word, my lady."

She knew he meant nothing by it, but she suspected if he ever held her hand for something other than to help her up or to dance, she might never let him go.

She swallowed and looked away sheepishly. Why could she not stop hoping for things that would never happen? She had given him plenty of opportunities and he had ignored her every time. He obviously had no interest in her, and it seemed his opinions were not likely to change.

Colin gently tugged her to her feet. But he did not release her hand immediately. Her heartbeat joined the tingles, dancing a dance that would surely redden the faces of the Patronesses of Almacks if they could see it. For a moment, she wondered if she'd been wrong. Could he feel something for her? Something more than just indifference?

As if sensing her thoughts, he dropped her hand and motioned her to the other side of the overhanging willow.

Biscuit sniffed the air and followed them, sitting in front of Colin, his tail thudding against the ground.

Colin grunted. "This won't do." He ripped off a piece of meat, which only proved to make Biscuit's tail thump harder, and placed it in Mariah's hand. "When I tell you, call Biscuit and show him the meat."

Mariah nodded, even as her nose scrunched up at the thought of what she was about to do. Did Colin have any idea the lengths she was going to just to be with him?

He picked up the dog and carried him to the other side before placing him back on the ground.

Biscuit lurched forward, but Colin grabbed him and held him in place.

Mariah could not tell how much training was actually happening. It seemed once the meat was no longer in their hands, the dog would go back to doing what he wanted. Perhaps it would serve Mariah better to work on training Colin instead.

# Chapter Twenty-Five

"Lady Mariah, call him to you." Colin kneeled in the grass across the way, holding onto the dog.

She sighed and patted her lap. "Come, Biscuit."

Colin released his hold, and the dog shot forward, running toward Lady Mariah.

She let out a yelp, her hand waving the mutton strip in front of her. But it was too late. The dog's paws hit her in the chest, and she fell backward onto the grass.

She twisted her head back and forth, trying to keep away from the animal's happy licks. When he couldn't reach her face, he moved to her hand, licking where the meat had been.

Mariah gagged. "It's on the ground, Biscuit. You need not lick at me." She pushed the dog to the side, and he sniffed the ground before lying next to her to devour his reward.

Colin pursed his lips tightly to keep the laughter in. But his smile faded as he noticed Mariah had not yet righted herself. He hurried over. What if she injured her ankle again? He would not have believed Biscuit could inflict such harm, but he could be wrong.

He hurried over and peered down at her.

She lay with her eyes closed, but her hand rubbed back and forth along the blades of grass.

Colin's grin returned. Was she trying to wipe off the dog drool? He extended a hand. "Lady Mariah! For a moment I thought you might have proven me wrong. I'm immensely pleased to see you are yet alive."

She cracked one lid open, though only to a slit. Was she scowling at him? "I do not believe I am completely out of danger. I may yet be in need of rescue." She opened her eye wider and sighed. "Or perhaps if Biscuit thinks me dead, he will leave me be."

Colin's lips twitched. "But I thought you loved dogs."

"But it does not follow that I wish to be drooled upon." Both her eyes opened, and this time he knew she was scowling at him.

She took his offered hand, tugging herself up to sitting. "However, my lord, I do not think it gentlemanly of you to remind me of my mistake continually." She scratched Biscuit on top of his head and under his chin.

"Then you admit you lied to me in the park?" His voice may have held too much triumph. "You have yet to admit it to me."

She shrugged, giving him a wide-eyed, exasperated look. "Very well. I lied."

He held her gaze. "Why?"

"Why what?"

He squatted down next to her. "Why did you lie to me?"

She dropped her gaze, twisting at the tips of her gloves. "It was the first time you had paid me any mind. You seemed so fond of Lady G. I thought perhaps if I said I like her, you might like me as well." Her voice sounded small. Then Reginald had been right? His pulse ticked up. She had wanted his attention. But why? Was it simply a flirtation? Did she do it with all the men she encountered? He pushed the thought away because he had seen no proof of it.

"And you did not think I could like you if you didn't like Lady G?"

Mariah licked her lips. "I had seen no evidence of that happening. At the time, it seemed a good course of action."

"And now?"

She looked up at him, her mouth twitching to the side. "While I know I should regret my actions, I find I cannot."

His brows rose high. "Oh?"

"I cannot see any negative that has come from it."

"How is that?" Could she honestly say that good had come from her lies?

"I do not believe Sarah and I would have healed our rift." She glanced up at him, her fingers still twisting at the tips of her gloves. "I do not know about you, but I cannot regret the time we have spent together this past week. And if not for my lie, you should never have bought me Biscuit. I cannot regret any of it."

He paused. He had not thought of it as she had. But now that he did, he had to admit he agreed. While he knew little about the reconciliation between Mariah and her friend, he had to agree with her on the other points. He would never have guessed that a lie could actually bring about good. But it seemed in this case, it had. He looked over at her.

She grinned, but he could see a hint of uncertainly in her eyes. "I have confessed my sin. Are you happy now?"

He grinned back. "Yes, I believe I am."

Colin stood up and moved over to the far side of the shade. "Can I really believe you like the dog?" He put a finger to his twitching lips. "You can't even stand for Biscuit to lick you."

She smirked. "I don't desire you to lick me, either. But that does not mean I dislike you." The smirk died on her lips almost immediately. "That is to say—"

Colin tilted his head to the side, his eyes alight with mirth. "Wait, a moment. You like me, but you don't wish for me to lick you?" He shook his head. "I do not know whether to be offended or pleased by that admission." He didn't even attempt to hide his grin. He snapped his fingers and called to the dog. Biscuit came running, immediately sniffing at Colin's hand.

Mariah folded her arms. "You need not tease me, my lord."

Colin rubbed at Biscuit's stomach. She liked him. He already knew as much. But what did it mean? Did she care for him in the same manner she cared for Reginald? Or was it something different altogether? Did he even want her to care for him in a different way?

He looked up at her, her face turned up with her eyes closed. The breeze picked up the small hairs at the back of her neck and his skin heated.

Yes, he did want her to think of him differently than she did Reginald.

THEY HAD WORKED with Biscuit for nearly an hour, calling him to come and rewarding him periodically with a piece of meat. The dog was a quick learner.

But now, the dried mutton was gone, and Biscuit seemed content to sit in the grass and chew on a shoe.

Colin motioned to it. "You should not let him chew on that. It will only make him believe he may chew on others."

Mariah grinned coyly. "Oh, it's not mine. It's Reginald's. He may chew on any of Regi's shoes, and I care not a wit."

"I hardly think it will promote friendship between the two of them."

She frowned at him. "After all Reginald has done to you, you do not wish to teach him even a small lesson?"

He looked down at the dog, his lips pushing out in thought. Mariah had a point. Reginald had acted quite high-handed regarding the dog—forcing Colin to help with the training. Perhaps he deserved to lose a shoe or two. Although—he glanced over at Mariah—Colin could not say he was angry about that anymore.

Colin shook his head at her. "But he'll not know which shoes are yours and which are Reginald's. Do you really wish for him to be in the habit?"

She released a heavy sigh as she stood and hobbled over to the back of the garden. Moving aside some flowers, she pulled out a stick. She grabbed the shoe from between Biscuit's paws and replaced it. "Here you are, Biscuit. Lord Heatherton says you may not have Regi's shoes."

Colin shrugged. "You may allow it if you wish. But I should not like to hear you complain when all of your slippers have teeth marks."

Mariah's stomach growled, and she placed a hand to her middle. "Biscuit is surely full from all the meat strips. But I am famished."

She limped over and took the napkin bundle off the branch, gently lowering herself down onto the grass. "Would you like a pasty?" She glanced up at Colin through her lashes.

Colin's own stomach churned, and he dropped to the grass beside her. Stretching out his legs, he leaned back on his hands. "Indeed, I wondered when you would allow us to eat."

Mariah untied the knot, pulling back the corners to reveal the contents. "Which kind do you want?"

He reached forward and grabbed a venison pasty, breaking off a piece and popping it into his mouth. A quiet moan sounded from low in his throat. Mrs. Leach was truly gifted.

They both chewed in silence, a soft breeze blowing through the willow branches.

Mariah reached forward and lifted out another pasty with an *A* browned on top. "Are you too full for dessert?"

"I am never too full for dessert." Colin waggled his brows and reached for the pasty.

Mariah pulled it back. "I did not hear the proper word—"

Colin frowned. Proper word? What proper word? He dropped his hand but looked up at her in realization. "Ah, yes. I apologize. May I *please* have a pasty, Lady Mariah?" She was teaching him about saying please? It was curious how things had changed.

She grinned and handed it over to him. "Much better, my lord." Picking up her own, she broke it in half, placing the other half on the napkin. "I'm full, but I cannot consider putting this aside without even a taste. It was the one I wanted to begin with."

She took a bite, and apple juices mixed with cinnamon, nutmeg, and cloves dribbled out the side of her mouth and down her chin. She leaned forward, wiping her mouth with the corner of the napkin.

Her face pinked when she caught him watching her. "I should have brought extras." She glanced away and took another, much smaller bite. She was so different from what he'd thought her to be. She was not a child anymore, that was for certain. But neither was she so proper as to be boring. Ragsdale might think her propriety was lacking, but Colin found her refreshing.

He put the last bite in his mouth and quickly reached forward, taking the other half of Mariah's apple pasty.

Her hand shot out, grabbing hold of his wrist. Heat prickled his skin, nearly making him drop the pastry.

"What do you think you're doing?" she asked.

He swallowed hard and looked at her with wide eyes, but his lips quivered slightly. He had seen that look before. "You said you were too full to eat it. I did not wish for it to go to waste."

She released his arm and scowled at him, but she didn't really look angry. "You have not changed a bit."

He paused with his hand halfway to his mouth and stared at her innocently. "What do you mean?"

"You're always stealing my desserts."

He sat back and popped the rest of the pasty into his mouth. "*Always*? When have I ever done such a thing?" He knew the circumstance he was thinking about. But was it the same as hers?

"When I was twelve, you came to our estate on holiday. It was the first time my mother allowed me to have tea outside of the nursery, and there was one biscuit left at the end of tea. I wanted that biscuit, but you took it."

Colin scratched at his cheek, pretending to think. It surprised him she remembered the incident. Indeed, it was one of the few real memories he had of her before last year. But the menacing look she had cast in his direction was difficult to forget. He had wondered if she might not poison his tea before he left the estate. He put his finger to his lips and shook his head in confusion.

She folded her arms across her chest. "It was when Regi came home for grandmother's sixty-fifth birthday."

Colin nodded and bit down hard on his cheek. She was growing vexed just thinking about it. "Why did you not just ask for it?"

"And have my mother hear? She would have banished me to the nursery until my come out. No, it was better to hold my tongue and hope you would leave it behind. But you didn't. And worse still, you ate it in one bite!" Her mouth twitched slightly.

He grinned at her. "But it was a delicious biscuit, and I had hoped it might induce you to say something. But alas, you just sat there. I wondered if I might not have been wrong about you wanting it. But when you cast me dark looks for the rest of my stay, I knew I had been correct."

"You knew and ate the biscuit on purpose?" Her eyes widened.

Colin lifted a shoulder and grinned sheepishly.

Her grin matched his own. "Now I do not feel so guilty for calling you Biscuit Thief for all these years."

"That is how you have thought of me?" He feigned indignation. She'd even given him a nickname for what he'd done. The thought made him look at her a little closer. Is that how she still thought of him?

Colin grinned rather wickedly at her. "Perhaps I shall give you a name also."

"Oh, and what would it be?"

Colin put his finger to his lips in thought. And then the wicked grin was back. "Perhaps I shall call you the Pretty Little Liar."

Mariah sucked in a breath. "That is not kind, my lord."

He raised his brows. "And Biscuit Thief is?"

She shrugged. "But it was true."

He tilted his head to the side, staring at her knowingly, but said nothing.

She fought the smile that seemed to be forming on her lips. Then she was not so very angry with the name? He *had* called her pretty. The old Mariah would have been offended at the name, he was certain. But could the new Mariah see he meant it as a name of endearment? It stemmed from a shared experience between them. Besides, he now knew why she had done it and he held no ill will toward her.

Biscuit rolled over onto his back, and the stick dropped to the back of his snapping jaws. *Wait a moment.* Colin raised a brow. "Tell me, my lady. Just how did the dog earn his name?"

Mariah looked away from him, but not before he glimpsed mirth dancing in her eyes. She put her hand to her mouth, obviously trying to stop her laughter.

Colin froze for a moment. His stomach jumped into his throat, and his skin tingled. Lud, the sticks and leaves in her hair that he had so admired were nothing to seeing her genuinely laugh. Even if it was at his expense.

"He got his name after stealing the last biscuit off the tray." She tipped her head to the side. "I named him after you. But in my defense, I haven't thought of you as Biscuit in many years."

Colin stared at her. He had an overwhelming desire to pull her into his arms and kiss her until she genuinely laughed again. He frowned and shook his head. Why did he continue to think such thoughts? He had decided long ago he did not want a woman in his life. At least not yet.

She sobered. "I'm sorry. It was wrong of me, I know. But I was angry that you gave me the dog out of spite." She looked back at her hands, twisting again at her fingertips.

He dropped his gaze to his own hands. "It's any wonder you should not like for me to lick you. I have treated you very ill." He winked at her when she glanced up. Their story was a rather absurd one. They had done nothing but try to vex each other over the years. Or…was he the only one doing the vexing? Did it really matter? In the end, they had become friends. He frowned at the word. Were they friends?

She leveled her gaze at him, but her lips still turned upward. "Perhaps we should begin again." She dipped her head to him. "Lord Heatherton, it's a pleasure to meet you."

Colin shook his head. "No, I do not believe I would like to begin again. I rather like our history. I do not believe I would feel so comfortable around you if we had only just met." He grimaced. "Perhaps that's why I act so abominably around you. I feel as though I'm among family."

Her smile fell, and her face blanched. "I suppose you're right." She pushed herself up with the help of her cane and brushed at her skirts. "I'm certain I have kept you from your business. I won't keep you any longer." She glanced over her shoulder at the dog. "Come along, Biscuit."

Colin frowned at her back. What had he said to make her

leave? "I shall come by tomorrow, and we will work with Biscuit some more."

Mariah nodded, but there was no excitement in her. "If you feel it's necessary." She turned away and limped toward the terrace, looking very weary.

Colin watched after her. As he stared at her back, he realized he'd grossly misspoken. His thoughts of Lady Mariah were nowhere close to being like those he had for his family.

# Chapter Twenty-Six

MARIAH SAT IN A CHAIR WATCHING OUT THE FRONT WINDOW. Colin had sent a note that he would come around to collect her for dog training at the park. She had gathered her spencer, bonnet, and gloves in anticipation.

A carriage came into sight, and her stomach fluttered. She pushed it down as she had every time it happened when she thought about Colin. He thought of her as a sister. Nothing more. She was very near to giving up trying to convince him of something he did not believe or seem to want. They would complete the training of Biscuit and the Season would end. Perhaps she should return to Oakdale and take the summer to lick her wounds and prepare for next Season.

The carriage passed their house, and Mariah grumbled. She had worked herself up over nothing.

"Good morning, Mariah." Sarah came up from behind.

Mariah shot a quick smile over her shoulder. "Good morning, Sarah."

"Are you waiting for Lord Heatherton?"

Mariah sighed. "Yes, we are to take Biscuit to the park for his training today. I am hopeful he has learned enough that he will not run off once he sees a squirrel or butterfly."

"But that is not what has you out of sorts, is it?"

Mariah's shoulders dropped. "I am out of time. Parliament closes tomorrow next and Lord Trenton's ball follows. I am no closer to securing his affections than I was in May when he returned."

Sarah moved beside her and stared out the window with her. "Do not give up yet. I don't believe your cause is lost completely."

Mariah snorted. "You have not been with him. He retreats at every chance."

"And yet, he still keeps coming back."

Mariah's head shook. "Only because he has to. Regi is forcing him to complete Biscuit's training."

Sarah shrugged. "I think you would find that if Lord Heatherton truly wished to be finished, Reginald would excuse him from the task. But Heatherton has not requested it since that first day." She cast a look at Mariah. "Which tells me he wishes to be here, at least to some degree."

Mariah puffed out her lips. "It is likely only because he adores Biscuit. Or that he is a loyal friend to Reginald and will not go back on his promises."

Sarah patted Mariah on the arm. "Just please promise me you won't give up on him yet."

Mariah nodded and sighed as Colin's carriage came to a stop in front of their house. "Very well. But if I do not concede soon, I might never do it. Indeed, I fear my heart is already irrevocably his. Even if he does not want it."

Sarah smiled. "I think what he wants might surprise you." She clasped her hands in front of her. "Are you taking Miriam with you?"

Mariah nodded. "Yes, much to her chagrin, I am certain. While she does not say it, I believe she is tired of being forced to walk all over London. I think she will be happy to return to Staffordshire."

"Her trials are nearly at an end. I am certain she can suffer through the next few days without complaint."

*Next few days.* Why must her lack of time be constantly brought to her attention? "Miriam never complains."

"It is why she will go far. It should not surprise me to see her as a housekeeper in time." Sarah kept glancing over her shoulder toward the door. Finally, she smiled. "Ah, at last."

"Lady Mariah, Lord Heatherton is here to see you." Maxwell's deep voice sounded at the doorway.

Both Mariah and Sarah turned around at the same time. Mariah's smile was instant and unconsciously given.

"Good morning, Lord Heatherton." Sarah dipped her head.

"Lady Stoke. It is good to see you." Colin smiled, but his gaze did not linger on Sarah for long. He looked to Mariah, staring intently at her.

Sarah glanced over at Mariah and raised her brows knowingly.

"Lady Mariah, are you ready?"

Mariah chuckled nervously. Her palms turned instantly damp. "I still don't know if Biscuit is ready for the open grounds of Hyde Park."

Colin shrugged. "How will we know until we test him?" He looked around the room. "Where is my namesake, anyway?"

Mariah grinned, even as Sarah turned confused eyes to her. "Come, Biscuit." Mariah snapped her fingers and Biscuit jumped up from his spot under a nearby table.

"Ah, there he is."

Mariah leaned over and rubbed Biscuit's side. "Are you ready for your test, Biscuit? I hope you do not disappoint." She muttered to herself. When they began training Biscuit, she would have hoped the dog would fail the test, for it would surely mean more time with Colin. But now, the more time they spent training, the guiltier Mariah felt for forcing him into this position. If Biscuit was a dismal failure at the park, Mariah would simply have to allow Colin to quit. It was only fair.

He approached and bent over, picking Biscuit up and holding him under his arm. He motioned to the door. "Shall we, my lady? We want to be there when it is not crowded with people."

"Then you must not dally any longer." Sarah shooed them toward the door. "I will make certain tea is waiting for you when you return." She smiled broadly at Mariah.

"Thank you, Sarah." Mariah knew Sarah was only trying to help, even if it was surely only making it harder for Mariah to let Colin go for good.

Hyde Park was not completely devoid of people, but it was significantly quieter than it would be in another three or four hours. A dozen riders occupied Rotten Row, but only a handful of people were within sight of where Colin stopped and looked around. "This should serve our purposes."

A bench sat a short distance off, near the walking path. Miriam moved off in that direction without a word.

Colin pulled a handkerchief from his pocket and unfolded it. Several meat strips lay within. He took a breath and looked at Biscuit tucked safely in her arms. Not for the first time, Mariah felt a burning jealousy for the attention the dog received.

"Now, Biscuit." His voice held a feigned seriousness, as did his face. "You have trained for this moment for over a week. You have learned much. And I have faith in you and your abilities. Please, do not prove me wrong."

Biscuit barked and squirmed, nearly setting Mariah off

balance. It was not a good indication of his impending success.

"I will walk a few paces off and call him. Let's see if he will come." Colin walked several rods before stopping. He turned around and Mariah stared at him. Could it be he grew more handsome each time she saw him? Or was it simply that she had grown to know him better? She now knew that he was kind to most everyone he met and loyal to those he cared about. What was she going to do when they returned to the country and she no longer saw him every day? Her heart pounded painfully in her chest. Perhaps she should tell him that afternoon that the training was finished. Every day they were together, the thought of being away from him was harder to accept.

"Lady Mariah, set him down and let me call to him." Colin beckoned.

Mariah leaned over, setting the squirming animal on the ground.

"Come, Biscuit," Colin called.

Mariah released her hold and Biscuit shot across the grass. He stopped at Colin's feet and sat, his tail beating the ground in anticipation of a reward.

COLIN SQUATTED DOWN on his haunches and scratched the dog's ears. "Good dog, Biscuit." He held out his hand with the piece of dried meat and Biscuit snapped it up without pause.

Colin looked up at Mariah and smiled. "He did well, did he not?"

Mariah nodded. "I am surprised but pleased." She hobbled over slowly so her walking stick did not catch on any divot or hole in the grass.

When she reached them, Colin handed her two strips of meat. "Why do you not keep a few pieces? Then you will not need to come over every time. We can simply call him back and forth."

"Oh, yes. That sounds like a fine idea." She tried not to sound disappointed not to be standing next to him the whole time.

They took turns calling Biscuit to them, and each time he came without even looking in another direction. Colin walked over and stood next to Mariah. "Perhaps we should try to take a turn with him. Make certain he can do it when there is not a set destination."

Mariah smiled. She both longed for and dreaded their prolonged time together. Why could they not return home, and she could set Colin free once and for all? She had told Sarah she would not give up just yet, but Mariah did not think she could do it any longer.

Sarah could not understand how much it hurt to love someone and know they did not love you in return.

They walked on the grass between the Serpentine and Ring Road. Biscuit walked beside them, sniffing at each tree and bush they passed.

"He is doing well. I think we were successful." Colin sounded like a proud father.

"Yes. And you claimed you did not know what you were about." Mariah gave him a side look.

"I will have to thank Mr. Jones, our huntsman, when I return to Ravencliff next week. I confess, I only did what I had seen him do with my pointers."

Biscuit let out a bark and, before either of them could react, took off running.

"Biscuit, come back here this instant," Mariah yelled after him. But the dog paid her no heed. He charged after a squirrel running frantically just out of Biscuit's reach. The squirrel ducked into a patch of tall grasses beside the Serpentine and Biscuit went in after it. A splash sounded.

Mariah raced over to the water's edge in time to see

Biscuit's head break the surface. "Colin, he is drowning. Help him!" She looked at him with wide eyes.

Colin shook his head. "No, dogs are fine swimmers."

She shook her head. "No, look at him. He is struggling. Please, help him." Tears filled her eyes. How was it she had finally come to love the little beast and now she was going to lose him? "Please, Colin."

Colin looked fleetingly from her to the dog and back. Without another word, he unbuttoned his coats. Shrugging out of his tailcoat and then his waistcoat, he handed them over to Mariah before tugging off his cravat and then his Hessians. Giving her one last look, as if to ask if she really wished him to move forward, he dove into the lake. When he came to the surface and brushed away the water from his eyes. He looked around as water dripped from his hair, down his brow and cheeks. He spotted Biscuit, and with two strokes, reached the flailing dog.

Biscuit barked and pawed at Colin's chest. He wrapped an arm around the dog, but Biscuit squirmed his way loose. Swimming away from Colin, Biscuit climbed onto the bank and out of the water. He sniffed at the tall grasses the squirrel had disappeared into as he shook the water from his fur.

Mariah hobble-ran over to Biscuit and picked him up, snuggling him close to her—not caring that he made her clothes damp. "Oh, Biscuit. You are safe. Don't scare me like that again."

She felt Colin stop beside her. "Is he harmed?" He did not sound as if he thought it to be true but wished to hear Mariah's opinion on the matter.

She turned and flung her arm up over Colin's shoulder, burying her face in his neck. "Oh, Colin. Thank you for saving him. I don't know what I would have done should something have happened to him." She released a shuttering sob.

Colin's arms came up around her back, pulling her in

close. "Don't be sad. Biscuit is fine." His head tilted slightly, resting his cheek on her hair.

They stayed that way for a moment until the wetness seeped through Mariah's spencer and gown. She pulled slightly away and looked up at him. Her breath caught in her throat.

His hair was in complete disarray, drops of water still clinging to the tips. He smiled down at her, even as she saw concern in his eyes.

Gads. How could someone look so desirable and so disheveled all at the same time?

She dropped her hand from his neck and rested it on his chest. "You are no longer able to say you have not saved a life," she whispered.

He sucked in a jerky breath. "Even if he did not need saving?" His voice was as quiet as hers.

Mariah looked down at her hand, only then seeing how very transparent his shirt was. She swallowed. Slowly, her eyes traveled from her hand up to his chest, and to the open neck of his shirt. Finally, resting on his slightly parted lips.

Never had she wished so badly—and she had wished it many times over the years— that he would kiss her. What would it feel like?

Her body shivered, but she could not be sure it was only because of her wet clothes.

Colin wiped a drop of water from her cheek. "I should return you to Berkeley Square before you catch a chill." He whispered, and for a moment, Mariah almost wondered if he wanted the kiss as much as she did. But if he did, why had he not done it already?

She lifted her chin. Why must she wait for him? Her time was running out and she would not have the whole of the summer to wonder what it would have been like to kiss him if only she had been brave enough. She was brave, and she was determined. If her heart must be broken, at least she would have something to remember with fondness. And had she not promised Sarah she would not give up? If he would not do it, then she would.

She leaned in closer and stretched taller. Without another thought, she pressed her lips to his.

She thought he might immediately pull away when he froze at her touch. But then he wrapped his arms around her again and pulled her closer to him, taking over the kiss. He put a hand on her cheek. His thumb rested on her jawline, slowly brushing back and forth.

Her skin rippled with gooseflesh.

Mariah put her arm back around his neck, her fingers clutching at the back of his collar, almost as if to hold her up.

He tightened his hold on her, as his lips moved over hers.

In all her imaginings over the years, none of them had been even close to what was happening now. The chill she had felt disappeared as contented warmth spread from the crown of her head to the tips of her toes.

His lips were warm and soft and fit perfectly against hers. Indeed, she did not know how she had lived for so long without them. And now how was she to live without them, knowing they were out there in the world?

Gracious, what had she done? Was this the curse Pandora found when she opened the box? Because Mariah could not think of anything worse than not being able to feel his lips on hers ever again.

Biscuit let out a yelp, and Colin took a step back. His eyes widened, and he looked around them as if searching for anyone who might have seen them.

Indeed, it was likely wise to discover that. But must that be his first thought? Was he worried about who might think they had an arrangement?

Mariah pinched at the bridge of her nose, closing her eyes against the tears that were forming. He regretted what had happened. He must surely think her the most untoward woman he had ever encountered. Whatever hope she'd had of forming an attachment disappeared like steam in a warm room.

Biscuit squirmed in her arms and dropped to the ground. "Sit, Biscuit," she called in a shaky voice.

Colin scooped up his discarded coats and cravat, shoving his feet into his boots, all the time muttering under his breath. "Come, Biscuit. It is time to return you home." Colin did not look at Mariah. He looked at Biscuit or straight ahead. But never at Mariah.

# Chapter Twenty-Seven

COLIN LEANED OVER THE BILLIARD TABLE, LINING UP HIS SHOT. He pulled the cue back and struck the ball, sending it spiraling across the table and bouncing off the side cushion.

"What is wrong with you? I have never seen you miss such an easy shot." Ben leaned against the wall, waiting for his turn.

"Nothing is wrong." Colin snapped, then tempered his tone. "Why should you ask?" His mind went immediately to the park the morning before and the kiss he had shared with Mariah. She had called him Colin when she embraced him—just before she had kissed him. The sound of his name on her voice had echoed through his mind all night.

Rags looked up as he lined up his shot. He squinted at Colin as if he were trying to see something deep within. "I agree with Ben. While I see no difference in your billiards, you have been acting strange of late." Rags pulled his cue back and struck his ball, sending it crashing into the red ball which rolled softly into the corner pocket. "And that is what they call a red hazard." Rags said with a grin on his face.

Ben rolled his eyes. "We are all familiar with the terms, Rags. You need not tell us how to play."

Rags shrugged. "I thought our good friend, Colin, may have forgotten. He has not made a winning hazard yet."

Ben leaned forward for his turn. "Which is why I asked what was wrong. It is not common for you to play so abominably."

Colin smirked at his friends as he took a sip of his drink. "I am not playing abominably. I'm simply not as competitive as the two of you."

"Since when?" Ben raised a brow.

Rags put the broad end of his cue on the floor, clasping both his hands together around its tip. "Yes, since when have you not cared about winning? You are nearly as annoying about it as I am."

Ben's striking ball sent both the red and white ball into the pocket.

Rags growled. "A canon. Thunder and turf, Ben. Perhaps I should question you about what the matter is. You have never landed a canon."

Colin grasped hold of the change of conversation. "Yes, Ben. What has happened? Have you been practicing of late?"

Ben shot them both an irritated look. "I have landed a canon before." He narrowed his eyes at Colin. "You will not change the subject so easily. Now, what is the matter? I do not believe that nothing is bothering you." He glanced at Rags. "You can tell us, can he not, Rags?"

"He has likely already discussed it with Reginald." Rags glanced at Colin. "He does not need us."

Colin looked away from him. While he would normally share these types of things with Reginald, it was not as if he could this time. How would he even begin? *By the way, Reg. I kissed your sister. I hope you do not mind.* Reginald would surely land him a facer. And Colin could not blame him if he did. He had kissed her and left her with no promises or agreements. What kind of man did such a thing?

"Wait, you have not talked to Reg about it?" Ben stared at Colin. "Why?"

Rags groaned. "Do not say what I think you are about to say."

Ben's brows shot up. "The only thing you could not speak to Reginald about would be something about his wife or…his sister."

Colin's face heated, and he knew that without saying a word, he had confirmed his friend's suspicions.

"What did you do?" Rags nearly spat out.

Colin glanced out the door into the sitting room of Brooks's, making certain Reginald had not come when they were not looking. "I kissed her." Colin leaned forward to line up his shot, so he would not have to look at his friends' faces.

"You did what?" Ben stepped over next to Colin and grabbed hold of his cue, prohibiting him from making his shot.

Colin straightened. "That isn't completely true. She kissed me first. I simply…"

"You did not put a stop to it?" Rags demanded. "You know she has had a tendré for you for years. Of course she is going to kiss you if given the chance. It was your responsibility to put an end to it."

"Wait, you knew she had a tendré for me? Why did I not know?"

Rags glowered. "Because you are an idiot, obviously."

Colin shook his head. "I know I should have stopped it. But—." But he had not wanted to stop it. Indeed, if Biscuit had not barked, he might have stayed there kissing Mariah for heaven only knew how long. He had enjoyed nothing so much while also knowing it was completely wrong. Although, how could something so wrong feel so right? It was as if he had found a part of him that had always been absent. There was a joy, not just passion, but complete and utter contentment he had felt while holding Mariah in his arms. And yet, even now, as he thought about it, it scared him.

"Kisses bring complications. Did you forget that?" Rags leaned forward, his hands spread out wide on the table. He stared at Colin with irritation and hurt—that did not seem congruent with Rags—in his eyes.

"I know kisses bring complications." Colin nearly shouted. He leaned on the table opposite of Rags, only a foot or less keeping their noses from touching. "Do you think I planned this? I didn't. And now I have done it and I don't know how to undo it."

"Do you want to undo it?" Ben's voice was low and calm.

Colin shrugged. "I don't know."

"What do you mean you don't know? Only a fortnight ago you were telling Reg of all her shortcomings. And now you don't know if you wish to undo kissing her? What is wrong with you?" Rags' face was crimson, and his brow glistened with perspiration. He was furious.

"She isn't like that. I was wrong when I said those things about her. I was speaking from ignorance." Colin set the cue to the side and leaned against the chair positioned in the corner. "Since spending time with her, I know her better. She is nothing like I thought. She *is* kind. And funny. As well as brilliant and quick-witted." He frowned. "And she fits quite perfectly in my arms."

"But what about her giggles and eye fluttering you found so annoying." Ben leaned onto his cue.

Colin lifted a shoulder. "I do not mind them so much anymore."

"Egad. You are in love with her." Rags shook his head, looking as if Colin had just described eating maggots. He dropped his cue on the table. "I can't believe this is happening again." He looked at Colin. "We all promised. And now you are breaking the promise too." He turned and sulked out of the room.

Colin ran a hand through his hair. Rags had accused him of being in love with Mariah. Surely, not. Yes, he enjoyed being with her. And he did enjoy kissing and holding her. But love? That could not be true. Colin enjoyed being a bachelor. He did not want to give it up in favor of a wife. He sighed. But nor did he wish to give up Mariah. Before the week's end, she would be returning to Staffordshire, and he would not see her for a month. *A month.* A lump formed in his throat.

Ben came over and stood in front of him. "That went better than I thought it would."

Colin gave him a half grin.

Ben's brow rose slowly to his hairline. "But he did make one very interesting point."

Colin pretended to shrug it off, but he looked away. When had his friends become so perceptive? And why must they now use it on him?

"Are you in love with her?"

Colin dropped into the chair, resting his elbows on the arms and steepling his fingers. Did he love her? He had never been in love before. But then, he had never felt what he felt for Mariah. He shrugged. "I don't know."

"Don't you?" Ben twisted his head to the side. "I think you do, but you are simply refusing to acknowledge it."

"Why would I not acknowledge it?"

"Our little league of friends has not looked favorably upon marriage. Or love. I suppose it takes time to overcome that thinking. But Reginald did. And I believe he is better for it. I can see it whenever his wife enters the room."

"Or even when he speaks of her." Colin nodded. "I have noticed it too. He is happier."

Ben nodded. He was quiet for a moment before he lifted his eyes to Colin. "May I make an observation?"

Colin shrugged. "If you must."

"Cort, Ponsy, Charlie, and I have noticed the same thing with you of late. I cannot think it is a coincidence that it started when you began training that dog you gave Lady Mariah."

"You are wrong. I have always been happy."

"This is a different kind of happy." Ben raised a brow. "Indeed, the dog should have been our first clue to your feelings."

Colin shook his head. "I did not buy her the dog because I loved her. I bought it because I was angry with her. I wanted her to suffer."

Ben tilted his head again. "Did you?"

"Of course I did."

"Or," Ben leaned against the wall, "you gave her the dog in the hopes she would learn to like it. And perhaps in turn like you."

Colin shook his head. Perhaps there was some truth to what Ben said. But was what Rags had said true also? Did he love her? The calm yet frantic feeling in his belly and chest, made him think perhaps the answer was yes.

"If I were to discover that I love her, what do I do?"

Ben blinked several times. "You have this conversation with Reginald."

"I was afraid you would say that." Colin grimaced. "Even the part about kissing her?"

Ben grinned. "I think you might be surprised at Reginald. But if he is angry, you might just want to remind him of a little incident that happened at Charlie's card party." Ben winked. "That should calm him down."

"And then I need to tell Mariah."

Ben laughed. "Yes, it is usually advisable to tell the young lady you love her at some point."

Colin pushed himself up and grabbed his cue. "Tell me, Ben. When did you become so wise in the way of love?"

Ben lifted his shoulder. "I am cursed to always see love for others, but never for myself."

Colin leaned over the table but glanced up. "That is too

bad, my friend. Because I highly recommend it." He waggled his brows. "Especially the kissing. The kissing is very agreeable." He pulled his cue back and struck his ball. It crashed into the white ball and then the red, sending them both into the side pocket. "I think I am better now." He grinned widely. "Thank you, Ben."

Ben frowned at the balls in the pocket. "Next time, I will keep my advice to myself."

Colin laughed. "I doubt there will be one anytime soon. The rest of you seem quite contented to remain bachelors."

Ben nodded. "It shall not be me that falls next. Of that, I can assure you."

Colin chuckled. "It would be ironic if it was Rags, would it not?"

Ben shook his head. "You know he refuses to marry while his father is alive. I think even if he should find someone he could love and who would love him back—"

Colin laughed. "That is the difficulty. Rags is not an easy man to love."

"No truer words have ever been said." Charlie walked into the room.

Colin shot a look at Ben. He dipped his head and Colin knew he would not speak of their conversation to anyone else. Rags, however, was just angry enough to put an ad in the nightly paper. Perhaps Colin should speak with Reginald at the Purdys' dinner party that evening, just in case.

# Chapter Twenty-Eight

MARIAH WATCHED AS COLIN SCRATCHED AT BISCUIT'S EAR. Since their kiss two days and approximately one hour ago, she had thought of hardly anything else. At first, she had thought perhaps he must care for her. Why else would he have responded to her kiss with such fervency? But as the hours ticked by, she realized he was a man. And his reaction had meant nothing.

At least to him.

To her, it meant everything. And she now realized what a mistake it had been. Now, instead of spending the summer wondering what it would be like to kiss him, she would spend the summer torturing herself with the memory of it. It would surely do her in.

Miriam had said nothing about the kiss. Mariah was uncertain if she was happy about that or not. She had not yet dared to tell Sarah. Would she chide her as she had with Lord Muckrake? Not that Colin could even be compared to that man. But still, Mariah had not felt ready to share it with anyone.

"Are you certain you do not wish to find a trainer to teach

him how to hunt when you return to Staffordshire tomorrow next?" Colin looked up at her.

Her stomach sank, and she put her fingers to her temple. *Tomorrow next.* How had time fled so quickly? It seemed like only yesterday Colin had placed the leash in her hand. And now it was time to return to Staffordshire. Without him. Why could Reginald not have planned the house party for next week? Although, what did it matter? Colin did not want her.

She closed her eyes for a moment. Two more days. That was all she had remaining to pretend that there was still a chance they could be together.

Mariah moved in front of him, her head tilted to the side. "Why do we not train him now? We still have two days."

Colin stood up and smiled. She loved it when he smiled *at* her. His smile had been one of the first things she'd loved about him. His cheeks creased on both sides, almost like a frame around a fine piece of art.

He tapped her on the tip of her nose with his finger, and she shivered, then chided herself. "And where would we train him? The fox is out of season, and there is no wide-open space for it."

She took a step closer.

Colin's Adam's apple bobbed.

Sometimes when she stood very close to him, she thought she might have an effect on him. "There is a large expanse of grass not far from here. Why could we not go there?"

His brow furrowed. "The only expanse of grass close by is . . . Hyde Park." He shook his head, his lips only half grinning. "After my last visit, I am a little leery."

She raised a brow. "Then you are never to go to Hyde Park again?"

"Perhaps I might if—" He looked at her then shook his head. "Besides, there are no foxes in Hyde Park."

Mariah looked down at her hands. "Please? If we go now, before the fashionable hour, I see no problem with it."

Colin dropped his head to the side. "But surely there are things that must be acquired before we even begin."

She wanted so badly to put her hand on his cheek—feel the smoothness of his skin. But she had gloves on.

And she was trying to forget him. Lawks, she always seemed to forget that part of the plan.

"And where will we find a fox?" He asked.

She reached up and tapped the end of his nose. "I have seen to that. You don't wish to end the training before it's complete, do you?"

He sighed exaggeratedly, and Mariah hoped it meant he did not really oppose the idea. Or Hyde Park. "I suppose not." He stared at her for a moment, and she thought he might have more to say. But he kept silent.

MARIAH HELD the bag and Biscuit's leash tightly in one fist and her cane in the other.

He pointed to the bag in her hands. "I assume that is what we need?"

She nodded. "When you mentioned fox hunting several days ago, I enquired of Mr. Bland, our gardener. While he was an undergardener at Oakdale, he did help the huntsman on occasion. He had a limited knowledge of what we need to do." He had also told her to leave the training to Mr. Humphreys. But she had disregarded that piece of information.

She opened her sack and Colin peered inside. He reached in and pulled out a stuffed fox. It was not the most realistic-looking creature, as Mariah had made it herself. Had she had the proper time, she was certain she could have done a more proficient job. But she'd done the whole thing in an evening, afraid that it would not be ready when Colin did this part of Biscuit's training.

He frowned at the creature in his hand. "Is this supposed to be a fox?"

Mariah snatched it from his grasp. "I should like to see you do any better."

He grinned and her toes curled inside her half-boots. He lifted out a small corked vial and held it up between his thumb and forefinger. "And what is this?"

"It's fox scent. We sprinkle it on the stuffed fox and hide it. Then we send Biscuit to look for it." It had seemed simple enough when Mr. Bland explained it to her.

Colin uncorked the vial and gagged. "Lud, that smells terrible."

"I am not suggesting you dab it behind your ears, my lord. It's for Biscuit." Mariah gawked at him.

"And I'm eternally grateful for that. Just be careful where you apply it." Colin turned up his nose as he handed the vial back to her. He looked around the park. "How do you wish to start?"

Mariah shoved Biscuit's leash into Colin's hands. "You hold this while I put the scent on the fox." She set her cane to the side and sat down carefully on the ground.

Uncorking the vial, she held it out over the grass, just in case any spilled. Dribbling a few drops on the fox, she replaced the cork. She took the leash back from Colin and nodded to the fox laying just in front of her. "Now, you go hide it. Make sure it's not too hard, but also not too easy."

Colin's nose crinkled. "Why must I touch the smelly thing?"

Mariah tilted her head and fluttered her lashes at him. "It is not as if I can hobble around to hide it. Besides, you're a gentleman and would never think of asking a lady to do it."

He narrowed his eyes at her, but his lips quivered. "You are a devious creature, my lady." Pinching the tip of the fox's tail between his fingers, Colin held it out in front of him. He glanced back at her over his shoulder, and Mariah covered her mouth with her hand.

She bent down and scratched Biscuit's ears to distract him from watching Colin. She didn't wish for him to cheat and know where the fox was. "There's my good Biscuit. Were you happy to see Colin today? Yes, so was I." She crooned to the dog like he was a child.

"You were happy to see me?" Colin stood at her side. He looked down at her with a look she could not quite describe or interpret.

"Of course. You know I always enjoy our time together."

"As do I." He sank down to his haunches. "It's hidden. Now what?"

Mariah bent low and uncorked the vial. She held it under Biscuit's nose. The dog sniffed, and she replaced the cork. Patting him on the rump, she gave him a little shove in the direction Colin had gone. "Go on, Biscuit. Find the fox."

The dog stood staring at her.

"Go on, Biscuit. Find the fox." She looked over at Colin. "What is wrong? Why is he not finding it?"

Colin chuckled. "I think you missed a step."

Mariah frowned. "Mr. Bland didn't tell me another step." She handed him the leash and some meat pieces. "Perhaps we should lead him to it the first time. Then maybe he'll understand."

Colin shrugged. He led Biscuit to a bush not far off. Biscuit sat down at the base, his tail wagging as he waited for a treat. "No, Biscuit. Get the fox." Colin motioned to the bush. Finally, he bent and pulled the fox from the tangle of branches and shoved it under the dog's nose. Biscuit sniffed at the fox. Then looked up eagerly for his reward.

"Good boy, Biscuit." Colin gave the dog a chunk of meat.

He led Biscuit back to Mariah. "Keep him busy while I hide it again."

Colin sighed, and again she wondered if he wanted to say something. But he just walked off in the opposite direction. A few moments later, he yelled. "It's hidden."

Mariah held the vial under the dog's nose again. "Go find the fox, Biscuit."

The dog sat obediently at her feet, his tail smacking the ground.

Colin came over and stood next to her.

"Why is he not going after the fox?" Mariah whined.

Colin grinned. "Perhaps he does not know we mean it to be a fox."

She glared up at him. "It is a very fine fox."

He kneeled down in front of her and picked up the vial from beside her. "Perhaps there is not enough scent on the *fox* for Biscuit to pick up the scent."

"Lady Mariah? Is that you?"

Mariah turned around to see Lord Muckrake coming from behind. Lawks. Did she have to speak with him?

Colin put out his hand to help her up.

"What are you doing in the park so early?" Lord Muckrake eyed Colin with disdain.

"Lord Heatherton is helping me train my new fox terrier."

Lord Muckrake looked at her. "Where is your whip?"

"Whip, sir?" Mariah raised a brow.

He guffawed. "You don't think to train the dog properly without a whip, do you?"

A lump formed in her throat. "I learned of a technique which did not require the whip."

He grunted. "It isn't an effective way, I assure you. Your huntsman will not appreciate your interference. Foxers are meant to be hunters, not pets." His nose wrinkled, and he took a step back. He looked her up and down before tipping his hat to her. "Good day, my lady." He glanced at Colin. "Lord Heatherton."

Colin sneered at Muckrake but said nothing.

Once Lord Muckrake was too far away to hear, Mariah turned to Colin and narrowed her gaze. "Why did it suddenly smell of fox, my lord?" she asked.

Colin shrugged. "Perhaps the cork came loose, and it spilled on Muckrake's boots."

"You didn't." Mariah's eyes widened.

Colin shrugged. "I don't know what you are speaking of."

Mariah grinned. "You're a wicked man, my lord."

"Anyone who would think of whipping this dog should smell like a fox." Colin looked in the direction Muckrake had walked.

Mariah lifted her hand to touch his face but dropped it to her side. "You're right. He should." She turned away, unable to control her feelings for him. If she was not careful, she would kiss him again. And she did not think she could manage another rejection. "Come, Biscuit. Let's go find the fox." She hobbled with the dog to the bush where Colin hid the fox, but Biscuit didn't seek it out. "Perhaps if we said *tallyho*?" She did not really think it would help the matter, but she was at a loss as to what else to do.

She heaved a sigh and leaned to pull the fox from the bush. Biscuit jumped up, putting his front paws on her thigh. Suddenly, branches came at her from all directions. She let out a gasp.

"Mariah!" Colin called, but it was too late. She was already tangled in the bush.

"Let me help you." He reached out his hand, and she grabbed hold, but as he pulled, twigs and branches tugged at her hair and dress.

"Ouch," she cried.

"Hold on, Mariah. Let me untangle you first." It seemed like only a moment as Colin's fingers slid through her hair, separating it from the twigs and branches. If her ankle had not pained her so badly, she might have wished for it to continue indefinitely.

He pulled her free of the bush. But when he saw her gently lift her injured ankle off the ground, he put his hands under her knees and around her back and lifted her up into his arms. "You've injured your ankle again, have you not?" Concern laced his voice.

"It is only twisted." Mariah laid her head on his shoulder and thread her arms around his neck. She did not think she would ever tire of being there.

"I've heard that before." Colin sighed and looked down at her. His creases smoothed out and a grin appeared. "You know, I think twigs and leaves are my favorite hair accessory for you."

Mariah swallowed. His heart thumped rapidly beneath her ear. Could he possibly feel the same as she did? Or was he simply worried about telling Reginald she had injured her ankle again?

He stared at her for several heartbeats, but then shook his head. "I should get you to the carriage. This surely does not look proper." He walked quickly toward the entrance. "Miriam, please bring Biscuit."

He said nothing as he walked. But he did periodically glance down at her. Or he did until he stumbled. Then his gaze stayed straight ahead.

They arrived at the carriage much faster than Mariah would have liked. He set her down on the ground and then helped her climb inside.

She settled on the seat and waited for him to join her. But he didn't. He must be waiting for Miriam. It did not surprise her that he would wait for the maid. But it disappointed her. She had hoped they might have a moment alone together.

Finally, Biscuit scampered into the carriage, followed by Miriam and then Colin. Miriam sat next to Mariah, and Colin took the seat across from them. He rapped on the side of the carriage, and it lurched forward.

No one said anything, but Colin watched her the entire

ride. His features alternated between concern and a small smile. What was he thinking about? Was he wishing they had shared another kiss, as she was?

The carriage stopped, and Colin sprang out onto the walkway.

He held onto Mariah's hand, his other arm around her waist as he helped her down. She leaned heavily on him, her ankle not as sore as when she had first sprained it, but much sorer than it had been in recent days. "You are coming in for tea, are you not? Sarah will be very disappointed if you don't." Mariah did not include her own disappointment, even though it would surely be worse than Sarah's.

"Of course. I should not like to disappoint her ladyship." Colin sucked in a breath. "Lady Mariah? May I speak with you alone, before we join your sister-in-law for tea?"

Mariah swallowed. What could he wish to say? Her pulse thundered in her ears as she thought about what she hoped he would say. She nodded, hoping her expression looked appropriately light-hearted. "Of course. Why do we not stop in the Yellow Parlor? It is just off the entryway."

He nodded.

"Miriam, will you please take Biscuit to the back garden and let him run around?" Miriam dipped a brief curtsy and shuffled off toward the rear of the house.

Colin opened the door to the parlor and motioned Mariah inside.

She moved slowly, limping toward the sofa.

He closed the door and swung her up into his arms before she knew what was happening.

She let out a squeal of delight, the pain in her ankle forgotten. He carried her twice in one day. Surely that meant what she thought it meant.

He walked to the couch but did not set her down. He simply stared down at her. "Oh, Mariah." Her name—her

Christian name—came out in a whisper. Almost as if it pained him to say it.

She timidly lifted her hand to his hair, smoothing down the curls in the back.

He sucked in a stuttering breath.

Was he angry at her? She really should remove her hands from his chest and hair, but they did not seem to listen to her.

Neither of them moved—just stared at one another. His heartbeat still hammered beneath her hand. Indeed, it may have even increased.

His mouth opened as if he wished to say something. But then his brow furrowed, and his lips pursed shut.

Mariah pulled in her bottom lip between her teeth.

He groaned and his pulse increased.

She could think of something else he could do with his mouth if he had nothing to say. If she had her way, he would drop his head slowly and kiss her again, as he had at the park. She closed her eyes, allowing herself, if only for a moment, to remember it. She could almost feel his breath on her cheek . . . feel the warmth of his skin against hers.

Her breath stuttered out of her at the feather-light touch of his lips on hers. Lawks, when had she developed such a vivid imagination? It felt so real she threaded her hands deeper into his hair.

He groaned again and the kiss intensified. As he trailed tiny kisses along her jaw, Mariah realized it was not just her imagination. Colin was kissing her. It was as real as the sun shining through the window. And it was even better than before—which she had not thought possible. He had initiated this kiss. Not her. He was not simply responding to her kiss but was taking the lead.

He gently sat on the couch, placing her on his lap as he continued to kiss her earlobe.

"Mariah," he whispered against her lips. "You are everything I want in a wife. I cannot imagine my life without you. Please say you will marry me."

Mariah froze. What had he said? She was everything he wanted in a wife. While the words should have made her happier than she had ever been, they did not. Indeed, they sent a cold wash over her skin, and she pulled away. What had she done? She could not marry him. It was all lies. She was not what he wanted at all.

"I suppose I should call you out for what you're doing to my sister."

Colin and Mariah spun around. Mariah fell off Colin's lap onto the couch rather haphazardly.

Reginald stood just inside the door, his arms folded across his chest.

Colin looked nervously at his friend. "Reg, it's not what you think. I just asked Mariah to marry me."

Reginald's face split into a grin.

Mariah shook her head. "I'm—I'm sorry, Colin. But—I—I can't accept."

Colin's smile fell, and his brow creased. "But I thought—"

"Yes, as did I. But I realize now that I cannot accept. I am not the woman you think I am. I tricked you…again."

She tried to stand, but her ankle gave out. Drat the injury. How did one make a hasty retreat if they could not even walk?

"What do mean you tricked me?"

"Yes, what do you mean?" Reginald stepped forward.

Mariah tried to push back the tears threatening to erupt at any moment. But when she opened her mouth, she could not stop the sob. "I heard what you said in Regi's study about me. You said I pouted too much and was unkind. I used that knowledge to become the kind of woman you wanted. But that isn't really me. I am naturally unkind and rather spoiled. I was just doing what I thought would draw your attention to me." She released a rather slobbery, snotty sob.

Grabbing for her walking stick, she pushed herself up and hobbled around the couch. She paused a moment and turned back to Colin. "I am so very sorry. I never meant to hurt you."

Colin just stared at her. She turned back and limped as quickly as she could from the room. Even Reginald did not try to stop her.

# Chapter Twenty-Nine

Mariah had said no? Although, that was not the only surprise she gave him. She had tricked him on purpose. After all they had spoken of over the last two weeks, she still lied to him?

Colin shot a look at Reginald.

His brow was knit in confusion.

"Did you know about this?" Colin spat out at him.

"Did I know about what?" Reginald shook his head. "I had no idea she was listening at the door."

Colin dropped his head into his hands. What was he to do? He had fallen in love with a fraud. Lud, he would never hear the end of it from Rags. Not that he cared much about Rags just then. What was he to do now? His chest ached and his mind spun with all the conversations that they'd had. Was there a point when he should have realized it was not real?

Reginald came and sat on the couch. "I don't believe it."

Colin sneered. "You don't believe what? That your sister could concoct a plan to try and trick me into marrying her? Was the lie about Lady G not enough to convince you?"

Reginald shook his head. "But it makes no sense."

"It makes perfect sense. She pretended to be a kind and

generous person when I was around so that I would fall in love with her."

"But that is just it. She did not only do it when you were around. She has been kind to the servants for weeks even when you were gone. Maxwell mentioned it to me. And Mrs. Leach told me that Mariah insisted all of Mrs. Leach's sister's medical fees be sent to Mariah. She has been paying for them with her pin money." Reginald shifted and looked hard at Colin. "While it may have started as a means to be what you wanted her to be, I do not think it is that now. I think she has become that person."

Colin frowned. "Regardless. It still began as a trick."

Reginald pursed his lips.

"I know you wish to say something. Do not hold back." Colin could barely look at his friend. Was this not what he had worried about when Reginald spoke of Mariah's tendré? Was he to lose his friendship with Reginald?

"I think you are being too hard on her." Reginald sat on the far end of the sofa but kept some distance between them.

"Why must you defend her? Why can you not see how ill she has treated me?"

"But has she treated you so very ill?"

"Indeed, she has. She has lied to me at nearly every interaction we have had."

Reginald shook his head. "That is what I question. Was it all a lie?" He paused for a moment as if gathering his thoughts. "Is there nothing you have improved upon since being with her." He sighed. "It is what I noticed with Sarah. I improved because I wished to be worthy of her. So in a sense, I did the same thing as Mariah. Should we not all want to grow and become better? Indeed, I should think that is the measure of love. When we want to become what our loved one sees in us."

Colin sat back. Was that true? Had Mariah changed not

because she was trying to trick him, but because she wanted to be better for him?

"Indeed, does not her confession add to her defense? If she had only been doing it for the proposal, do you not think she would have accepted you?" Reginald stood up and clapped Colin on the back. "I am not trying to convince you out of your anger at Mariah. Her history surely must make you leery. But I would not be truthful if I said I was not pleased to hear you might become my brother." He sighed. "You have much to think on and I will leave you to it. I will give Sarah your regrets for missing tea."

Colin stood up. Reginald was correct. He did have much to think about. But he could not think clearly in Reginald's parlor. Indeed, the rosemary, lavender, and vanilla scent still hung in the air. He would never be able to make a clear decision while standing there. He must go where he made all of his best decisions. He must go to Brooks's.

Mariah hiccupped into her pillow. Her ankle throbbed as it had not in nearly a week. But it was nothing to the pain squeezing at her chest. While she had always hoped for it, she had never really believed that Colin would ask for her hand. And she could barely fathom that she had declined his offer. Had she not worked for months to draw his attention? And when the moment came to seize all her dreams, she said no.

But how could she not? How could she accept his honest, good faith offer when she had been nothing but deceitful? And while it hurt more than she could imagine telling him no, she knew it would hurt even worse had she accepted. She loved him too much to make him miserable for the rest of his life. Which he surely would be if he married her.

A knock sounded on her door, and Mariah wiped her eyes on the pillow. "Enter," she called in as normal a voice as she could muster.

Sarah poked her head in the door. "May I come in and speak with you?"

Mariah did not wish to speak with anyone. Indeed, she was content to lay in her bed and cry until they returned to Staffordshire. But she did not think Sarah would allow it. Mariah may as well get the talk over with. Once Sarah and Reginald left for the Kirkpatricks' card party, Mariah could wallow all she wanted.

"Of course." Mariah sat up and rested her back against the headboard.

Sarah pulled a chair close to the bed and sat down. She did not speak immediately. "You look sad," she finally said.

Mariah swallowed. Should she tell her everything? Reginald likely already had. It was an irritation of her best friend being married to her brother. Mariah was rarely the first to share anything with Sarah anymore. "I injured my ankle again while at the park."

Sarah glanced at Mariah's disheveled appearance. She must have assumed it all happened with the kiss—as Reginald had surely told her about it. "Oh? What happened?"

Mariah sighed. "We—I was teaching Biscuit to find a fox. But he refused to find it. When I went to fetch the fox from out of the bushes, Biscuit jumped on me and I lost my balance."

Sarah's hand went to her mouth. "Oh, Mariah. I'm so sorry. Is it much worse?"

Mariah shrugged. "It is not as painful as when I first sprained it. But it is worse than it was yesterday."

Sarah frowned. "Drat it all."

Mariah sucked in a breath. Sarah was not usually one to use such words.

"My apologies. But I was hoping your foot had healed

enough that you might come to Lord Trenton's tomorrow evening. Even if you could not dance many sets, I had thought we might have a lovely time of it."

"I'm sorry, Sarah. That would have been delightful."

Sarah pinched her lips together. "I wonder at your ankle being the only reason for your tears." She sighed. "Shall we talk about it? If not, I understand. I do not want to force you to do something you do not wish to do."

Mariah smiled. Since they had mended their friendship, Sarah had been very cautious about advising Mariah overly much. She could only assume Sarah was trying not to mother her anymore.

Mariah dropped her head. "I made a terrible mistake."

"Oh?" Sarah leaned forward and took hold of Mariah's hand.

Mariah pushed her lips out. Should she tell Sarah what she had done? It was rather lowering to admit she had been listening at the door. It was another reason for Colin to add to his lengthy list of complaints against her. And it would mortify Sarah. As well, it should. Thinking about it brought a degree of embarrassment to Mariah. But she had already told Reginald and Colin. It would not be long before Sarah knew the whole of it—if she did not already know.

"While you were away, I happened to hear Colin speaking to his friends in Reginald's office."

Sarah grimaced. "Oh, you didn't."

Mariah nodded. "I was only going to listen for a moment—try to discover something I could use to catch Colin's attention. But as I was listening, he mentioned that I was very handsome."

Sarah smiled. "That is very good, is it not?"

"Yes, I was pleased. But then he went on to tell them all the things he opposed about me."

"That was most unkind of him." Mariah smiled at the

look of annoyance on Sarah's face. She truly was the best of friends.

Mariah shrugged. "In his defense, he did not know I was listening." She sighed. "At first when I heard him say that I pouted too much and was unkind to those I thought beneath me—."

Sarah's brows rose as if she understood something she previously did not. "I see."

Mariah looked down at her hands in her lap. "At first I was angry at what he had said. He was calling me unkind just as he was behaving unkindly toward me. But the more I thought about his words, the more I realized he had given me the key. I knew what I needed to do to gain his attention. And so, I changed."

"Yes, you have. Many of us have noticed." Sarah spoke quietly, as if she wasn't certain Mariah would receive her words well.

Mariah shook her head. "But it was all a trick. I used what he said to become what he wanted. It was no different from telling him I loved dogs." Her lids filled with tears again. "That is why I had to decline his offer when he asked for my hand. I could not accept. He would learn in time that I tricked him, and he would come to despise me."

Sarah sat holding Mariah's hand for a long time, not saying anything. Finally, she sat forward. "Mariah, I believe you are treating yourself too harshly."

Mariah pished. "I do not believe I have ever treated myself too harshly. It is likely why I rarely think of others needs before my own." She shook her head. "Besides, you are only defending me because you are my friend and sister."

Sarah raised a shoulder. "Perhaps, in part. But I also have a unique perspective. When I left London, you were very much the girl Lord Heatherton described."

Mariah jerked her head up but then nodded. "I know."

"But what you don't seem to realize is that when I

returned, I found a very different Mariah. A kinder Mariah. And I have not seen your practiced pout since I returned."

Mariah released a mirthless laugh. "That is only because I was trying to be what Colin wanted."

Sarah nodded. "And in the process, you have become that person. While I cannot speak for Lord Heatherton, I can say that I do not think it matters why you changed. Only that you did. You have become a kind and caring person. Several members of the staff have noticed."

"But where does that leave me? Now that Colin knows, he will surely withdraw his offer."

Sarah squeezed Mariah's hand. "It leaves you a better person. The person you were meant to be. The person your parents would be proud of."

Mariah's lips quivered. "Being a better person does not make my heart hurt any less."

"No, but perhaps it will give you more understanding of when others are hurting." Sarah stood up and leaned over and embraced Mariah. "You are what a gentleman should want in a wife. If Colin cannot see that, he is not worth your tears."

Mariah nodded as tears ran down her cheeks. "But it still hurts."

Sarah tilted her head to the side. "Do you want to come to the Kirkpatricks' with us tonight? I am certain Reginald would carry you up the stairs."

Mariah shook her head.

"Then I will send my regrets and stay home with you."

"No." Mariah shook her head fiercely. "I will be fine. Indeed, I have cried enough that I will likely fall to sleep early."

"Are you certain?"

"Yes. Go enjoy yourselves at the party."

Sarah made a face. "It is cards, and it is the Kirkpatricks'. How diverting can it really be?"

Mariah gave her a watery smile. "I will expect a detailed report."

"I shall take copious notes." Sarah smiled and then left Mariah alone.

She made a fist and pounded it into her pillow, only in part trying to make it comfortable. Why could she not have realized what Sarah said before she declined Colin's offer?

She sighed. She could not think on it a moment longer. Her eyes burned and her head ached. Even her throat was tight from holding back her tears. She closed her eyes, telling herself it would only be for a moment. But instead, she drifted off into a fitful sleep.

# Chapter Thirty

Sarah sat in the chair next to Mariah's dressing table. Miriam finished braiding Mariah's hair and swept it up into a knot at the crown of her head. When she picked up the tiny pearls, Mariah looked at Sarah in the mirror. "I don't see why it is necessary for me to dress for the ball when I am not attending it."

Sarah smiled. "Reginald has shut you up in this house for weeks, missing all the pleasures London offers. I thought it might lift your spirits if you dressed in a fine gown with pearls dotting your hair."

Mariah released a mirthless chuckle. "Yes, I want to be finely dressed to read my book this evening."

"Are you certain you do not want me to remain at home with you?" Sarah asked.

"Yes." Mariah nodded her head. Would Colin attend the ball? Reginald had said he had accepted the invitation. But would he dance or spend the night in the cardroom? Mariah wanted to ask Sarah to watch and give an account of every lady he danced with. But she really didn't want to know. That seemed a whole new kind of torture for her to endure. And she was uncertain she was up for it just yet.

"You have waited the whole Season to attend this ball. I will not hear of you missing it." She smiled. "We set out for Staffordshire tomorrow next, and we will have the rest of the summer together."

Miriam stepped back and Mariah looked at her reflection one last time. "It looks lovely. Thank you, Miriam." A tug of regret tightened in her chest. Miriam had done fine work with Mariah's hair. It was not sticks and leaves, but it would do. It was a pity she was wasting it on Biscuit and a very mediocre book. Would Colin approve? She shook the thought from her mind. She had tried very hard not to think of him, although she was failing miserably.

She stood up and reached for her walking stick. "I suppose it is time for my gown."

Sarah stood up and motioned to the chair she had vacated. "Sit down first and let Miriam wrap your foot."

Mariah frowned. "But she already wrapped my ankle."

Sarah gave an exasperated look. "But we will be gone all evening. What if you wish to move to a different room? Reginald thinks it best to wrap your ankle extra, just for added support."

What was wrong with Sarah and Reginald tonight? They were treating Mariah as if she were an invalid. She would sit on the couch the whole of the evening until she retired to bed. Why did she need extra support for sitting on the couch?

Sarah dropped her head to the side and pouted, as Mariah had taught her all those years ago. It was a look Sarah rarely used. Only when she was teasing Mariah.

Mariah flopped down into the chair. "Oh, very well. If it means you will go to the ball and enjoy yourselves." She lifted her foot while Miriam wrapped another stiffer strip of fabric around her ankle.

When the task was done, Mariah stood and was surprised at the support it gave her. It almost made her change her mind about staying home from the ball. Almost. She smiled at Sarah. "Reginald was right. It does feel better. Thank you."

Sarah nodded and looked at the clock. "It is almost time for us to leave." She twitched her lips to the side. "Are you certain you do not wish us to stay?"

Mariah lifted her arms as Miriam dropped the gown over Mariah's head and settled it on her shoulders. "Yes." She nearly shouted. Pushing her arms through the sleeves of the deep green gown, Mariah shooed Sarah toward the door. "Go and enjoy yourselves. As always, please return prepared to give me a full accounting."

"You know I shall." Sarah leaned over and placed a kiss on Mariah's cheek. "We will miss having you with us."

Mariah nodded. "And I will miss you. Now go. You do not want Reginald to come in search of you."

"You are too late for that." Reginald's voice carried in from the corridor. Sarah swept over and opened the door. Reginald stepped inside, a soft smile forming on his lips as he caught Mariah's gaze. "You look lovely, Mar."

Mariah ran a hand down the front of the gown. "Thank you, Regi. I am uncertain it was necessary, but I am happy to be out of a day dress for once."

Reginald nodded. "Yes, this will do very nicely."

Mariah's brow creased. "I beg your pardon?"

He shook his head. "Sarah said this might help to lighten your mood, and it seems to have done just that."

Mariah looked at him. It felt as if there was more to his meaning, but she could not guess what it might be. Perhaps she was just allowing her feelings of restlessness and despondency to cloud her judgment. "Yes, yes. I am very light, indeed."

Miriam tied the ribbon at the back of Mariah's gown and set to brushing it. Mariah raised her hand. "You need not worry about that, Miriam. I do not believe the couch will object to a piece of lint clinging to my gown." She smiled at her maid. "Thank you. I appreciate all this. Even if it is for naught."

Miriam curtsied. "It made you smile, my lady. That makes it worth it." She ducked her head and scurried about picking up discarded clothing.

Mariah clutched the top of her cane, leaning on it for support. "May I ask for your assistance down the stairs before you leave?"

Reginald nodded. "I can carry you if needed."

"No." The thought of Colin carrying her down the stairs came to her mind. She did not need to relive that memory with Reginald as a replacement. "I am able to walk if you will help me."

Reginald nodded as if he knew the reason for her objection. How long would it take before the pity left his and Sarah's eyes? "Then let's be on our way."

Mariah released a breath. This was the last event of the Season, then they could all return to Oakdale. And Mariah could begin to forget Colin in earnest—at least until he visited. But hopefully, by then, she would be past the worst of it.

Colin stepped from the carriage and straightened his coats as he looked up at the front of Reginald's townhouse. Lud, it had been nearly three weeks since he stood there on the night of their ball. He would never have guessed how his life would change. Although, it might be too early to make such assumptions.

He strode up to the front door and rang the doorbell.

Maxwell appeared and smiled. "Good evening, Lord Heatherton."

Colin smiled nervously. "Is Lady Mariah at home?"

Maxwell nodded. "Yes, Lord Stoke told me of your visit. Lady Mariah is in the library." He motioned toward the corridor. "I believe you know the way?"

Colin nodded. "Indeed, I do. Thank you, Maxwell."

He walked down the corridor and paused outside the library. From where he stood, he saw Mariah sitting on the couch reading a book. His breath hitched in his throat. What was he doing? She had already declined his offer.

Charlie, Cort, Ben, Ponsy, and Reginald had all encouraged Colin to return and ask Mariah for her hand again. It was a misunderstanding, they said. She would surely accept him this time, they said. He frowned. They had said many things. But why had Colin listened to them? What did they know? Apart from Reginald, none of them could boast any degree of knowledge about women.

What if they were wrong? What if he asked Mariah for her hand again and she rejected him a second time? Could he endure the pain? Yesterday had been the worst day of his life. He had found new hope after speaking to the gents, but all his doubts and insecurities came flooding back.

He stared at Mariah, her head tipped to the side and her finger playing with the curl laying at her cheek. How could he not take the chance at being with her forever? If there was even a minute chance she would accept him, he had to take it, did he not?

He closed his eyes and gathered his courage. Everyone but Rags—and perhaps Mariah—seemed in favor of them marrying. There was no sense in delaying any longer.

He stepped into the library and moved quietly over to the couch. There was no reason to alert her to his presence any sooner than he had to. He cleared his throat and bowed deeply before her. "Lady Mariah, I wondered if I might claim the set you owe me."

Her gaze jerked up to meet his. She did not smile, which

did not seem in his favor. She studied him for a moment. "I do not recall owing you a set, my lord."

Colin straightened but motioned to the couch next to her. She nodded, and he sat a proper distance away. "Perhaps it is because you did not give me the opportunity to ask."

She raised a brow. "Oh? And why is that?"

He shrugged. "I intended to ask for your first set after supper at Lord Cleverly's ball. But then you went and injured yourself after the very first set. You left the ball early and denied me my opportunity." He smiled at her, hoping to earn at least a flicker of a smile.

"If you know of my injury, then you should know I'm unable to dance."

He nodded slowly. "I confess. I was aware of your predicament. It is why I searched for you here, instead of Lord Trenton's."

Her chin trembled slightly, and the pain in his chest sharpened. He had upset her. Lud, he was an idiot.

"If you know those things, why are you asking me to dance?"

"I understood your ankle was wrapped especially tight tonight." He winked at her. "But I also know of a special way to dance where your feet need never touch the floor. It should not bother your ankle in the least."

"Why are you doing this?" She whispered. "Please know it is nearly killing me."

"The last thing I wish is to distress you." He settled against the couch back and ran a hand through his hair. "I had hoped we could settle things between us."

She twisted at her fingertip. "And how do you propose to do that?"

"I thought perhaps if you consented to be my wife, it would start things in the right direction."

She looked over at him. "But how could you still want me after everything I did?"

He shook his head. "I realized it did not matter why you changed. The fact was that you changed. Is a butterfly any less beautiful because it once was a rather ugly caterpillar? It does not really matter how it happened, only that the butterfly is a better version of what it once was." He scooted next to her. "I want the butterfly."

A tear fell over her lashes and down her cheek. "But what if inside I am still the caterpillar?"

Colin shook his head. "I think it is the opposite. Deep down, you were always the butterfly. You simply needed a reason to change." He wiped the tear off her cheek. "I feel rather privileged to have helped you discover your true potential."

"I'm afraid I will disappoint you." Her chin continued to quiver, and she looked away.

Colin chuckled. "I am certain you will disappoint me at one time or another. Just as I am certain I will disappoint you. That is just being human. But we will work through it together." He took her chin between his fingers and drew it back to look at him. "I love you, Mariah, and I will grow with you if you will grow with me."

She nodded. "I can think of no other place I would rather be."

Colin grinned. "Then we are engaged?"

"I believe we are." She pulled her lip between her teeth.

Colin leaned forward. "Why must you do that? Do you have any idea what it does to me?"

She shook her head.

"It makes me wish to do this." He leaned forward and gently brushed his lips against hers, his hand cupping her cheek.

She leaned into him and smiled beneath his lips. "I had no idea it did such things to you."

"I nearly lost my mind keeping my lips away from yours." He wound her curl around his finger.

"Thank the heavens you no longer have to try." She kissed the tip of his nose. "Did you not promise me a dance?"

He jumped to his feet and held out his hand.

She stood and limped toward him.

"Forget about the extra wrapping," he said as he swept her up into his arms. "Is this not the best kind of dancing?"

She wrapped her arms around his neck and snuggled into him. "But there is no music."

He looked down at her. "The only music I need is the beating of your heart next to mine."

# Epilogue

STOKE-ON-TRENT, STAFFORDSHIRE, AUGUST 1815

COLIN WALKED down the corridor but stopped before the entryway. Voices sounded, and they did not sound as if they were having a pleasant conversation.

"What do you mean you're leaving? You have not even been here three days." Berwick's voice ticked up a notch.

"Yes, well, two days was all it took for Papa to become ill. I told you it would happen if we traveled, did I not?" Lady Amelia replied.

Colin crept to the end of the corridor and peered around the corner.

Ben's stance was rigid, and his hand clenched at his side. "It is barely a cough, Mia. Surely it does not warrant you quitting the party completely?"

Lady Amelia nodded curtly. "But it does. Ben, you know I was not in favor of coming, yet against my better judgment, I relented, because my father and you persisted. And now my fears have happened."

Ben shook his head. "No, they have not. You are simply

using your father as an excuse. He has not even kept to his bed. He just returned from shooting with the men."

"An activity he should never have participated in. You should hear him. His cough is rattling as I have never heard it."

Ben's head continued to shake. "I heard his cough—if you could even call it that." He clasped his hands behind his back. He looked from side to side. "Where is your father? If you are to depart immediately, I wonder what is keeping him."

Lady Amelia narrowed her eyes at Ben. "His delay should indicate just how unwell he truly is. It is not like Papa to dally."

"Or perhaps it is because he wishes to stay." Ben took a step forward. "Please don't go, Mia. I thought we were having a pleasant time."

Lady Amelia released a sigh. "Our leaving has nothing to do with you, Ben. Indeed, if it were not for Papa's health, I should stay. But I cannot risk his cough worsening."

Colin noted, as he was certain Ben had, Lady Amelia's gaze dropped to the floor when she stated she should like to stay. Colin did not know the lady well, but even he knew it was an utter lie.

"I will watch after your father myself if you stay." Ben's voice lowered.

Lady Amelia shook her head. "You are most kind to offer, Ben. But my father is not your concern. And I can take care of him better back at Hedlund Hall." She lifted a hand, as if to offer some comfort to Ben, but then dropped it back to her side.

"It seems there is nothing I can say to change your mind." His voice was clipped.

Colin raised his brows. He rarely heard Ben angry. It was interesting the person causing it was the same person Ben was trying to convince to stay.

"I'm sorry, but there is nothing that will convince me. I do hope you will call on us when you return to Northumberland." She turned away from Ben and looked up the staircase. "Now I must fetch my father. I am concerned he is worsening, and that is why he is taking so long."

Ben nodded. "I wish you safe travels, Mia." He turned and headed toward the very corridor in which Colin stood lurking.

Colin moved several steps backward, before turning and jogging to the nearest open door. He looked around. Ah, the billiard room. It would do nicely. Grabbing a cue, he leaned over the table, as if he were playing a solo game.

He felt Ben enter the room. The entire feeling of the room shifted from frantic to discontented.

Colin looked up. "Ah, Ben. I was wondering where you were. Indeed, I have seen none of the gents this afternoon."

Ben's jaw worked fiercely. He sucked in a breath and grabbed a cue. "Are you content to play alone, or do you mind if I join you?"

Raising a brow, Colin swept his hand toward the table. "I should be happy for the company." He clasped both hands around the top of the cue and leaned into it. "Although, from the dangerous look on your face, it might not be a wise decision."

Ben shook his head. "I am fine," he grunted.

"Yes, you seem fine. Or you would if you were Rags. The look on your face is one I usually associate with him, not you." Colin tried to look innocent. "What has you so vexed?"

Ben growled in his throat. "Lady Amelia. She and her father are leaving for Northumberland."

"Oh? When are they to depart?" As if he didn't already know. But he could not let on that he had been eavesdropping on Ben's conversation with Lady Amelia.

"Even as we speak, they are on their way." Ben thrust his stick forward, sending the balls scattering around the table.

"But they only just arrived."

Ben growled again. "I am very aware of when they

arrived. Lady Amelia is concerned about her father's cough." If Colin had not heard the conversation, he might think Ben agreed with Lady Amelia's rash decision.

Colin frowned. "His cough? I did not detect any cough when we were out shooting this morning."

Ben flicked up a brow. "I heard him cough once or twice. I should have known this would be her response. She has always been rather protective of her father."

Colin leaned against the wall and crossed one foot over the other. "If you knew this was her tendency, why do you seem so out of sorts about her leaving?"

"I am not out of sorts. I am simply disappointed, that is all. I believed, as did her father, that this house party would be good for her. But she has not been here long enough to enjoy it or make any friends."

"And you feel she needs friends? I thought *you* were her dearest friend. Do you wish to change that?"

Ben shook his head and motioned to the table. "Are you to take your turn or just offer me advice on a matter that does not need any?"

There was obviously something Ben was not telling Colin. But what was it? Colin leaned over and took his shot, landing the ball in the corner pocket. "I was allowing you a chance to play without feeling the pressure of my superior skills." Colin grinned at his friend. "Did you not just see my red hazard?" He placed a lazy grin on his face. "And I will have you know I offered you no advice. I simply inquired about your sour-looking expression."

Ben sucked in a long, slow breath through his nose, as if he were breathing away his frustrations. Although, why he was frustrated, Colin was uncertain. He would surely not be so grumpy should one of the gents leave early.

Ben grinned across the table. "I was simply giving you a chance, for once. But it looks as though my kindness might have led you to believe you had a chance of winning. Which you must realize is complete nonsense."

Colin smiled. That was more like the Ben he'd known for more than a decade. "Then you are not distracted by Lady Amelia's removal to Northumberland?"

Ben shrugged. "Lady Amelia will do what she wishes. I should know by now that I cannot change her mind." He leaned forward and shot, landing the two balls in the pocket. Ben shook his head sympathetically. "You are no match for me, Colin. But thank you."

Colin shrugged. "Why are you thanking me? Do you think I lost on purpose?"

"I am confident I am more proficient than you. But you always know how to lift my spirits." He put the cue back in the corner. "I have some correspondence I have been putting off. I shall see you later this afternoon." He clapped Colin on the shoulder as he passed on his way out the door.

Colin put his cue away. He need not pretend to be absorbed in the game any longer.

"There you are. I thought perhaps you had come to your senses about me and run off." Mariah stood in the doorway with her arms folded across her chest.

Colin smiled wider. "Never, my pretty little liar."

Mariah shook her head, but smiled up at him as he slid his hands around her waist. "People will think you do not truly love me if you continue to call me that name."

He placed a kiss on the tip of her nose. "No one who sees us together will ever think anything of the sort. You need only ask one of the gents. They will tell the truth of it." He pulled her closer to him. "And you are the only one I care about. Do you believe I do not love you when I use that name?" He leaned down and placed a kiss on the nape of her neck. "Because I do not think that of you when you call me Biscuit Thief."

She shook her head and shivered beneath his touch. "I am

certain you love me, Colin. And as long as you know I will never lie about loving you, I do not see a problem." She laced her fingers through the hair at the back of his head. "And what lady does not like to be called pretty?"

He chuckled and pulled her farther into the room, kicking the door closed behind him. He nuzzled his face into her neck. "Oh, Lady Heatherton." His heartbeat quickened. "Have I ever shown you how to play billiards?" He winked down at her before swinging her up and setting her on the table's edge.

She pulled her bottom lip between her teeth. "I thought one played the game while standing on the floor."

He waggled his brows. "I'm going to teach you a different way to play." He leaned forward but stopped just short of her lips. "Trust me, you'll be proficient in no time."

# Author Notes

Thank you for reading *Lying to a Lord.* I hope it was as fun for you to read as it was for me to write.

Unlike most of my historical books, the lines between what was considered proper and what was not may have been blurred a little in this book. It was done consciously, for the sake of the pacing and the storyline. I hope that as a lover of historical novels, you can set aside those proprieties and still enjoy the story as it was intended—for fun.

If you would like to get a peak at all of the League of Gentleman, you can check them out on my Pinterest Board https://www.pinterest.com/MindyBurbidgeStrunk under the League of Eligible Bachelors.

# Acknowledgments

A huge thank you-

To my editors Jolene Perry and Brandalyn Seaman for fixing all my plot holes and poor grammar—because I know it is there.

To my proofreaders: Patti Knowlton and Rose Hutchison for catching all those pesky typos that seem to slip through.

To my great writers' group: Laura Beers, Sally Britton, Anneka Walker and Laura Rollins! Thanks for all the help you give me to tighten my storyline and help me improve on my ideas! You guys are the best!

To my great ARC team. Thank you for all you do to help me be successful! I couldn't do it without you guys.

And last and most importantly, to all my boys—big and small. Thanks for not complaining when you were out of clean clothes or get pizza for dinner…again. For reading over my shoulder and telling me you thought my story sounded 'really good.' And for encouraging me—telling me I 'made a good job choice to become an author.' I love you, tons! Especially to Christopher for supporting and helping me push through when it just felt too hard and for making sure I had the tools I needed to make me successful. You are my great cheerleader! I couldn't do this without your support! LY

# *About the Author*

Mindy loves all things history and love, which makes writing romance right up her alley. Since she was a little girl playing in her closet "elevator," she has always had stories running through her mind. But it wasn't until she was well into adulthood that she realized she could write those stories down.

Now they occupy her dreams and most every quiet moment she has.

Her kids are used to being called names they have never heard and they now use words like vexed and chagrined.

When she isn't living in her alternate realities, she is married to her real-life Mr. Darcy and trying to raise five proper boys. They live happily in the beautiful mountains of Utah.

You can connect with her on her website mindyburbidgestrunk.com.

# Also by Mindy Burbidge Strunk

**Regency House Party Series**

Mistaken Identity

Miss Marleigh's Pirate Lord

**Scoundrels, Rakes and Rogues Series**

Reforming the Gambler

Rake on the Run

The Secrets of a Scoundrel

**Unlikely Match Series**

*Saving Anna*- prequel novella

An American in Dukes Clothing

The Baron's Rose

A Princess for the Gentleman

**Bells of Christmas Series**

Unmasking Lady Caroline

Thawing the Viscount's Heart

**Hidden Riches Series**

The Mysteries of Hawthorn Hall

The Treasure of Owl's Roast Abbey

**League of Eligible Bachelors**

Engaging the Earl

**Top Flight Series**

Bear: A Fighter Pilot Romance

Mustang: A Fighter Pilot Romance

**Stand-alone books**

*Just as You Are-* Novella

Want more? Sign up for Mindy's newsletter here to receive updates, deals, and new releases. f you want to listen to the audio books you can find them on my Youtube Channel: https://www.youtube.com/@mindyburbidgestrunk7846 Or your preferred audiobook retailer.

Made in the USA
Coppell, TX
09 June 2023

17908524R00166